Murder at the Bad Girl's Bar & Grill

Also by N. M. Kelby

Whale Season
In the Company of Angels
Theater of the Stars

N. M. Kelby

MUR
at the Bad Girl's

DER
Bar & Grill

a novel

Shaye Areheart Books

NEW YORK

Copyright © 2008 by Nicole Mary Kelby

Published in the United States by Shaye Areheart Books, an imprint of
the Crown Publishing Group, a division of Random House, Inc., New York.
www.crownpublishing.com

Shaye Areheart Books with colophon is a registered trademark of
Random House, Inc.

Library of Congress Cataloging-in-Publication Data
Kelby, N. M. (Nicole M.)
Murder at the Bad Girl's Bar & Grill : a novel / N. M. Kelby. —1st ed.
1. Police—Fiction.   2. Eccentrics and eccentricities—Fiction.
3. Florida—Fiction.   I. Title.

PS3561.E382M87 2008
813'.54—dc22   2007049105

ISBN 978-0-307-38207-8

Printed in the United States of America

Design by Lynne Amft

10 9 8 7 6 5 4 3 2 1

First Edition

For George and Sally Kelby—always

The secret source of Humor itself is not joy but sorrow.
There is no humor in heaven.

— MARK TWAIN, *Following the Equator* (1897)

Murder at the Bad Girl's Bar & Grill

Chapter One

It was the hissing that caught his attention. Like a tire going flat, like a snake giving warning—but loud. Almost deafening. The security guard was making one last pass before dawn when he heard it. Then saw it.

At first, Wilson thought it was just bats. Laguna Key is home to hundreds of them, maybe even thousands. It's not one of the features mentioned in any of the retirement community's brochures, but every night clouds of bats come screaming out of the mangrove forest, fly low along the beach, bank over the tennis courts, cast shadows on the moon, and slip into dreams.

But this was different. Louder. Angry. It made him uneasy. He followed the noise, the hum of it, back behind the bar, back to the Dumpster—then stopped. The air reeked of salt and death.

And there were wings.

Wildly flapping wings. They covered the Dumpster. Made it seem alive, as if it were some sort of a new creature. Iridescent in the blue-white glow of vapor lights. Menacing.

Vultures.

Their hissing seemed to vibrate through his body.

At this point, Wilson thought he screamed. He wanted to. He might have. He believed he did, but the vultures did not move. Hungry, they were trying to push their way inside the Dumpster, hissing at each other, unaware that Wilson was standing there. Or uncaring.

Wilson had a horrible urge to laugh. Sweat slipped along his spine.

A single bald red head turned toward him. The wrinkled neck, the sharp curve of its beak, the cool eye. The frenzy stopped.

Not good, Wilson thought.

The vultures all turned, their crinkled bloodstained heads bobbing in unison.

Wilson's heart beat hard. A single bird broke away, flew slowly around him. Sniffed. The bird was so close Wilson could smell blood on its breath.

It swooped in even closer. Hissed. When the tips of its wings lightly brushed his forehead, Wilson flinched and the other birds began, again, their hissing. Spat at him. Bits of undigested flesh covered his shirt, turned the cool morning air acid.

Really not good.

And so Wilson did the only thing that a man in his position could do. He sang "Surfer Girl."

"Do you love me . . ."

Apparently, the vultures did not. They fled.

Wilson took a deep breath. He was unsure. Uneasy. A little cold. The smell of blood, the rot, was overwhelming.

Carrion, he thought. The polite, less graphic name for roadkill. Then he leaned into the Dumpster.

He was, unfortunately, very wrong.

Chapter Two

Two days later, despite the fact that it will soon be sunset, or maybe because of it, the sky is preening in its blueness. It is bluer than any suede shoe or wandering eye. But even though the sun is still out, there's a soft warm rain. It dusts, not falls. Pisses Wilson off.

"Man," he says under his breath.

"Man, what?"

Sophie is sitting behind the privacy wall, on her own deck, knitting. She has very good hearing.

"Just man," he says. Disgusted.

The problem is that the rain adds up and puddles on the felt. Makes it tough to break the rack, tough to hold the cue. Blue chalk runs like mascara.

"Three in the left pocket," he says.

"Easy shot?"

"Maybe for you."

Sophie is blind, so she laughs. "It's just a little rain," she says. "Don't be such a sissy."

Sophie has an unnatural love of water, or at least Wilson thinks so. She sits on her side of the deck day and night, rain or not, and listens to the ocean. Knits.

A landlocked mermaid, that's how he thinks of her.

Wilson sets the shot and tries not to think of Sophie knitting in the rain, just a few feet away, stubborn, her long blue-black hair cascading down her back like a waterfall at night, her dark unseeing eyes. The clicking of knitting needles makes him twitch.

"What's the shot again?" she asks.

"Three in the left, " he says, and shoots. Quick. Careless. Misses the ball completely. The cue slips out of his wet hand, flies across the table, and, just as he called it, bounces off the left corner pocket, spins for a moment like an Olympic high diver, and then clatters to the ground. Spent.

Nice, he thinks.

"Should I call ESPN?" she says. "Or 911?"

Wilson sighs. He picks up the cue again, leans across the table, and aims. *Tap the three ball,* he thinks, *just give it a little topspin.* Then reconsiders. The rain changes everything, makes it difficult to know how the ball will slide across the slick felt.

He'd like to double-check his options, get a surer shot, but *Byrne's Complete Book of Pool Shots* is lying open on the hammock chair and taking on water like shame. Its pages are soaked down to the pulp. He's afraid to pick it up. Afraid it will fall apart. Can't have that. Wilson needs that book. Of all the things he inherited from his father—the soft chin, the neckless-linebacker body, the undying love of anything made with lard—the pool-shark gene was not one of them.

Ray, Wilson's father, was a hustler—and a good one. He played the circuit for a while when Wilson was in junior high. Ray tried to teach his son, but it never worked. Wilson was more interested in his electric guitar and girls.

"Pool teaches you nerve, boy," his father would tell him.

Now he's gone.

So Wilson wants to learn nine-ball, his father's game. Pool was his language. Wordless. *The perfect music of the clack, Jack.* That's how Ray always described it, cigarette hanging out of his mouth like some sort of exclamation point.

Wilson wants to understand that perfect music down to his bones, so he bought an all-weather table and put it on the deck. It was the only place in the town house large enough for it.

Now he spends every waking moment out there practicing. And he still isn't very good.

But he doesn't want to think about that now. He's decided to make the three ball in the side pocket and kiss it back off a frozen seven ball with a backspin, and he needs to find the page that tells him how to set the shot. The rain is picking up. The hammock chair shakes as he turns the soggy pages. Some of them tear slightly in his hand.

Wilson's problem is simple. The pool table is designed for the outdoors. Guaranteed waterproof.

The book is not. And Florida is a subtropical climate.

Details, Wilson thinks. *Details will bite your ass.* And then he begins to hum "California Girls." It's a tic of his. It's also part of the reason he was asked to leave the FBI Academy at Quantico. Makes people nervous. Makes them think you don't take things seriously. Makes them remember that you grew up in a place where people usually take a vacation.

"Insubordinate"—they'd written that word in his file so many times, Wilson thought it was his middle name.

It's just not easy to be Brian Wilson, live on the beach, and know all the words.

"What's the shot again?"

Sophie loves the simple perfect clack of ball against ball. The dull thud when it hits the rail.

"Three in the left pocket."

"Mulligan?"

"That's golf. But no. Topspin this time."

She sighs—and it's not an encouraging sound. He knows it's stupid, but he hates to let her down. Even in little things.

Sophie is his. At least, that's the way he sees it. In a sense, it's true. Wilson's primary job is to keep an eye on her, and on the town—in that order. Sophie's father, Mr. Whit, owns most of Laguna Key.

Whitless, Sophie calls him.

Once a day, Mr. Whit drives his silver Vespa into town, surveys the property, and waves at the locals like an aging rock star. The scooter is retro-styled and underpowered, barely street legal. Mr. Whit wears old-fashioned racing goggles and a long silver silk scarf that matches his helmet and the bike.

"We're selling style here at Laguna Key," he told Wilson.

Shoot me if I get that crazy, Wilson thought.

So Wilson is all Laguna Key has in the way of law enforcement. Three times a day, he gets into a bright yellow golf cart and makes his tour of the perfectly manicured streets. Just to keep an eye on things. Stops by the Bad Girl's Bar & Grill, the only thing Whit doesn't own, to check up on some of the fellas at the bar—make sure they don't drink too much. Wilson worries about them, with all the meds they take.

Sophie is more of a challenge, a little harder on the heart. She's been blind since December, less than a couple of months. She and her husband were scuba diving off Key West when apparently something in her brain just popped, like a bubble.

The doctors said she was lucky. It was caught in time. Not too much damage, just the blindness, they told her. They would have told her husband, too. But, according to Sophie, when the police came to question him, he was gone. They'd only been married six months.

Sophie suspects Whit paid him off. So she doesn't answer the door when her father visits. He's stopped coming around.

"You only have one father," Wilson wants to say, but doesn't.

The endless knitting really bothers him. She's not making anything in particular. The project has grown long past the desired length for a scarf. Sophie says the only important thing about the piece is that it is blue—shades of blue, like the water of the reefs. "I like to run my hands through its blueness."

He watches her feel it in her hands, make her way through it as if it's a deep-sea tangle. She works it as a diver does, as she once did.

A landlocked mermaid, Wilson thinks. *Wicked sad state of affairs.*

"Hey, are you going to take that shot or not?" Sophie now says. So Wilson shoots and a miracle happens. The four ball goes into the corner pocket. The three bounces off the eight and follows suit. It wasn't the shot he was going for, but he laughs with pleasure anyway.

"Three ball?" Sophie asks. She's stopped knitting.

"Damn straight," Wilson says, triumphant. Then his cell phone rings. Instead of a tone, it plays "I Get Around"—Wilson's always been hopeful when it comes to women.

"Get your ass down here."

It's Danni from the Bad Girl's Bar & Grill. In times of stress, manners are sometimes not her strong point. Danni, also known as Danni Keene, Slasher Queen, was the 1980s goddess of schlockmeister horror films. She's now somewhere in her midforties, depending on what bio you read. She's at the age where she hopes age doesn't matter but knows it does. A movie critic once described her as "the workingman's Sharon Stone" and it stuck. The resemblance is striking: the classic face, the wicked eyes, and that peculiar alchemy of a woman who is bad and beautiful and should never be underestimated.

Danni is Laguna Key's newest and only celebrity—and that's not saying a lot. Even she's quick to admit that. For more than twenty years, Danni's scream was her claim to fame, which was disturbing to her parents because they paid for her to go to Juilliard.

"It's my day off," Wilson says.

"Don't jerk me around," she says in that throaty there's-a-guy-hiding-in-my-closet-with-a-knife-and-I'm-going-to-have-to-shoot-him kind of voice. "I got some of your people here chained together with bike locks."

"They're not my people."

"They're pissing me off."

"Any reason for that?"

"Buddy. Buddy broke into a rap version of 'Copacabana.' "

Buddy is the Barry Manilow tribute artist whom Danni recently hired to appease the residents of Laguna Key. Since the Laguna Key development encircles the bar and the sound of music carries, some of the residents are pushing to pass an ordinance that will ban live music after 7:30 p.m. *Wheel of Fortune* comes on at 7:30 p.m.

A town has to have its priorities.

But Danni wants live music. A bar doesn't seem like a bar without it. Since she opened the place two months ago, she's tried several acts, but the complaints kept growing worse.

Two weeks ago, she hired Metallical, a heavy-metal Metallica tribute band from Strasburg, North Dakota, Lawrence Welk's hometown. It seemed to be a great choice. Before every song, the lead singer would shout, "And a one and a two . . ." and then slam into "Leper Messiah" or another Metallica classic. Like their hometown hero, the band made a solid attempt to appeal to a wide audience. Once, they slipped into a Welk homage featuring the famed bandleader's own version of Del Shannon's "Runaway" as a waltz.

Danni thought it was quite haunting in a heavy-metal, dip-and-twirl sort of way—the sweep of the electric guitar, the shimmer of the drums, the side-step crooning beating down on you at 110 miles per hour and the ear-shattering decibels—"I wah-wah-wah-wah-wonder why, why why why why why she ran away . . . my little runaway, run-run-run-run-runaway."

Quite haunting, but apparently it was the last straw.

Later that night, somebody lit Danni's Hummer on fire. Sent her a note: "Next time it's the bar."

"Apparently, these people *really* like to watch *Wheel of Fortune*," Wilson told her.

Since the burning of a bright yellow Hummer falls under the terrorist threat guidelines of the Patriot Act, the FBI is looking at the incident—more or less. The agent assigned, Gayle Hennessey, a tall, toothy redhead who once sat behind Wilson at Quantico, kept shaking her head and saying, "The heavy-metal band played 'Runaway' as a waltz?"

Wilson just shrugged.

After that Danni hired Buddy. He hasn't quite been there a week, but it seems like a lifetime. He never breaks character. Wants to talk about his Vegas years. Has a shih tzu named Mandy.

Right now, Wilson can hear him trying to channel Snoop Dogg as he sings, "Her name was Lola. She was a showgirl. Dig?"

"How bad is it?" Wilson asks.

"Your people have chained themselves to Lono."

"Lono?"

"The tiki god of fertility."

Too much information, Wilson thinks, and suddenly has a visual of the scene. He imagines leather-skinned men in pastel plaid shorts chained around the obscenely endowed hand-carved tiki, who is smiling for good reason.

"I just hope that grass skirt holds," Danni says. "They could get us on an obscenity charge, if you know what I mean."

Wilson does, and that's why at times like this he wishes he carried a gun, mostly to use on himself.

"I thought this Buddy person would be okay," Danni rambles on. "But he doesn't even know 'Margaritaville.' Man. Still, he's really into the Manilow thing. Your people love Manilow, don't they?"

"Would you stop saying that? They're not *my* people." Wilson is now whining and he hates it when he whines. "Wait a minute," he says. "You hired a guy who doesn't sing Buffett? Isn't there a state law against that? Even those Metallica wannabes knew 'Margaritaville.' "

Wilson once heard "Cheeseburger in Paradise" played on a lute at the Renaissance Festival. He knows that there has to be a law.

But before Danni can answer, a dog, which Wilson believes to be the tiny Mandy, begins to howl. Over the painfully tinny miniature wail, Wilson recognizes the jingle for a State Farm commercial: "Like a good neighbor . . ."

"Oh no," Danni says. "Three pink buses just pulled up and there's a crowd of people outside and Buddy's doing that jingles medley again. I told him never to do the jingles medley. You better get over here before he gets to the McDonald's part. There's something about the phrase 'You deserve a break today' that really pisses people off."

And she hangs up. No good-bye.

It's times like this that Wilson wants to jump into his little deuce coupe and drive away forever. Unfortunately, he can only afford a GTO.

Chapter Three

Sòlas MacKay and his two assistants, otherwise known as the Rose and Puppet Circus, arrive in a cloud of exhaust and hope. Their ancient buses shudder to a halt, toss pistons like pennies to be left on the sidewalk.

The buses are pink. Well, rose, actually. But they look pink.

When Laguna Key Association CEO and de facto president of the Chamber of Commerce Bill Bryon walks out of the bar and sees the great expanse of pink—*A hippie color if there ever was one,* he thinks—he calls security. Wilson's line is busy. So Bill calls the Florida Highway Patrol.

"Pink," he says with great portent.

There is laughter. The line goes dead.

The buses are covered with childlike drawings of hearts, the color of worn velvet, and hands, seemingly made of sky. THE ROSE AND PUPPET CIRCUS is painted on the side of each one, along with each bus's name: SILENCE, GRACE, and WATCHFULNESS.

Definitely hippie fodder. Bill calls the National Guard. Then FEMA. He has them both on speed dial.

"Hippies," he says. No one seems to care.

Inside the buses are life-size puppets. Their clay faces, smooth as river stones, smile simply, seem content as the moon dreaming of itself. Some seem to wave. Some cover their unseeing eyes. At the back of the bus named GRACE, two are posed as lovers locked in an embrace.

So Bill calls the American Automobile Association. "Tow trucks. It's an emergency."

Bill's concern is understandable. No one in Laguna Key had ever seen anything like Sòlas MacKay and the Rose and Puppet Circus before.

And Sòlas has never seen a place like Laguna Key. Everything seems bleached to the bone: the people, the streets, the sidewalks, the endless miles of picket fences. Makes him squint.

The gathered crowd is as well manicured as the grass. They hold manhattans, martinis, and Chablis—it's cocktail hour, after all.

Sòlas slowly opens the door of his bus. He is a carved wooden figure of a man with nickel-plated hair and eyes that, in a certain light, are the color of crushed violets. He is the last living member of the warrior tribe of Clan MacKay, the Highlanders whose motto was *Manu forti,* "With a strong hand."

His kilt is the color of the sea. He can trace his lineage back to Macbeth—the real Macbeth—the former king of Scotland who, some claim, was darker than any of Shakespeare's imaginings.

But Sòlas, the last MacKay standing, is a circus clown.

Apparently, the cosmos has a wicked sense of humor.

Dazed, weary from driving day and night nearly fifteen hundred miles on the road—and yet regal—Sòlas feels moved to address the crowd. He wants to set them at ease, wants to say something profound, wants to tell them of the great spectacle that the Rose and Puppet Circus will be. Wants to dazzle them with his loquaciousness, charm them until they weep—but all he can think to say is "Something wicked this way comes!" which he shouts in Gaelic, his father's language, Macbeth's language. His voice is filled with peat smoke, raw wool, and sorrow.

The moment would be majestic and somehow beautiful—the wild-eyed handsome Scot has an undeniable charisma—except for the fact that Sòlas trips and hits the sand, face-first.

The crowd is silent.

And so, as if on cue, the two ancient assistants, Marie and Klara, twin puppeteers from Sweden, pop out of the doorway of their own buses, click the heels of their red shoes twice, and shout, "Ta-da!"

"Ta-da?" Bill says.

"Ta-da!" they say again.

It is nearly the only English they know. Their Gaelic is also a little rusty.

Since the traditional language of the Gaels, the race of Celtic Scots, is not often heard in Florida, the irony of fair warning is lost. The women in the crowd run to help Sòlas. The men know they are in trouble.

And Bill has no one else left to call.

Overhead a kettle of vultures circles. *Hiss.*

Sòlas crosses himself and says a prayer.

It was no heart attack, he thinks, even though the police told him they believe that's how his brother died. Natural causes.

No man conveniently dies in a trash bin.

They wouldn't listen. And so, Sòlas is here. Grief-stricken. Determined.

He has always been a reluctant MacKay, a clown by training and disposition, but he's come to Laguna Key to avenge his brother's death.

It is his destiny, after all, uneasy as that is.

And the vultures, apparently, are waiting.

Chapter Four

B_y the time Wilson arrives at the Bad Girl's Bar & Grill, Sòlas has been carried inside and is lying on the bar. His kilt is fanned out like a peacock's tail. His ankles are modestly crossed. A sign over the bar reads IF IT'S TOURIST SEASON, WHY CAN'T WE SHOOT THEM? Sòlas looks wan, ready to be plucked.

Surprisingly, his assistants don't appear concerned. The two ancient Swedish puppeteers, twin crones, are intensely focused on the NCAA men's basketball game on the television at the other end of the bar. Gators versus Bulldogs—or, if you don't speak sports, the University of Florida versus the University of Georgia. Either way, it's a classic match and the crones are enraptured.

They point. Cackle. Their long gray braids sway behind them like the tails of parrots. When the ball hits the backboard, then slowly rolls around the rim and falls in, they cheer—no matter what team scored.

Fast breaks make them squeal with delight. And when one or the other team commits a flagrant foul—gives a nasty shove or jabs at an eye just for fun—the twin crones slap each other on the tops of their heads, mutter something in Swedish, and spit on the floor.

It's clear that the two are either avid fans of college hoops or are just quite fond of watching young men wearing shorts.

At least, Wilson thinks, *the god Lono and his grass skirt are safe and the threat of a riot is long forgotten.*

Once Sòlas arrived, Buddy, the Barry Manilow tribute artist, stormed off muttering something about puppets being "chick magnets."

"How can I compete against freakin' puppets?"

It didn't seem as if Buddy was coming back anytime soon, so the protesters unlocked themselves and ordered a drink as if nothing had happened.

All is good, Wilson thinks.

Nearby, clusters of women hover over Sòlas. They fan him with anything they have—their hands, their electric bills, their check-books, their copies of the Victoria's Secret catalog—anything to make him comfortable. Danni has her back to him. She's pouring a large tumbler of whiskey and water—both at room temperature "to take advantage of the full bloom of the fruit of the peat," as Sòlas explained.

"And a cup of coffee with about an inch of cream," he says to her as she pours. An afterthought.

"Coffee?" Danni says. She doesn't even turn around. When she says the word, it sounds as if it has been squeezed out of her, not spoken. "There's coffee right next to you. Self-serve."

That's the way it always is. If you want a cup of coffee at the Bad Girl's Bar & Grill, you get it yourself. There's always a pot at the end of the bar.

Danni spent too many years as a struggling starlet fetching coffee for producers, directors, and actors who thought they knew, beyond a doubt, that they were better than she was.

And she will tell you this until her face turns red, or yours does, or both.

To her, the act of getting someone coffee is "an insidious form of domestic terrorism—the last vestige of the cold war between the sexes."

And Danni wants no part of it. She pours the water into Sòlas's tumbler of Scotch. Stirs it with a tiki swizzle stick.

"I just brewed the pot. It's fresh," she says.

"Ah," Sòlas says, and sits up a bit. Leans on one elbow. Shaky. "Then it would be so lovely with an inch of cream floated on the top. And two teaspoons of sugar."

Danni is cool-eyed, the Scotch and water in one hand. It's not clear if she's going to toss the drink or hand it to him.

This is not good, Wilson thinks.

"Look out," Bill whispers.

"If you don't have cream," Sòlas continues on, blithely, "whipped cream will do. I don't partake in the nondairy stuff, though. Organic is preferred."

Wilson cringes. Danni's eyes narrow. The tumbler of Scotch and water shakes slightly in her hand. It's obvious that she's counting to ten.

Wilson turns away. He can't bear to watch.

Everyone knows that there are rules at the Bad Girl's Bar & Grill. They are written in very large letters over the door on a sign that reads THINGS YOU SHOULD KNOW. They are very specific and include a preamble:

Bad Girl is a philosophy of life. It is genderless. Anyone can be a Bad Girl—even boys. In fact, Bad Girl Boys are the most interesting boys of all.

To be a Bad Girl all you have to do is lead with your heart.

To drink in this bar, however, you must follow these rules:

1. *No "isms"—this includes racism, sexism, and ageism.*
2. *Practice civility.*
3. *Loiter attentively.*
4. *Flirt.*
5. *Cultivate fun.*
6. *Be generous in heart, spirit, and time. Tipping is good, too.*
7. *Get your own damn coffee.*

Number 7 had always been Danni's favorite, but when she hands Sòlas his Scotch he looks at her with those violet eyes.

Amethyst. Orchid. Grape pop.

Danni isn't quite sure what shade his eyes are exactly. The color seems to shift.

Heliotrope. Blackberry. Eggplant.

The tumbler nearly slips from his hand. "Still a bit woozy," he says. "Wouldn't ask otherwise, because I *can* get my own damn coffee." Then he laughs the warm throaty laugh of conspiracy. "Very nice sign, by the way. Very legible."

Indigo.

"Two sugars?" she says, and can't believe she heard herself asking that. Neither could anyone else.

He nods. "Thanks, love."

Then Danni sighs.

"I'll be damned," Bill says.

"Ditto," says Wilson.

It is now clear that this puppeteer, this Scot, despite the fact that he is relatively prone, disheveled, exhausted, and smells like a herd of wet sheep, is working his considerable charm on all things female. Even Mandy, the tawny shih tzu who bears a remarkable resemblance to Barry Manilow, is licking Sòlas's limp hand. The marmalade cat has slid by to purr.

The men of Laguna Key sip their gin and tonics and watch the master at work. "Bottle that. Make a fortune," Bill says. Sounds wistful.

Wilson shrugs, looks out the window. The rain is now torrential. *Damn.* He remembers that he left *Byrne's Complete Book of Pool Shots* on the pool table. It will be mush by the time he gets home. He'd really like to leave, mostly to check up on Sophie, to see if she's inside—sometimes she sits in the rain for hours and that scares him—but he can't. He's got three international visitors driving pink buses and Mr. Whit will not like that at all.

Bill leans over, loudly whispers to Wilson, "Frankly, I don't know what all the fuss is about. Look at him. He's wearing a skirt and his eyes are purple—that's the fruitcake color. Everybody knows that."

"Sh," one of the women scolds.

"Tell us about your home country," another asks Sòlas.

"What's there to say about Mars?" Bill says under his breath, giving Wilson a wink. Wilson laughs.

Danni gives them both an ugly look and hands Sòlas his coffee. "Two sugars with an inch of real cream," she says.

"You're a good woman," Sòlas says, and takes a sip. Coughs. "Lovely. Now, could I trouble you for a pillow?"

"Pushing his luck," Bill mutters.

"There's a couch in the corner," Danni says.

"Hard is better," he says. "I just need a little lower lumbar support to keep the pressure off my wings."

For a moment, everyone in the bar stops everything.

Wings? they all think.

"Wings?" Danni says.

Wilson wonders if they covered this type of situation at Quantico after he left.

The women titter. "I told you he was an angel," one says.

"Not even close," Sòlas says. "Just wings. Not very fancy. They're actually quite small."

Danni's hands sweat. The only wings she's ever seen took the special effects guy eight hours to apply. "You're kidding, right?"

"No," Sòlas says. "Wings run in my family."

His charming lilt makes it seem like a joke, but he is perfectly serious. Everybody, even Mandy the dog, takes a step back. The marmalade cat makes a run for it. In an elegant move, Sòlas pulls his shirt over his head with great flourish, a showman, and turns his back to the crowd.

"Wings," he declares.

His two puppeteers turn away from the boys in shorts on the TV and point to the small of Sòlas's back. "Ta-da!" they shout. Smile broadly. Wildly applaud. "Ta-da!"

The cautious crowd moves in for a closer look.

Indeed, at the base of Sòlas's spine there are two small wings. They're not birdlike, not covered with soft down. Nor are they as fragile as a butterfly's. They instead look like tiny webbed hands, the hands of a baby reaching.

Everyone—even Bill, who always has something to say about everything—is silent. Shocked.

On the television, someone scores. The crowd cheers. The sound is faint. The crones do not turn away to see what's happened. They are still pointing at the wings.

"Ta-da," they both say sadly, as if to suggest the burden of useless wings; how they serve as a constant reminder that you are different, but not different enough to soar.

Danni leans in closer. Much closer. She is so close that she can see tiny bones through the translucent pink skin. Instead of horrifying her, unfortunately, the sight of the two handlike extremities kicks her primal networking skills into high gear.

Ever the actress, Danni has never passed an outstretched hand without shaking it—that's just good business. And so, as a reflex, she squeezes the one closest to her. Gives it a firm shake. It feels cool in her palm. Dry as marble. Not at all what she expected.

Sòlas shivers. "Ah, lass," he sighs. Then laughs, but his voice is filled with remorse. "You've done it now. Legend has it that if you touch the wings, you have to be my bride."

The wing flutters slightly in her hand.

Everyone, including the Swedish crones, turns to look at Danni. She is unreadable. She stands very still, holding the small wing in her hand.

"Bride?"

She repeats the word slowly, as if trying to make sense of it. *Bride, love, marriage*—these are not lucky words for Danni.

"Bride?" she says again.

"Bride," Sòlas confirms. "But I'm a very good cook, if that's some comfort to you, darling."

"Bride?"

The word has finality. She releases the tiny wing. She now understands. Fully. And so, like a woman who has seen all manner of horror—some created by latex, some created by three ill-fated marriages—Danni does the only thing she can do. She screams.

It is not just any scream, however. World-class virtuoso that Danni Keene is, her scream is still a masterpiece—pitch-perfect, with a bold arc of fear and an appropriate coloration of titillated horror. It is the famed scream that Danni once delivered in the 1982 classic remake *I Married an Alien from Orange County, New Jersey— And He Never Picks Up His Socks.*

"They don't make screams like that anymore," esteemed drive-in movie critic Joe Bob Briggs once wrote of it. "Check it out!" And he was right. The years have not diminished its sheer genius. The scream's perfect glory rings in the ears of all within a two-block radius. Mandy, the great howling shih tzu, looks on in admiration, and is inspired to howl along. Wilson is moved to applaud, as are the two ancient Swedish puppeteers. They point at Danni's open mouth. Smile. Shout, "Ta-da!"

Sòlas makes a note not to take it personally.

Chapter Five

Sòlas MacKay's parents were famed clowns who worked for all the great gilded circuses in Europe—Circus Knie in Switzerland, Cirque d'Hiver in Paris, and Circus Krone in Germany. They had an F. Scott Fitzgerald air about them, brilliant and doomed. They performed in harlequin dress with tight black leather suits quilted in the traditional diamond pattern, bloodred lips, and shocking white faces.

Thrilling and reckless, they crossed the lines of all traditions. They were, by nature, harlequins (*arlecchini* in Italian, *arlequins* in French, and *Harlekine* in German), creatures with dark pasts.

Some say the origins of the name lie in Dante's *Inferno*, XXI, 118: one of the devils is called Alichino. In France, it is said that harlequins are emissaries of the devil, determined to chase damned souls out of the body with fear and laughter. Mostly fear.

In that sense, Sòlas's parents were true to the art. They twisted, turned, tumbled, crept, balanced, and swiveled. They threw themselves against walls, hoping to stick. They knotted themselves around each other in a sinuous embrace while elephants rolled them around the stage as if they were a ball. They set themselves on fire with bottles of Napoleon cognac.

Their violent grace was frightening.

But sometimes, they stood silent in the spotlight and watched the audience watch them. Their black leather suits faded into the darkness of the stage. Their shocking white faces and ripe lips seemed to float in space. And then, as if they were moved by a great innate sorrow, a single black tear would fall at the same time and at the same speed on each of their faces.

Their pain seemed so real that it often caused the tenderhearted to faint.

The press was amazed. Dubbed it "the Harlequin's Sorrow."

It was not at all what you'd expect from circus clowns, but that was precisely why they were famous.

Just before Sòlas turned twenty-two, his parents died in an accident while driving from the Carnevale di Venezia through the Alps. It was February. Snow. Ice. Steep winding curves. Their MG slid off the sheer side of a mountain and into an ice-capped lake. When told, Sòlas imagined his mother and father airborne in their small white car, the spoked wheels spinning snow-blind and aimless; the look of surprise on their pale harlequin faces, the two black tears falling.

It haunted him. He couldn't sleep. Being the elder of his parents' two sons, Sòlas inherited everything, which was a surprising amount of money. His parents were paid well and invested wisely. So Sòlas put his younger brother, Peter, in a boarding school and came to America to create his own art his own way.

As soon as Sòlas arrived, he began to forge a new kind of circus employing only puppets. These were not children's toys. Instead of being animated by strings or wires, or worn on the hand, they were huge solemn beasts, forged from clay, bamboo, and his own fancy. They were either carried or worn as a coat. They seemed to be alive.

As with most circuses, every performance began with a parade that featured exotic creatures walking the streets. But when the Rose and Puppet Circus came to town, instead of bejeweled pachyderms, there were puppets. Blocks filled with puppets, including a two-story Mother Earth—a towering ghostlike figure with a sad face holding a globe in her enormous hands. She was held up by dozens of people with poles, volunteers from the town itself. They made her dance.

The Rose and Puppet Circus was not so much a performance as a community event. Towns would pay Sòlas to help them build the circus of their dreams. It was, in the spirit of Dr. Seuss's *If I Ran the Circus,* their very own Circus McGurkus. It was also great fun. Sòlas and the people of each town would design the parade themselves and make their own masks. Each parade was different: there could be groups of townsfolk wearing elephant heads and riding unicycles, or marching as tigers in top hats, or driving as dolphins on motorcycles.

Whimsy always ruled the day.

When Peter was finally old enough, he joined Sòlas in America but announced that he had decided to study at the Ringling Brothers and Barnum & Bailey Clown College in Florida, thousands of miles away from his brother and his troupe in Vermont.

Sòlas was confused. He loved Vermont: the beauty of it, the clean air. It reminded him so much of the highlands of Scotland, but Peter wouldn't have it. He demanded that Sòlas divide their parents' estate, which had grown through the years, and give him his fair share.

Sòlas tried to reason with him. It wasn't about the money, he said. It was about legacy. "Clown College is beneath a MacKay," he told Peter. "They will teach you to be crass, obvious."

Although the college was quite famous at the time, rigorous and as difficult to enter as Harvard, the instructors taught an American style of clowning based on slapstick. The European approach is stylized, elegant, and sly.

"The money was given to me to do with as I see fit. I will not give our parents' money to you to throw your talent away," Sòlas told him. "If you walk out that door, you walk out penniless. Not one cent."

"You don't understand."

"No," Sòlas said, "you are the one who doesn't understand."

Then he took his brother into the ancient barn where all the puppets were kept. It was winter—well below zero. Brittle winds wailed through the slats in the barn's walls. Where horses once stood, the floor buckled into waves that the coming of spring would lessen, but only so much. Still, it was an amazing sight. Everywhere you looked, puppets and masks hung from the rafters, or were set in amused repose at make-believe tea parties, or sunning themselves on imaginary beaches, or standing silent as language waiting for the moment of use. It seemed like a small village. Waiting. The clay eyes watching. Throughout the cavernous space, the puppets moved in the fog of cold, animated themselves. No one was willing to give them life. Not now. Not in the bitter air of winter.

The two brothers stood so closely together that their breathing fell into the same rhythm. Their two broken hearts beat as one.

"What I understand is this—pageantry, elegance, heart. That's the world of a MacKay, that's our world. Not lapel flowers that squirt."

Peter was silent for a moment, and then said, "Your beasts are magical and beautiful, but I can't live under our parents' shadow any longer."

Sòlas was confused. "The circus works in the European tradition, as our parents did, but—"

"That's not it," Peter said, and picked up a puppet of an old woman. She was wearing a dress made entirely of bright yellow tissue-paper sunflowers. She was sitting in an armchair with smaller puppets, like children, at her feet. "What do you see?"

"La Nona, the Grandmother."

Peter shook his head.

"And those?" He pointed to a couple, two puppets in tuxedos and silk, placed as if in midwaltz.

"I call those Joy and Sorrow," Sòlas said.

Peter was insistent. "But what do you see when you look at them?"

"The dance of life. Sorrow takes the lead, but Joy is always there."

"But their faces. Who do you see when you look at them? Really look."

Sòlas had no idea what his brother was talking about. He shrugged. "I see my heart."

Peter was furious. "Don't you see? They all look alike. All the puppets' faces look exactly alike."

"Well." Sòlas shrugged. "That is to be expected. This is my style, my vision."

"No," Peter said. He was red-faced, shouting. The brittle winter winds rattled the boards of the old barn. Sòlas had no idea why he was so angry. His response seemed disproportionate to the situation. "Look closer," Peter insisted. Picked up another puppet and started to shake it. "Don't you see? Don't you see who these look like?"

"They look like the world in my head."

"Wrong," Peter shouted and threw the puppets to the ground. "How can you not see?"

Then he touched a single finger to the corner of his own eye; then to Sòlas's. And then, at the same time, and at the same speed, he traced an imaginary tear on each of their faces.

The Harlequin's Sorrow, Sòlas thought.

Peter's violet eyes, their mother's eyes, were unblinking. He whispered, his breath hot, "Every puppet—every beast, child, man, and woman in this barn—has our parents' faces. You re-create them over and over again.

"I can't live in their shadow any longer," he said.

Sòlas was stunned. He'd never realized. He pulled La Nona, the Grandmother, into his arms. Peter was right—the elegant line of her slender nose was his mother's. Overwhelmed, he didn't know what to say.

Peter left him in the barn, weeping. Sòlas never saw his brother again.

After a time, Sòlas contacted the college, but they had never heard of Peter. He had never even applied. Sòlas searched for him everywhere, but had no luck. Eventually, the memory of those violet eyes became a sorrow Sòlas just couldn't shake.

When Peter's body was found in Laguna Key—eyes and hands missing—the starving vultures had picked a good part of him clean. The only way the police could identify him was from an old driver's license in his wallet. He also had a slip of paper with Sòlas's phone number at the circus and a Web address, www.thehomelesssoul .com, written on it.

The Homeless Soul is Peter's website. It's one of those free sites filled with pop-up ads, but fairly sophisticated. It has a bulletin board where visitors post information about shelters, free health care, and day-labor opportunities. There's a chat room, links to the National Coalition for the Homeless, and a donation box, where you can give money to Peter using PayPal.

Sòlas hadn't expected poverty to be so high-tech. The Rose and Puppet's website is only slightly more advanced. The crones designed it and maintain it. All Sòlas knows about it is that they wanted something called Flash, which makes the puppets magically pop out and perform.

Secretly, Sòlas thinks the site is beautiful. It's wonderful to see Flash animation make his puppets come to life on their own—no strings, no one holding them. They dance and laugh. It's charming. The site is designed to attract an audience and keep the revenue stream going. The crones recently added an Internet gift shop, where they sell limited-edition prints of the circus's posters, Swedish folk art (mostly hand-carved statues of Elvis that a cousin of theirs makes), and Scandinavian techno-pop music—it's an odd mix but it's bringing in more cash than the performances do.

Still, there's something about the idea of a website that feels unseemly to Sòlas, too public.

For example, when Sòlas was awarded a MacArthur Fellowship, the website made life impossible. Often called genius grants, the fellowships come with a stipend of $500,000, paid out in equal quarterly installments over five years. The money allows artists to work without financial constraints.

It's an important award for an artist, the kind of thing you'd put on a website.

But a week after it was awarded, Sòlas's phone began to ring. Investment counselors, former girlfriends—it didn't stop ringing day or night. He had no idea why until he visited the site.

On the home page, the crones had created banners that read: "Sòlas named genius! We're rolling in kronor! Free money! Call for details!"

It was their idea of a press release.

And so, unlike the crones, Sòlas has a love-hate relationship with the Internet.

However, it's clear from his brother's website that all across the libraries of America, many of the poor and homeless embrace technology. They surf the Web, build sites, IM each other, and blog. Righteous Poverty Dude from Fresno wants to know where there's a day-labor gig near St. Stephen's shelter. Dragon Slayer of Memphis is looking for a car to live in that's not too close to the freeway— maybe a late-1970s model with a bench seat. And the Homeless Soul—Sòlas's brother, Peter—was chronicling his life, a life that Sòlas had not been part of.

It was all very surprising. Peter wrote about snorkeling off the Florida Keys and roasting crabs for dinner like a modern-day Huck Finn. But there were also other entries, like one about a friend who went back to Wisconsin and froze to death or how Peter had lost a toe to gangrene, that unsettled Sòlas.

According to his blog, Peter worked off an old laptop given to him by Catholic Charities and pirated wireless connections from the lobbies of hotels and coffee shops. He made short films with a digital camera that he bought with his income from PayPal contributions. His brother lived in a world that Sòlas never imagined.

What was most surprising to him was that Peter had a following. His readers would post comments, some of them hopeful, some helpful. Some very angry.

"You are a disgrace," wrote the Avenging Angel. "You talk about the need for rights for the homeless, but you have a better life than most middle-class Americans. Get a job."

Then there was Peter's photo.

The image was grainy, ghostlike. After all those years, Peter still wore wire-rimmed glasses and had that permanent bemused look on his face. His hair and beard had turned into wisps of clouds. His face was too tan and ridged with age.

Twenty years is a very long time not to see your own brother. Sòlas had no idea who his brother really was—but those violet eyes, their mother's eyes, were still kind, still laughing.

Peter's last post read:

> *The word "homeless" is not quite accurate. Abandoned cats and dogs—these are the truly homeless. Those of us who eat what you do not want, wear what you no longer need, and stand on the street corners with open hands—we are not homeless. We are the lost, yes. But our home is with you.*
>
> *We are the lost among you.*

One month later, a security guard named Wilson found Peter, his body tossed away in the trash.

Chapter Six

According to Buddy's research, Barry Manilow doesn't eat red meat. He loves almond ice cream. His favorite drink is water, although he enjoys the occasional glass of white wine. He is also partial to a Snickers bar, roast chicken, and shrimp cocktail.

Buddy doesn't care anymore. There's a busload of puppeteers in town. When they pulled in, Buddy pulled out. You just can't compete with puppets. He knows that. The gig is over. So on his way out of the Bad Girl's Bar & Grill, he lifted a bottle of tequila and the rack of ribs that Danni had set aside for her own dinner.

He now sits behind the Dumpster, pork grease and barbecue sauce glazing his face, holding the unopened bottle in his hand, contemplating his next move.

Flies buzz around his head. Thoughts, too.

Everybody is inside the bar fussing over the puppet people. Every now and then he can hear a laugh, or two. They don't even notice that he's gone. *That's okay,* he thinks. It's quiet out by the Dumpster, nice. The security light is easy to unscrew and so he does. He likes the darkness; it calms him.

Perfect place to kill a fella, he thinks. *That homeless guy must have really pissed somebody off.*

"It was a real pro at work, gentlemen," Buddy tells the flies. He wipes his face on his sleeve and applauds a hit well done by saluting the heavens with a rib bone.

Then he tosses it into the trash.

Because the Dumpster is still off-limits, the bone bounces off the crime-scene tape and lands back at Buddy's feet. The flies cover it, greedy.

"Perfect place. Great choice," Buddy says to them and feels a pang of professional jealousy.

Buddy is a part-timer in the hit world. The rest of the time he's unemployed, so he hopes to make it big someday—but it's going to be difficult. After the mishap in Albuquerque, word got around. Referrals are not as robust as they once were. And it's really unfair, too. How was Buddy supposed to know that there are forty-six species of snake found in New Mexico and only eight are poisonous? Who knows that kind of thing?

To Buddy, a snake is a snake. You fly into town, go out to the desert, turn over a rock, grab a bagful, then fling them—fling them hard, fling them fast—then run. It's that simple. That's the way anybody would do it.

Anybody who isn't some sort of snake Einstein—which, unfortunately, the mark was. He took one look at his lap, laughed, drove over to Buddy's employer's house, and ran him over with his SUV.

But how was that Buddy's fault?

Buddy warned the guy, pop 'em and run. That's the way to go. None of this poetic shit like snakes.

"I can guarantee you this—poetry will only kill you if you have to listen to it being read by some sissy. I know this for a definite fact," he said.

But the guy wouldn't listen. So Buddy threw the snakes—he followed the contract to the absolute letter—and then his employer's widow wouldn't pay up.

Unfreakingbelievable.

It still raises his blood pressure to think of it. The lack of venom was not Buddy's fault. It was a technical difficulty. He explained that. It's not like she couldn't afford to pay—she was rich now that her old man was knocked off. She was rolling in dough. She should have been ecstatic.

Yet, somehow, she was mad at Buddy. It just didn't make sense to him. He tried to reason with her. "Hey, face it. Your husband was a loser. What kind of a guy pays to have snakes dropped on the lap of his wife's boyfriend?"

That's when she called the police.

POP AND RUN it says on Buddy's business cards, and that's what he does the best. Or used to. Now, he's killing them with karaoke.

And he doesn't even look like Barry Manilow. Buddy looks more like a Chia pet, stout with unruly hair growing all over his body. That's why he had to buy the dog—that Fitz-Zoo, or whatever the hell it's called. But the dog is a good cover. Damn thing could be Manilow's twin: that is, of course, if the famed crooner were a lot shorter and canine.

But it now appears as if it's Albuquerque all over again.

Busloads of puppets, Buddy thinks. *Damn. Everybody loves a ventriloquist. I'm screwed.*

He really hasn't been the same since *The Ed Sullivan Show* was canceled and Señor Wences died. All Buddy needs is a wig for his fist and some lipstick, and he's right there again—an eight-year-old with a blue-light TV tan.

Ventriloquist Envy—it's not a pretty thing.

Buddy is convinced that they'll be lining up to see this Scottish ventriloquist, even though Sòlas is not a ventriloquist. Of course, Buddy doesn't know that but even if he did, that doesn't matter. Ventriloquist Envy impairs all rational thought.

Ventriloquists are a damn huge draw, Buddy thinks. *Better than heavy metal. And ventriloquist lovers are a thirsty lot. Big boozers, everybody knows that. Danni will be printing money with that crowd.*

Mr. Scooter will definitely not be pleased.

Mr. Scooter is Buddy's code name for his actual employer on this current gig. The one thing Buddy knows for sure is that when you're a professional enforcer like himself, even a part-timer, you need code names.

For example, Buddy is not his real name, either. He's cagey that way. His real name is Florence. He was named after his father.

Some people think this explains a lot.

"The mojo of ventriloquists is omnipotent," he tells the flies. They buzz in agreement, continue to gnaw the wayward rib bone.

Buddy knows he must do something preemptive soon, or he and that bone will have a lot in common. *But what?*

"Because I could not stop for Death," he recites to the flies, "He kindly stopped for me. The carriage held but just ourselves and immortality."

Poetry, even though it won't really kill a guy, helps Buddy think. And that's his little secret. He closes his eyes for a moment, lets the words soak in.

"That's that Dickinson dame," he says to the flies. "Killer stuff.

If there was justice in the world, I could just spew that at you and you'd fall over flat."

Buddy goes flush, feels a trifle sheepish about exposing his love of nineteenth-century verse to a group of insects. But he can't help himself. "It's punchy stuff, man," he explains.

The flies seem to understand. One of them lands on his hand. Buddy looks into its tiny green eyes.

"Yeah," he says, gently. "She's that 'I heard a fly buzz when I died' broad. She liked you guys."

The fly makes a grateful sound, a warm buzz, like a sigh. Seems to understand. Tilts its head, curious.

Then Buddy swats it. Flicks its dead body onto the ground.

At that moment it comes to him. His salvation. He knows how to get out of this one. It's a classic. He will do exactly what he always does when life deals him an Albuquerque.

Blackmail.

Sounds good, he thinks. Perfect, in fact.

What's he got to lose? He was hired to close that Danni woman down, so he torched the car, but that didn't work. And now he's singing with a damn dog.

"And I hate that dog," he explains to the flies. "Hoppin' mop of a mongrel."

And now there are puppets.

Buddy twists open the gold seal on the tequila. He knows he should get up and get Mandy from the bar. He left her tied around the bottom of the Copacabana sign. *Dogs like that ain't cheap,* he thinks. *And you can't buy them by the pound, like 84 percent ground round.*

But Buddy doesn't move. He'd rather sit with the flies and rue his fate.

"These ventriloquist guys got the life," he tells them. "Señor Wences was a hundred and three when he died. He was a god. They named a street after him. Right next to the damn Ed Sullivan Theater in New York City. Damn Señor Wences Way. Nobody ever named a damn street after Barry Manilow."

The flies have no comment on this injustice. Buddy watches them buzz the Dumpster and is suddenly struck with one of the undeniable truths of the world.

"If Manilow would get a damn puppet, he could have his own damn street," he says, and, in the excitement of the revelation, the flush of the moment, Buddy takes a slug of tequila. Then spits it out. Coughs.

"Tastes like dirt."

He's never had tequila, rarely drinks. Since everybody wants him to sing "Margaritaville," he's trying to figure out what the draw is.

"Damned if I know," he says, and tosses the bottle aside. Buddy makes the famed Señor Wences fist. "Tequila I can live without, but every man needs a puppet.

"Puppets are soulful shit."

Buddy imagines the golden lights of the Ed Sullivan Theater. Imagines the hound-dog host smiling in the wings, the words *Really big shew* still ringing in the rafters, and that plate-spinning guy getting ready to go on next. Buddy is overwhelmed, lost in the moment. And so he closes his lips and sings through his teeth, "I write the songs that make the whole world sing."

And somewhere around the second chorus, with Manilow's lyrics vibrating against his clenched molars, Buddy suddenly understands their profound implication.

"I am music," he belts, "and I write the songs."

The words give Buddy a cosmic shiver, just like Dickinson does. He suddenly feels filled with righteous fervor.

"Man," he says, "if Manilow had a puppet, he'd be a god."

Then he picks up his cell phone. *Blackmail time.*

An hour later, Buddy understands just what a bad idea this is.

Chapter Seven

Happy hour is over. The early bird specials are no longer valid. Tonight's *Wheel of Fortune* is just a memory. The tiki bar is open, but the god Lono, in all his manly wooden splendor, is the only one there. All over Laguna Key, residents count out the next day's prescriptions, surf the Internet, let the dog out, have a smoke, finish the crossword, and lock up for the night—it's 8:00 p.m. and their world is silently winding down.

The rain has stopped. The air smells new.

The oatmeal, however, is cold.

"I'm sorry," Danni says. She is standing at the door of Sòlas's old school bus. Its name is SILENCE. The Rose and Puppet Circus has set up camp in her parking lot for a while. It only seemed right. It was late. They'd come a long way. The engine in Sòlas's bus was shot. He could fix it, but he needed parts and there isn't an auto store in Laguna Key, or nearby. In fact, there's not much around at all. No stores. No hotels. No cafés. No campground. No public beach. No public anything—Danni's bar is on the only land in town that isn't owned by the Laguna Key Development Corporation. Until morning, there was really no place else for Sòlas and his troupe to go.

Besides, she thinks a circus could be great for business. Hopes she can convince them to stay and perform.

Danni is having Cirque du Soleil dreams, with $200 tickets and two-drink minimums. She can already hear the eerie operatic cyclone of circus music and see the old Swedish crones hanging upside down under the big top, as those in Cirque do, performing a version of the Spanish web, tethered to the tent top with bungee cords, hanging over the rapt audience, spinning around each other in large languorous arcs, their bodies wrapped in long white silk as if they were elegantly reedy Chinese acrobats rather than "Ta-da!" kinds of clowns.

But Rose and Puppet is just not that kind of circus.

Danni doesn't know that, so she is standing at the door of Sòlas's bus, bowl in hand. The briny air has the edge of a chill. The sun has set. The interior of the bus, softly lit with candles, feels warm, friendly. The last bus, WATCHFULNESS, is dark; it's filled with supplies. But the next bus over, the one named GRACE, is where the crones live. They are singing a simple Swedish folk song. One is fiddling. One plays the button accordion. Their voices are so sweet, and the music is so plainly lovely, it makes Danni itch.

"For you," she says, and thrusts the bowl of oatmeal into Sòlas's hands.

He sniffs it. Cautious. "And this is?"

Up close, in the candlelight, Sòlas's eyes take on a luminous quality. *Lapis,* she thinks. *They look like damn lapis.*

"Oatmeal," she says, and blushes—which is an unfortunate

turn of events. Every ill-fated marriage started with Danni blushing like an idiot. And here she is again. And that makes her angry. And when Danni's angry, she likes to break things. As did her characters.

In *The Well-Bred Zombies of Beacon Street* Danni once broke an entire china service for twenty-four, complete with sugar bowl and creamer. It hyperextended her elbow, but she won a Razzie for her performance. "Never has so much Mikasa given its life for so little," the Golden Raspberry Award Foundation members wrote.

It made her oddly proud. And now, she's angry in a china-free zone and is not sure what to do about it. She has an overwhelming urge to put her fist through a window, but is pretty sure that unlike in the 1979 remake *The Teenage Vampires of P.S. 101,* the bus window is made of real glass, not sugar. And Danni's pretty sure that real glass really hurts.

Civilian life sucks, she thinks.

Sòlas, seemingly unaware of Danni's emotional maelstrom and the imminent plate tossing that it might portend, sniffs the bowl again. "And you are bringing me oatmeal because . . ."

"It's your national dish."

"Ah." He seems surprised.

"A peace offering. Didn't mean to scream—"

"Ah," he says, again.

Oatmeal is obviously not Sòlas's national dish. He gently sets the bowl down on the driver's seat of the bus. "I'll save it for later," he says. Danni cringes. Even in the candlelight it looks like a bowl of gritty cement.

"It was a very nice scream, you know," Sòlas says. "Wonderful pitch. You have quite a gift."

"Thanks."

"No. Thank you."

"Thanks."

"And thanks for letting us stay. Very kind."

"Thanks."

"Thanks."

"Well."

"Yes."

Sòlas and Danni have now exhausted all small-talk opportunities they have, so they stand quietly for a moment and listen to the Swedish crones singing.

Sòlas is barefoot but still wearing his kilt with a clean white T-shirt. His famed wings are hidden, but the shirt is loose around the waist. In the glow of candlelight he looks kind, gentle, and, unfortunately, handsome.

"Do you have anything I can break?" Danni asks.

"Yes, as a matter of fact, I do," he says. "I have a mixed set of china in the back somewhere."

"You do?"

"I like to toss them about when Scotland enters the World Cup. Break a few plates, good for the soul. Gets very frustrating. We're the world champions of elephant polo, you know, but football is not our strong suit."

"Elephant polo?"

"Masterful game!" he says, suddenly animated. "Used to be a bit of a player myself. It's more dangerous than that sissy horse polo the English are so fond of."

Sòlas is a man who knows his large herbivorous mammal sports, she thinks.

"Did you know that elephant polo was cofounded by a Scotsman?"

Danni did not. She now, however, understands how a thing like that could happen. After all, the Scots invented golf, a game that appears to be about trying to hit a very small ball a very long distance with a very expensive stick. Elephant polo makes complete sense.

"You know what the biggest problem with elephant polo is?" he asks.

There are just so many possibilities that Danni doesn't even know where to begin. So, "No," she says.

"You need a damn speedy elephant to pull it off!"

Luckily, before more beast polo chat ensues, the crones break into a loud song with a silly popcorn beat. The fiddle and the accordion play tag within the melody.

Jag älskar min Mac för den är så uppenbar, så användbar, så underbar Den är det enda jag vill ha.

"Some ancient song?" Danni asks.

"Love song," Sòlas says.

Just my luck, she thinks.

He translates, "I love my Mac," he sings, his voice Broadway pure. "Because it's so obvious, so usable, so wonderful. It is the only thing I want."

"Mac? Your clan?"

"Our computers. My assistants are crazy about the Internet. They're always in the chat rooms. Can barely get them out."

Sòlas smiles at Danni like a man who understands the power of his own charm.

Danni looks over his shoulder and into the bus. In the center of a thicket of puppets there is a hammock hanging with a glowing laptop on it. The puppets seem bemused.

"Our laptops are rigged to a wireless satellite system."

"Really?"

"We Scots are not just a mystical race, lass. We are a technologically advanced society whose menfolk just happen to look good in plaid skirts."

She laughs, for the second time that night.

"You have a good laugh," he says. "It's strong and decent. Lilting as your scream."

"Don't try your charm on me. I know charm. Keene is an Irish name. We Irish invented charm."

"Is that what Keene means?"

"It means wise—as in we are wise to guys like you."

Sòlas laughs. "Fair enough."

"MacKay?"

"Mak-CUR-ee is how you'd say it in Gaelic. SOH-lus Mak-CUR-ee."

"And it means?"

" 'The people who specialize in infuriating their neighbors until they finally knock us all off,' " he says, and then he laughs, although it's a sad laugh. Danni can tell he's not joking.

"Everybody's gone?"

He nods. "An occupational hazard of warriors, I suppose."

Danni thinks of her bright yellow Hummer burning in the parking lot. "Well, I'm not that popular with the neighbors myself," she says.

The two are standing very close together. It's then that Danni notices the small ornate knife slipped into a garter on his leg. "What's that?"

"Ah, *sgian dubh*," he says. "Black knife. At formal occasions, you wear them tucked into the sleeve of your shirt. Some wear them in a garter. But it must always be hidden."

"Hidden from who? Or is it whom?" She laughs. But Sòlas is serious.

"The English," he says without hesitation. It is as if the answer is genetically encoded into him.

Danni pulls it from its scabbard to get a closer look.

Quickly, Sòlas takes the knife from her hand and slices his palm. Puts the knife back into the sheath.

The moment is shocking. "Why did you do that?" Danni says.

The cut is deep. Blood runs down his arm. Danni pales.

The crones have stopped their singing. The night feels too quiet.

"The blade can never be drawn without the taking of blood," Sòlas says plainly, as if it's a fact, nothing more. His hand is bleeding profusely. He looks at it a moment, and then wipes the blood onto his kilt.

"That'll stain," Danni says, but she can see by the look on Sòlas's face that, somehow, it already has. He takes off his clean white shirt and winds it around the wound so that it stops bleeding.

"Good night," he says, and turns away from her. In the small suns of the candlelight, she sees his wings flutter, aimless, all flesh and tiny bones, earthbound.

Chapter Eight

A faux-pearl moon hangs low and large over the Gulf of Mexico. Even with the naked eye, you can see its many silver seas: Serenity, Tranquillity, Crises, and Vapors. If you squint, you can see that they form a cameo pattern, and look a lot like Wilma Flintstone, the Queen of Bedrock, in the prime of her celebrity.

But Sophie does not squint. Blind, she just keeps walking. Her knitting, a near ocean of a shawl, is wrapped around her shivering body.

In the moonlight, she is Venus; hues of blue swirl around her, down the length of her, trail along at her feet.

Sophie has taken off her shoes; they were soaked, weighed her down. The sand is packed hard, like cement. She'd forgotten it could be like that. It hurts her shins to walk. The shore seems wider than she imagined. Five cars deep, she thinks. She'd once been to Daytona and saw the cars parked along the beach as if it were a shopping mall parking lot. She knows her condo is not too far away, but how far is at question.

She'll worry about that later. *He'll be here soon.*

The water feels cold against her feet. This time of year, without a storm in the gulf, the surf is weak. A recent outbreak of red tide has turned the gulf toxic, scattered the shore with fish gone belly-up. Every now and then, her feet slip on them. The air burns, feels thick in her lungs. She starts to cough hard.

"Why am I doing this?" she says. Hopes no one is around to hear.

She can't turn back, though. Not yet. Not until he comes back.

Each step is difficult. Sophie has to be careful. And she is, but it's easy to misjudge. What feels like a plastic bag is a jellyfish. Still alive, it curves under the arch of her foot. She slips. Hits her head on the ragged edge of an old mast from a sailboat.

"Damn it."

The wood is rotted, soft, but she hits it hard. Splinters dig into her scalp.

"Damn it all."

She has no idea what she landed on, but the pain is profound. Sophie lies still for a moment in the heap of dead fish, rotted wood, and broken shells. In the moonlight, she looks as if she has washed ashore, too. Her long blue shawl is tangled in seaweed and wicking up water. A hermit crab scurries between the curls of her long black hair.

If Wilson were to step onto his deck right now, he would see that he is right—she is, indeed, a landlocked mermaid, dreaming of the sea and yet drowning in it.

She thinks of him and imagines what Wilson would say if he saw her like this.

"Don't be such a drama queen."

He tells her that all the time. "You're blind—which means you'll never know that your socks don't match, so life is good."

Sophie now laughs at the thought. *Where the hell is Wilson when you need him?*

Home, she thinks. Snoring. Can't tangle him up in this mess. Still, surprisingly, she misses him.

Her head throbs. She can feel a thin line of blood run down the back of her neck; it gives her goose bumps. Underneath her, tiny crabs scurry deeper. Coquinas bury themselves. She can feel them shift in the sand: it's unnerving. A cold wave laps up against her left hand, feels like an electric current. Panic is not an option. She takes a few deep breaths and smells the rot of the wood from the mast that's underneath her body. Feels it carefully.

"Okay," she says. "I can do this."

Sophie tries to picture the scene in her mind. Her occupational therapist told her to do this, to help her get her bearings. The gulf must be to my left, she thinks. The condos, then, are behind me, to the right.

She slowly sits up. "It's fine. It's fine," she says.

And, for a moment, it is. She is nearly standing again when a large wave crashes around her, pulling her back onto the sand. She gulps for air. She was closer to the gulf than she thought. *Stupid.*

The undertow brings a school of stingrays. Dying, confused, slick as ice, they wash over her, frantic. They seem to be everywhere. Their tails slash out at her hands, face, and feet. Burn and slice. The rays are as blind as she, and twice as afraid.

But Sophie knows all about stingrays. All divers, even blind ones, know about rays. Stay calm, she tells herself, no quick moves. They don't mean to hurt. I'm just in their way.

Her skin is scored. The cuts burn. Saltwater stings.

"I must look like Carrie on prom night."

It's the only Stephen King book she's ever read, and she is only mildly pleased that she can make a literary reference at a time like this.

Sophie tries again to stand, but steps directly on a stingray's raised tail. The stinger breaks off in the arch of her foot. The pain is searing, as elegant as a razor's edge, but she refuses to scream. Acid rises from her stomach up to her throat. The rancid air of salt and rot overwhelms. But she will not scream. She will not panic. An infection will soon follow. She knows that. But screaming is weak, and doesn't help anything. And it might bring Wilson. That's the last thing she wants.

I can do this, she thinks, but feels the poison rise up in her leg. She pulls out the stinger, but the tip breaks off in the meat of her foot.

Then she hears it again: the sound of an airplane flying low, too low, the rumble of it.

"Coward," she says, and isn't sure who she means exactly. Maybe herself.

Since Sophie's father moved her to Laguna Key, she has heard that airplane buzz the beach outside her condo every Monday and Wednesday. It's very odd. There are no landing strips nearby. No airports of any size. At first, she thought it was a Coast Guard plane, but the station is too far away. She once asked Wilson about it.

"Must be somebody trying to get your attention," he said and laughed.

But Sophie wasn't laughing. Wilson was right. She's sure of it. The engine sounds so familiar.

It's Wednesday. So here she is. On the beach. Blind. Waiting. Obviously, it's what he wants.

The plane rumbles by. Low.

Sophie feels an edge of panic. She's wet and bloody, and the shawl around her is now filthy and drags her down. The poison in her leg is making it swell, go numb. She's vulnerable. Anything can happen. But she doesn't let herself think of that.

Sophie struggles to stand. Shaky, she finally makes it to her feet. She wants to continue walking on even though she has no idea where she's going. No idea where this beach ends, or what it looks like. She's never been on it before.

She doesn't want him to find her looking helpless. She doesn't need his help. Not anymore. Doesn't want it.

She is still standing when the plane takes another pass, but this time it sounds as if it's farther down the beach. Sophie panics. Wonders if he has the searchlights on and if he really is searching for her, or just seeming to. Wonders if it really is him.

He circles low again. Then closer. He's so low that sand kicks up into her face. The sound of his engine vibrates through her body. Sophie suddenly thinks about that homeless man. He died two days ago. Monday. Wonders if she heard the plane the night of his death. Mondays and Wednesdays.

Can't be, she tells herself, it isn't possible—but isn't sure she believes it.

But if there is a connection, it's too late now.

The airplane, she believes, is a Piper Tri-Pacer. If she's right, this one has had several run-ins with gravity and more with the law. This particular plane is a 1957 relic made of canvas and steel tubes and is flown by cables. It's a collector's plane, usually. This one is rusted, with cobbled-together patches. But it can cruise at about 120 miles per hour and carry about 643 pounds. It features four sets of radios, none of which work consistently.

Not exactly FAA approved.

When it buzzes Sophie for the last time, it is so low that it feels as if she can nearly reach up and touch it. The heat of that makes her flush. Her entire right side is now numb. She feels nauseous. Her shawl is so heavy that she can hardly hold it around her shoulders any longer.

This is stupid, she thinks, and coughs. Stupid to be blind. Stupid to be here.

"What the hell do you want from me?" she shouts, not so much at the airplane, but at heaven itself.

It's then that the pilot drops his payload—on Sophie.

Hundreds of silk rose petals fall down from the night sky, flutter in the silver light of the faux-pearl moon. Red as true hearts, they quickly cover her and the ocean of her shawl and mix with the dead fish beneath her feet, pile up over the dying stingrays that thrash wildly around her.

Sophie drops to her knees, exhausted, and rolls as if she's on fire. But the petals keep coming. Piling higher, deeper. Faster.

It feels as if she's drowning in them. And she is.

Chapter Nine

The best thing about key lime pie martinis is that they are suitable to be served with absolutely nothing. They make food taste wretched. They are designed for drinking's sake, no apology necessary.

The martini combines a nearly lethal dose of vanilla vodka, key lime liqueur from the Netherlands, a little pineapple juice, a little cream, and a tiny twist from a key lime. Then it's shaken over ice, poured into a toasted-graham-cracker-crumb-rimmed martini glass, and garnished with whipped cream—as much whipped cream as you want. Usually a lot.

And then you drink. Usually a lot.

At times like this, Danni likes to keep the commercial whipped cream dispenser handy and a box of nitrous oxide cartridges nearby just in case it runs out.

"This is not your mama's Reddi-wip," the restaurant supplier told her. And it isn't. The dispenser is big, nasty sounding, and silver. And, thanks to the nitrous oxide, this bad boy can shoot whipped cream down your throat faster than you can swallow it.

Danni knows. She's tried it.

"God bless nitrous oxide," she says as the whipped cream fills her mouth and makes her cheeks look like twin snowballs.

Danni knows that she has to be careful, though. Nitrous oxide can lead to "tragic physical consequences"—it says that on the order form. Brain injury tops the list and is closely followed by nausea, vomiting, disorientation, and a temporary loss of motor control.

Of course, the same can be said of key lime pie martinis.

Danni has already sucked back nearly half a can of whipped cream and a substantial amount of martinis—it's difficult to tell how many; she lost count after two. She's really not much of a drinker. Most times, she's just in it for the cream.

It's 1:00 a.m. The bar is officially closed, but no one's been in for hours. The lights are turned down low. Tiki music, with its bongo exotica beat, provides a goofy circa-1950s sound track. Every now and then there's a duet between an electric guitar and a xylophone, a male chorus booming the sacred Polynesian chant "Um ba-ba-hey-hey" and the ever-present drum machine mixing up a mai tai melody.

Danni isn't paying attention.

She can't stop thinking about Sòlas: those damn eyes, that charming lilt. Even that freakish little wing thing—she sort of likes that, too. And he likes to break china.

Damn, she thinks, how often can you find a guy who makes puppets, plays professional sports—okay, it *is* elephant polo, but still—and appreciates the fine art of breaking china?

But she can't fall in love with this guy. Can't risk another heartache. So, right now, she is reciting the litany of her husbands over and over again in her head. Trying to remind herself just how bad she is at love. She often counts her husbands before she falls asleep at night, like sheep. Black sheep.

They were all very handsome, all very charming, and all very good at leaving—and taking a good hunk of her money with them. There was Richard the First, the Older: winter wrapped around the curls of his hair. Phillip the Silent, the Youngest: his heat-resistant heart. James the Last: an eroding rocky coast.

The sentiment is not exactly hers. The litany is actually Danni's audition monologue, which came from an off-off Broadway show she did back in the days when she dreamed of working her way up from the chorus to the marquee and having late-night dinners at Sardi's and fans who waited in the cold alley behind the Majestic Theatre on West Forty-fourth for her to sign their *Playbill*. Back before she started screaming for a living.

A long time ago.

Still, Danni did have three husbands. Each one was "forever." Each one was a mystery. Each one was gone. It just sounds better when you toss a little poetry in.

So Danni is officially feeling sorry for herself—feeling old and ordinary—when Mandy, the small forgotten dog that bears a striking resemblance to Barry Manilow, bites her.

Mandy had no choice. Somebody let her off her leash a long time ago and she's eaten everything off the floor and has woken up from her nap and needs to go out. Biting is the only way she knows to get someone's attention.

"Where did you come from?"

The small dog bites again.

"Why are you biting me?"

Not much for small talk, the dog takes another nip.

"Stop that!"

Then another.

The yipping shih tzu named Mandy lunges repeatedly at the

drunken Danni in the way that only a small tawny dog can—all tiny teeth and determination.

The moment bears an uncanny resemblance to the 1981 sleeper hit *Yorkies from Mars.*

"What do you want from me?" Danni whines.

Mandy runs toward the back door of the bar. Scratches and whimpers—the universal canine sign for "I need to go out."

Danni understands.

"Good girl," she says. "Good girls go pee-pee outside." She grabs the nearby fire extinguisher, the one next to the kitchen. "I'll go out with you. Damn vultures are still looking for a handout."

She opens the door. It's dark, except for the moon and a scattering of stars. Mandy isn't going anywhere. Danni nearly trips over her. The door slams behind them. Locks.

"Shit," Danni says. Then hears a hiss.

The vultures, indeed, are back in the Dumpster. The bright yellow police tape has been torn away. Their slick black wings are beating. They turn to Danni and the small dog. The foulness of their breath is overwhelming.

"You guys remind me of one of my husbands," she says, but is too drunk to decide if it's number two or number three. "Maybe number one."

Either way, she thinks, this will be fun.

Danni laughs as she yanks the red safety pin off the fire extinguisher, aims the hose, and squeezes the lever hard. In an instant, foam and feathers are everywhere.

"Chickens!" she shouts after the fleeing birds. "You're nothing but a bunch of chickens with carnival-barker hair!"

Danni is not really sure what she means by this, but she likes the way it sounds.

"And by the way, you're not supposed to be nocturnal, so go to bed."

The vultures are gone, but Mandy is still whimpering, cowering at her feet. Danni turns her attention to the small shaking dog. Gets down on her knees. "It's okay," she says. Kisses Mandy's forehead. "Go pee-pee now. It's safe."

Mandy shakes even harder. Hides her head under Danni's arm.

The sight of such a small dog trembling breaks Danni's heart. "There's nothing in there. Just old meat and trash," she says gently. Picks her up and carries her to the Dumpster to prove it.

The moon is full overhead, but it feels oddly dark. Danni suddenly realizes why. The security light is not on. The bulb has been placed next to the Dumpster. She picks it up. It's not broken. She shakes it. It's still good. She turns around. Feels a chill.

Mandy begins to bark. "Sh. Sh," Danni says. Suddenly feels sober. "Everything is okay," she says but isn't sure she really believes it. As she leans into the Dumpster, she opens up her cell phone. The blue light is bright. "Sort of a flashlight," she explains to the small dog.

Then she stops.

Inside the Dumpster, Buddy lies faceup. What's left of his eyes seems to look to the sky. Mandy leans in. Licks her master's slack face.

For the first time in her life, the It Girl of Scream—Danni Keene, Slasher Queen—is absolutely silent. Her mouth is open, but there is no sound. She can't move. Can barely breathe.

Danni's never seen anyone dead before—really dead, not movie dead. It feels as though someone's thrown a switch inside her brain. On some level, that's true.

Chapter Ten

Danni Keene never wanted to own a tiki bar. She bought what is now known as the Bad Girl's Bar & Grill as a preservation project of sorts.

When it opened in 1954, the place was called Tiki Gardens. It wasn't just a bar, however. It was much more. It was, in fact, the South Seas. Or, at least, that's what owner Gordon Prescott was going for. He was stationed over there at the end of the Korean War and, like so many other vets of his time, came back a changed man—a Trader Vic kind of guy.

Tiki Gardens was Prescott's homage to Polynesia. He built it with love and the money he made running a casino out of the army's motor pool, in addition to a very creative application of the GI Bill.

Tucked into a nook on the west coast of Florida, Tiki Gardens was twenty-five acres of gulf-front property, including a vast mangrove forest knotted with banana, mango, and orange trees.

A huge surfing tiki, the god Kuka'ilimoku, greeted you as

you pulled in. Squat, toothy, and posed as if catching a wave, the square-headed icon, like most tikis, was a spiritual figure with a big mouth and several identity issues. For example, Ku, as he was familiarly known, was also called Ku'ulakai, or Ku of the Sea's Abundance, when he served as the god of fishing. But as the god of war, he was Kuka'ilimoku, or Ku, the Snatcher of Land.

It's an efficient, yet psychotic, system. Prescott used to tell people that his surfing Kuka'ilimoku was the god of fun—unless, of course, you tried to run out on the bill.

Beyond the wooden deity there was a village of tiny rental cabins with palm fronds glued onto tar-paper roofs. The sign that hung on a rusted hook read MODERN EFFICIENCIES, which meant that each tiny cabin had a tiny air conditioner wedged into the tiny window, each had a tiny refrigerator the size of a suitcase, and each had a tiny oven that was just the right size to reheat a rack of ribs or warm smoked mullet—both of which Prescott sold on-site—but nothing more. If you wanted to watch television, you'd have to go to the lobby. If you wanted to use the telephone, Prescott had one for emergencies only. The water was well water with a cranky septic system. Radios were not allowed. Shuffleboard was king.

But it was tiki heaven. There were gangs of wild monkeys—fringe-faced vervets—that stripped the mango trees bare, ate the peanuts kids bought for a nickel, and overturned trash. There were flocks of screeching wild parrots and schools of red carp swimming aimlessly in plastic lagoons. There were orchids, fat and fragrant, and Venus flytraps, toothy and waiting.

And, in the center of it all, in what is now the Bad Girl's Bar & Grill, the gift shop served free orange juice and sold lava lamps, authentic Hawaiian muumuus, saltwater taffy, and orange-blossom perfume. Sarsaparilla was served at the bar. Don Ho played on a continuous loop.

When she was a little girl, Danni and her parents would drive their Oldsmobile here all the way from Ohio for their summer vacation. Their car was black. The ride was long. And, because the air conditioner always overheated the engine, it was oven-hot.

They didn't care.

They cranked the windows down and drove as fast as they could through the red clay of horse country and its wood-smoke air; through the mountains, with their blue haze and falling rocks; through the city, with its cacophony of weaving cars and wide-turning trucks, to Tiki Gardens.

Gordon Prescott was an old army buddy of Danni's dad. She remembers everything about him: the ever-present pipe, his huge barrel chest, the well-cultivated resemblance to Hemingway, and the cackle of his laugh.

Prescott's wife left him while he was at sea many years ago, well before Danni was born. He never remarried, although he didn't seem unhappy about it. Through the years, he had a few girlfriends that Danni could remember. But what she remembers the most about Prescott was that he genuinely liked children.

When Mr. P. wasn't smoking mullet and ribs to sell to guests for lunch, he was leading safaris of children through the man-grove forest in search of the elusive Florida skunk ape, a creature that in other parts of the world is sometimes known as the yeti, and Danni loved to come along.

Back then, the forest seemed prehistoric, more like a swamp than anything, and was fully accessible only by boat. Fringed with trees, some five stories tall, it was dark and cool. Roots tangled around each other, reaching out like unsure arms. Flocks of squawking flamingos, pink as the shrimp they ate, hummed like so many didgeridoos. Albino egrets pecked and screeched. Spotted crabs took cover in the mud, nudged the oysters loose, and scared the snakes.

In the years that Danni and her family went to Tiki Gardens, she never once spotted a yeti. She saw the mating ritual of the frigate birds, how they puff up their red chests and gobble like a turkey. And she did meet a boy from New Jersey, who puffed out his sunburned chest when he gave her her first kiss.

But no yeti.

She did, however, learn how to snorkel, how to smoke mullet, and how to make coquina stew with the tiny slips of clams that burrowed on the beach.

She also learned the secrets of the thicket of land that is now known as Laguna Key.

"It's a sacred place," Mr. P. used to tell her. Never explained why.

In the end, Mr. P. was bullied into selling off parts of Tiki Gardens to the Laguna Key Development Corporation. Although he had no proof that the Development Corporation was behind any of the fires or dead monkeys, or the earthmover that appeared during the night and bulldozed the knots of banana, mango, and orange trees, it was difficult to think these were just random acts.

Eventually, all that remained was his rustic beachfront cottage, with its well water and cranky septic system, the dense mangrove forest, the gift shop—and his secret.

When Prescott finally died—a heart attack on the beach—he left instructions to his lawyer to sell Danni the property for a single franc of the Compagnie Française du Pacifique, the currency of Tahiti.

"You were always the bad girl," the note to her read. "Now do me proud. Get the bastards."

Then he explained the secret of Tiki Gardens. The note was odd and rambling, and at places it was quite confused. But it was clear to Danni that if exposed, the secret would have disastrous implications for the Laguna Key Development Corporation.

So the burning of her bright yellow Hummer was not a surprise. Danni is one of the last ones living who knows the secrets of this land. All she needs is proof—and to live long enough to do something about it.

Chapter Eleven

It is nearly dawn when the old man—a blues player, a Baptist turned Buddhist—comes upon Sophie lying in a sea of red silk rose petals, the tide rising around her, the waves crashing at her feet. He thinks she might be dead. Or at least dying. She is so still.

Not another one, he thinks. It was just a couple of days ago that they found that body in the trash, that homeless fella. *Sad state,* the old man thinks.

But the girl doesn't look homeless. Of course, neither does he. His well-worn shoes are impeccably shined. His three-piece suit, a winter-weight pinstripe, is only slightly frayed. The Marcel wave of his hair still has that brilliantine sheen.

"You okay, darling?" he says gently, and kneels beside her. His knees ache. The wool of his suit takes on water, sand. It's not quite dawn; still, he can see that her leg is swollen three times the normal size of a leg. "Can you hear me?" he asks.

Sophie's eyes remain closed. She slowly shakes her head.

The shawl that was wrapped around her is now a net filled with dead fish. *Malodorous,* he thinks. Slowly peels it off her clammy shoulders. Then feels her forehead: it's hot. An infection has taken hold. He lifts her into his tired arms. The fish rub against his last clean suit. Permeate the wool. He doesn't care.

"Am I dreaming?" she whispers.

"Dreaming dreams of a rose floating in a sea of petals," he says. It is what Buddha might say.

Sophie takes a wet silk petal and rubs it between her fingers. "Is that what this is?"

"Looks like."

"Are they red?" she asks. Her eyes are still closed.

That's when he remembers where he's seen her before. On the porch. Just up the beach. Not far. That blind gal.

"They are red as the blood of Aphrodite," he says.

"Bastard," she says.

Chapter Twelve

Up until the very moment that the three ball, traveling at a speed of about nineteen miles per hour, hit Wilson's sliding glass patio doors, he was of the firm belief that they were hurricane-proof.

The Florida building code requires that all new structures built on a Zone V floodplain, which means directly on the shore and at the highest risk, must have windows that would withstand an object being hurled at them at a speed of 140 miles per hour. That's the average speed that airborne particles, such as car doors, can come winging at you when a hurricane crawls onto shore. Impact-resistant windows have two layers of glass with a tough plastic laminate between them. Upon impact the glass might break, but the laminate remains and your house does not implode.

In a hurricane, the general rule of thumb is that imploding is never a good thing.

And, until that moment, Wilson had always assumed that Mr. Whit met the building code standards. But when the red ball hit the door with an enormous *crack,* the glass splintered. It wasn't even shatter-resistant. Wilson jumped from his bed. Looked at the clock: 6:07 a.m.

Sophie, he thought.

And there she was. Laid across his all-weather pool table, small fish tangled in her blue-black hair. She was seemingly washed ashore, the landlocked mermaid returned from the sea.

The deck was covered with broken glass, which shredded his feet, but Wilson didn't seem to notice. His hands were sweating as he picked Sophie up in his arms. She weighed less than he imagined, hardly anything at all.

"Took you long enough," she said.

He nearly smiled.

Chapter Thirteen

Opie is the first to arrive at the Bad Girl's Bar & Grill. It's 7:00 a.m., he's on time. He's always on time. Of course, it's easy for him. All he has to do is throw on a plaid shirt, paint a couple freckles across his nose, and gel his hair into a peak of a cowlick.

Gomer is next. "How-*dee*," he says when Floyd the barber strolls in with Thelma Lou and Barney. Aunt Bee, as usual, is a little late. Her Sunday hat has to sit just so—and it is not cooperating. Neither are her white gloves. Subtropical heat makes hands sweat and swell. The gloves are cutting off her circulation, which makes it tough to place the hat properly.

"My, my," she says over and over. The hat is precariously tilting to one side.

Humidity, even in the winter, is always a problem in Florida— lace collars curl, prim cotton dresses wilt like grocery-store roses.

By the time Laguna Key Association CEO and de facto president of the Chamber of Commerce Bill Bryon, as Sheriff Andy Taylor, finally comes through the door, most of Mayberry is milling among the tiki gods like lost cows. The 1950s exotica sound track is still on. There is no coffee. No coffee cake. Danni is nowhere to be seen.

"Andy! We need to talk," Aunt Bee says, and shakes her finger in Bill's face. "There's been a theft of my very own personal property and I know you know something about it."

"Andy?" Floyd says, tapping the face of his watch. "It is the first of the month, is it not? Did someone, who will not be named, forget to make the arrangements with Danni for refreshments?"

"Stuff it," Bill as Andy says to them both.

"Andy!" Barney snorts. "The use of uncivil language is against the rules. You know that. You drafted that rule yourself."

"Bite me."

The breach of decorum is understandable. The local chapter of *The Andy Griffith Show* Rerun Watcher's Early Morning Breakfast Club is under a little stress. First, there was last month's incident involving the reenactment of Episode 126, "Barney and Thelma Lou, Phffft," in which Thelma Lou used Gomer to make Barney jealous. Unfortunately, it was a spirited performance—a melee, actually. The unraveling began when Floyd took a few swipes at Bill/Andy just because he had always wanted to. Then Aunt Bee took a pop at Helen just because it looked like fun.

And now there's a dead body. Not just any dead body, but a homeless one. Things like that are not supposed to happen in Mayberry and/or Laguna Key.

"Let's just start," Bill/Andy says. It's obvious that he had forgotten the meeting. His sheriff's uniform is not pressed. His shoes are not shined.

Floyd is *tsk-ing*. "You did forget. Didn't you, son?"

"Are we going to start this meeting, or not?" Thelma Lou asks.

"Andy, we need our refreshments. Can't have a meeting without 'em," Deputy Barney Fife says. Then he sniffs, hikes up his pants, and adjusts his official Mayberry R.F.D. deputy sheriff's hat. "And I'm just the man to get Danni to fetch them for us."

"She's not in the kitchen," Opie says. "I already looked."

"I'm starting the meeting," Bill says.

"Danni's got to be out back, then," Barney says, sniffs again, pulls up his pants, and opens the back door out to the beach.

And there she is.

"Shazam!" Gomer shouts.

Nobody else says a thing.

Danni is pale, shocked, sitting against the Dumpster. Mandy, the small tawny dog, is still shaking, curled at her feet. And the man who, as part of a jingles melody, belted out "The Bathroom Bowl Blues" on a nightly basis is lying in Danni's lap, mouth slack.

"I killed him," she says.

Apparently, today's discussion, "Finding the Way Back to Mayberry: The Joys of a Simple Life," is just going to have to wait.

Chapter Fourteen

Right before Wilson left the FBI Academy at Quantico, he learned one thing that, even though it seemed useless at the time, he has not forgotten. According to the Justice Department, for an act to qualify as mental torture the "abuse has to cause psychological harm that lasts months or years."

He now has a clear understanding of how important that bit of information is.

Ever since Wilson found Sophie and drove her to the hospital in Naples, the song "Help Me, Rhonda" has been running though his head. *Help me. Help. Help me.* Three hours later, he knows exactly what those Justice guys were getting at. The happy hook, the soppy lyrics—if several hours of that is not the type of mental torture that has the ability to "cause psychological harm," then Wilson isn't sure what is. It's clear to him that he's driven himself insane with classic surfer rock. On some level, he always knew it would happen.

Of course, Sophie isn't helping. He wanted to have her airlifted, but she wouldn't let him. "I'm not getting into a damn plane," she said, and took a swing at him. So Wilson loaded her into his little GTO and drove her to the emergency room.

Get her out of my heart.

The song is annoying, distracting. He didn't even notice that they were being followed.

Wilson was often warned when he was at the academy that he needed to pay more attention. One lax moment can cause tragedy, his adviser told him again and again. So he's trying but he can't get that damn song out of his brain. And it's making him sloppy. Halfway to the hospital, he realized that he left his cell phone behind on his dresser. And, in his haste, he forgot to call Sophie's father. At least, that's his story and he's sticking to it. He has to. Mr. Whit will be furious and Wilson doesn't know how to explain what happened to Sophie. She won't tell him a thing. So, he has no idea how she got hurt but he does have a keen sense that he is completely screwed because he let it happen.

Whit does not exactly seem to be the kind of man to tangle with. He's taller than most. Leathered. Bored. Doesn't swerve for squirrels. "Darwin's law," he told Wilson. "That's why God created V8s."

Wilson suspects it's all talk, but when he writes Whit's name on the admittance form his hand shakes. Sophie's father is very rich and powerful, after all. More than a little nuts, too.

The nurse at the desk notices his hesitation. "It's only if she takes a bad turn," she says. "That seems to be a long shot."

That comforts him. *Besides,* Wilson thinks, *Whit won't even miss us. He won't even know I'm gone.* It's Laguna Key, not Detroit. What could possibly go wrong?

Chapter Fifteen

By Thursday noon, all the questions are asked and the body is taken away. The Bad Girl's Bar & Grill is deemed a crime scene until the final autopsy results are in—in about three weeks. Prescott's rustic beachfront cottage, where Danni lives, is also off-limits. They even wrapped "caution" tape along the well in back. It's an old-fashioned kind. If you want a bucket of water, you have to pump it.

They took a water sample, too.

When Sòlas finally finds Danni, she is sitting on the sand, staring off into the gulf, Buddy's small dog, Mandy, shivering in her lap. It pains Sòlas to see her like this—without a home, without kin, without comfort. Reminds him of his brother, Peter.

"I'm fine," she says, but is colorless.

Sòlas sits down next to her. She doesn't look up. The gulf is calm, gray. The winter sun is weak. Seagulls dive for pinfish. Herons peck at crabs.

Danni hasn't said much since they took Buddy's body away except "I killed him."

And so, after a time, she says it again.

"Everyone seems to disagree," Sòlas says, but there's question in his voice. Two deaths in three days, he thinks. She has to be involved somehow. It has to revolve around her. She must have known Peter. In the flat afternoon light, Danni's eyes are a dark, deepwater hue. Unreadable. Uncharted. The wind kicks up and she starts shaking.

Mandy begins to frantically lick her face as if to kiss her sorrow away, but instead it makes Danni cry. Sòlas hates to see that. Despite his suspicions about what she has to do with these murders, he puts his arm around her.

"Down," he says sharply to the dog.

Mandy is stunned. No one has ever spoken to her as if—well, as if she were a dog. The shih tzu, with its proud bearing and distinctively arrogant carriage, was bred for emperors as a prized companion and palace pet.

You don't mess with that.

So she flashes him her royal "lion dog" look, but Sòlas doesn't seem to notice. "Get down, dog. Now," he says. His tone is rough. He is frowning, stern.

Mandy wants a second opinion. Whimpers.

"You scared her," Danni scolds, and picks up the dog and cradles her in her arms, scratches behind her tiny tawny ears.

Mandy and Sòlas are now eyeball to eyeball. The small dog looks triumphant.

"Are you going to take her to the pound?" Sòlas asks. Mandy's ears prick up. Sòlas means this as a helpful suggestion. Danni has no real place to stay. She's not equipped to take care of a small and obviously spoiled dog. "It seems like the right thing to do."

Danni looks horrified. "I couldn't."

"Why not?" he says. "I'm sure that there are many charming matrons in Naples who are looking for a little dog that they can tote about in their pocketbooks."

Then Sòlas gives the small dog a well-meaning pat on the head, which is a mistake.

Mandy, although not fluent in Human, is clearly not pleased by the tone of this conversation. She places her tiny sharp teeth on Sòlas's hand and applies pressure. Snarls. It's a warning shot. Her dog eyes narrow. She appears to be calculating the distance to his jugular when Sòlas reconsiders and says, "Of course, you could always just keep her and rename her Cujo."

Danni suddenly perks up. "I loved that movie," she says. "Tremendous cultural implications. It's just like *Bambi* but, instead of Bambi's mother, the Ford Pinto represents modern industrial society and its role in the destruction of the nuclear family."

Mandy, confused, lets go of Sòlas's hand.

Sòlas, confused, uses it to scratch his head. "This is the film where the family canine eats the car, right?" he says.

"And so much more," Danni says.

Sòlas would like to know what she means by that, but just then she says, "You know, there was another man before Buddy. Just days before."

Sòlas's face goes hot. "Peter," he wants to say; my brother, Peter.

Danni continues on. "Homeless guy. But he had a laptop. Isn't that strange? Digital camera. He spent a lot of time sitting on the deck of the bar. It's closed for repair. I tried to tell him, but he just kept waving me off. Never spoke to me at all."

"Couldn't speak?"

"Wouldn't—that's all I know. He was pirating our wireless Internet connection."

"Anybody with him?"

"Maybe. Late the first night, I thought I saw somebody else, too. Not sure. I told the sheriff, but he said it was probably a heart attack. Case closed. Now this . . ." She trails off.

There's nothing more to say.

The two listen to the waves break against the shore. The world feels more quiet than usual. The sky seems darker. Mandy tucks her head into the crook of Danni's arm. Closes her eyes. After a moment, she begins to snore.

"She's so helpless," Danni whispers. "Like that homeless guy."

"Homeless guy"—every time Danni uses that phrase, Sòlas wants to break something, put his fist through a wall. He counts to ten and then says, "They aren't really homeless, you know. They've just gotten lost. They're lost among us."

As soon as Sòlas says this, the remorse in his voice is so deep that Danni knows that he's somehow connected to the victim—a cousin or brother or son—and that's why he came to Laguna Key.

She looks at him closely and is reminded of something that Prescott once told her: "Life is filled with moments of grace when we see our hearts in another's eyes and our lives are transformed."

And that moment, she can see her own heart, and her own sorrow, in his eyes. She takes his hand in hers.

It's clear that she knows. "He was my brother," Sòlas says. "Peter." The name feels like rust in his mouth.

"Peter."

She repeats his name gently, with dignity and honor. The wind kicks up again, harder. The sun will soon set. The moment is salt cold, wicks heat from the body. Danni holds Mandy closer. For warmth, Sòlas thinks, and notices she's just wearing a T-shirt and old jeans: the same clothes she wore yesterday. She obviously hasn't showered or changed.

"I'm so sorry," she says, nearly whispering. "About Peter."

"Ah, lass," Sòlas says, "what's done cannot be undone."

It's been a long time since acting class, but she knows that line well. "Act Five," she says. And thinks of Lady Macbeth, who had been driven so mad by guilt that she believed that her hands were covered in blood. Danni looks at her own hands.

"I didn't mean it like that," Sòlas says. Then he stands, slowly. The damp air makes him a little stiff. He reaches out to her. "Give me your hand," he says.

She hesitates. "This is somehow my fault, isn't it? "

"No," he says, and suddenly believes it, although he's not sure why.

"But," she says, "the Hummer. Your brother. And now Buddy. I'm the one thing they all had in common. Maybe your brother didn't have a heart attack." Then it suddenly occurs to her. "That's why you're here, isn't it? You think he was murdered."

Sòlas shrugs. Offers his hand again. "Come. It's cold."

Danni takes it and he pulls her up—and then, by accident, into his arms. The moment is filled with heat and sorrow. Mandy is between them, awake, wary, watching.

For a second, Sòlas leans in, by instinct. Nearly kisses Danni. She nearly lets him. The moment would have been romantic in a melancholic kind of way, except for the fact that they are standing close together and Mandy's dander makes Sòlas suddenly sneeze so hard and so many times that it seems as if he's gone into an epileptic seizure.

"For a man with wings," he says when he finally stops, wiping his nose on his sleeve, "you'd think I'd be a tad smoother with the ladies."

He pulls her back into his arms and they both laugh, which causes their noses to collide; that reminds Danni of her costar from *Todd Todd: The Demon Decorator of Fleet Street,* a man she often described as "honker-rific"—a trait that Sòlas shares.

All he needs is a meat pie, a color chart, and a swatch of silk dupioni in a winter shade and he could be Todd Todd's stand-in. And for that, Danni is grateful. She feels a little like her old self again, so she laughs her workingman's-Sharon-Stone sort of laugh—a cackle that's wicked, toothy, and bold.

Then he says, "Can I ask you a question of a personal nature?"

She blushes. "Sure."

He leans in again, even closer. "Ever build a clay oven?"

"No," she says, laughing. The word sounds like music.

"Well, then," Sòlas says. His voice is sexy and dark. "You're in for the experience of a lifetime, missy."

And at that moment they are both thinking what it would be like to kiss. Both wanting to, both wary. And so they lean in, giving in to the moment, and Mandy does the only thing a royal-bred shih tzu in her position would do—she gives Sòlas a nip on his lip. Draws blood.

Protection. It's in her job description, after all.

Chapter Sixteen

After spending several hours in the emergency room, and holding her hand though the administration of a couple of IVs, an enormous amount of antibiotics, and some rather nice pain relievers, Wilson learned one surprising thing about Sophie—she can't carry a tune.

"It's really easy," Wilson says. "Surfer girl. Surfer girl. My little . . ."

Wailing, screeching, an aimless meandering from F sharp to middle C—the product of Sophie's vocalizations were not so much songs as the senseless and wholesale destruction of both tone and lyrics.

So they are both laughing as the man slips into the hospital room. Wilson doesn't even turn around. Thinks it's a nurse, but it isn't.

Without a word the man Tasers him in the back. Electrified copper wires lash out. Fifty thousand volts hook into his skin. Snap. Crackle. Catch Wilson's heart between beats. Make it wiggle like a bag of worms. The electricity shocks the beat right out of its rhythm. It happens sometimes.

He drops hard.

Sophie screams, "What's going on?" Her hands are flailing, wild. She is drowning again in that blue ocean of her nightmares, but it is darker, deeper. Unfathomable.

Chapter Seventeen

By sunset Thursday, not even a week after Peter's body was found, with Buddy gone not even a day, the center of Danni's parking lot looks like an archaeological dig. Torches encircle small mounds of sand. Things are going well. The air is dry. The brick floor of the oven is laid and is proclaimed "even," which is crucial when baking bread. And that's exactly what Sòlas plans to do with the oven. Bake bread, and lots of it.

The gift of bread is a trademark of the Rose and Puppet Circus. Whenever they appear, the town and the performers always break bread together. The third bus in the caravan, WATCHFULNESS, is more like a moving pantry. It's filled with all sorts of grains and flours, stacked high in fifty-pound burlap sacks. There are also dried fruits, garlic, herbs from Sòlas's farm, and a small solar-powered refrigerator that holds the yeast, eggs, butter, and milk.

Sòlas usually makes a dense stone-ground wheat sourdough from a starter of wild yeast that he's cultivated from the Riesling grapes he grows in an arbor back in Vermont. Making bread for an entire community is a massive undertaking. Dozens and dozens of loaves must be made. Depending on the size of the town, the kneading alone can take an army of volunteers several hours.

The bread is always baked in an oven built on-site by anyone who is willing to lend a hand.

And right now, Sòlas needs a hand. Well, feet actually. The oven must first be built. So the clay needs to be mixed, and then shaped around bricks to form the beehive walls and ceiling.

And so the crones pull out their button accordion and fiddle and strike up a mazurka—a Swedish polka.

It's time to rouse the neighbors.

Sòlas plugs them into an old commercial audio system with Voice of the Theatre speakers. It's designed to rattle rafters. And it does. The button accordion booms, makes the buses shake.

Sòlas is especially hoping to rouse that security guard Wilson. Nobody's seen him all day and that's suspicious. Sòlas wants to talk to him. It's 7:58 p.m. *Wheel of Fortune* is nearly over. He cranks the sound on the speakers even louder.

And so, as Vanna turns over the last letter and a contestant spins the final spin, one by one the residents of Laguna Key leave the comfort of their homes with the sounds of Pat Sajak's boy-next-door voice still ringing in their ears. They arrive dressed in pastel shades and Rolex watches with cocktails in hand.

Bill, disheveled, still dressed as Andy of Mayberry, is the last to arrive. His wrinkled khakis are rolled up to his knees. He is barefoot, sandy, and drinking a large tumbler of bourbon, neat. He seems smaller, shaky. Worn down.

He must have been walking along the beach all day, Danni thinks, and feels sorry for him. The memory of Buddy scrapes away at her. *Must be the same for Bill.*

So, despite all the complaints that he has lodged against the bar, and all the times he's led the campaign to have her shut down, Danni feels a certain kindness toward him now that she had not felt before—an expansiveness, a kinship of sorts.

So, without thinking, she shoves him into the large pit of wet clay. She thought it would cheer him up.

For a movie star, Danni doesn't have a lot of social skills.

Bill goes down hard. The drink flies out of his hand. The crones stop playing. No one says a word. Everyone seems to be holding his or her breath. After all, the sight of an old cantankerous man dressed as the beloved sheriff of Mayberry lying in a pool of cold wet muck is shocking.

"Fun, isn't it?" Danni says, weakly. It's clear that, eventually, she's going to have to learn to think before she acts.

Lying in the cold mud makes something inside Bill snap. You can nearly hear it. His face contorts, lips purse.

He's going to blow in a Looney Tunes kind of way, Danni thinks.

And he is. He starts to sputter. His face turns red.

It is at this moment that Danni wonders what Wile E. Coyote would do. *Where is that dang Acme Company product line when you need it?*

An Acme jet-propelled pogo stick, the giant do-it-yourself rocket sled, earthquake pills, a smoke-screen kit—anything to aid Danni's escape would come in quite handy right now because it is extremely evident that the Laguna Key Association CEO and de facto president of the Chamber of Commerce, Bill Bryon, is about to let loose a string of obscenities that will be, in honor of their Scottish visitor, Shakespearean in both scope and verve.

But before Bill can say a word, Sòlas shouts, "Fore!" All golfers in the group duck and Sòlas pushes Danni into the cold glop.

It was the only thing he could think of to defuse the situation. "Oh, no!" somebody shouts.

Danni splats. Face-first. She nearly hits Bill. The clay swallows her up. For a moment she is motionless.

"She okay?" a man asks, and Danni rolls over laughing, wiping her face on her arm, because it is, after all, fun to be rolling around in the muck like a child and she is a gal who knows fun when she sees it. And despite the fact that she is covered in clay, her movie-star teeth shine like a billboard on Hollywood and Vine. She spits mud at Sòlas and then screams the primal scream from the 1989 remake of the thriller/horror/historical romance *La Brea Ghouls Gone Wild*.

It is the perfect scream for the occasion, a scream that the *Des Moines Register* once wrote was "primordial and oozing with some sort of undetermined, unfocused, and yet oddly heartfelt emotion—we're just not sure what that emotion is."

Everyone starts to laugh—except Bill. He is not amused. Mumbling, he pulls himself from the mire.

Sòlas jumps in. The crones, with their matching red-striped stockings and their silver Pippi Longstocking braids, follow. They strike up the polka again and pretty soon the whole town rolls up and rolls in. It looks like a muddy game of civic Twister.

There is something about being barefoot in red clay, stomping in it like workers turning grapes into wine, that apparently makes Sòlas feel philosophical. "Did you know that in Hebrew, the word *adam* means red clay?" he says. "That alone suggests profound implications for the serious task at hand."

"No, it doesn't," Danni says, and throws a handful of "adam" at Sòlas. The others join in. The clay flies.

Standing at the edge of the fray, Bill is still not amused. He shouts at Danni, "You will pay for dry cleaning, Miss Keene. You can depend on that!"

Even under the weak light of the surrounding tiki torches, she can see that Bill's clothes are ruined. The clay stains red. He is covered in huge splotches, as if he's hemorrhaging. It's going to take a lot more than dry cleaning to make this right, she thinks. As Bill stomps away, Danni jumps out of the clay, runs after him. She wants to make it better, wants to say she's sorry. But the clay has also permeated her clothes, which makes them heavy, and makes it difficult to run. So, like a La Brea ghoul gone wild, she hulks after him, lurching with each mud-heavy step, until she trips on a pile of sand at the edge of the bar's patio and hits something hard with her foot.

A bone. Femur.

Danni looks around quickly. Everyone is busy in the mud, so she kicks the sand back over it without a word, but it's clear that she's somewhat pleased. Feels lucky that no one sees her do this.

Well, nearly no one.

Chapter Eighteen

"It's a crazy idea."

That's what Laguna Key Association CEO and de facto president of the Chamber of Commerce Bill Bryon told Danni when she opened the Bad Girl's Bar & Grill.

Bill is a minority owner in Laguna Key, so he also put himself in charge of community development and informed her that opening the bar didn't make any economic sense and the project would fail. So she shouldn't do it.

"You need to sell this property to the corporation immediately."

Danni shrugged. "People used to pay me to scream for a living. This is as sensible as I get."

"But we've planned a tri-level Key West–style shopping mall for this space. With four boutiques just for shoes."

"Shoes?"

"Shoes."

Bill said the word gravely, as if Danni was supposed to understand the importance of it. She did not. He explained.

"Shoes equal widows. Everybody knows that. Widows love shoes. If we don't give them shoes, they're going to move to a planned community filled with shoes—and you do know what that means."

Danni did. She had, after all, been married three times. "At the country club dances, you'll have to draw straws to see who leads?"

"Exactly."

And then Bill shook the architect's drawings at her. As far as tri-level Key West–style shopping malls go, it was lovely. Danni had to admit it. The complex was humanly scaled and featured a beachside boardwalk with plenty of Adirondack-style benches where shoppers could commingle with nature—that is, watch manatees and dolphins play tag—while they slapped back some sushi to go.

Besides the abundance of shoe boutiques, Bill had planned three jewelry stores, an upscale ice cream shop, a boutique from Provence, two knitting shops, an art-film theater, and an olive-oil store.

It was widow bait, that's for sure.

And overkill for such a tiny development like Laguna Key, Danni thought. Unless, of course, Mr. Whit had expansion plans. Maybe cement over the mangrove forest. Sure, it's illegal, but anyone who complains would have to prove who was responsible.

It's done quite often. Crews come in the middle of night and cut down all the trees. Fill in the swampy parts. Cement them over, if need be. When the morning comes, the developer reports the "vandalism."

If a developer is stupid enough to get caught, he can be fined. But when you're selling homes starting in the millions, a million-dollar fine is just the cost of doing business.

When Danni asked Bill directly about the forest, he said, "Swamp, really. A hazard."

"The kind of thing that should be cemented over?" she asked.

"Exactly."

"No sale," Danni said.

She also had another offer from a mystery buyer. Her lawyer called and said that whoever this guy was, he was ready to pay seven million dollars, although none of it was liquid. Most of the funds were in the form of shares in Laguna Key, which is a publicly traded corporation listed on the OTCBB, or over-the-counter bulletin board. OTC is a catchall term for any security not traded on a recognized U.S. stock exchange.

Which means the shares are usually not worth the pink sheets they're listed on.

Danni suspects the offer came from Whit.

So now she's looking for bones. More bones, actually. Bones are the things that will save Prescott's mangrove forest from destruction. She'd hoped to find them somewhere else—like under the town houses or, better yet, under Whit's house. But Sòlas and the crones unearthed a bone under the bar by accident.

One femur found and a whole graveyard to go.

Bones are the secret of Tiki Gardens.

Gordon Prescott would be proud. And so would the founders of New Lulu, which is the real name of the abandoned town that Prescott bought and turned into Tiki Gardens.

At least, that's what his note said. It explained the convoluted situation in full detail.

"New Lulu was named after Lulu, near Gainesville. Apparently, you just can't have too many Lulus in a state like Florida."

Danni laughed when she read that, but Gordon was serious.

The original Lulu is the site of the last remaining slave cemetery in Florida. It's not a tidy city of marble, stone angels, and carved words of love—slaves were not allowed such things. Instead, most graves are marked by fists of daffodils, jonquils, and dwarf palmetto trees that now grow with abandon. There are rows of white seashells, which according to legend represent the world of the dead. The wildness is overwhelming. The graves themselves are lost underneath it all.

And so that's why Danni is looking for bones—and bottles, and old lamps, and broken dishes, and bed frames, and mirrors, and white chicken feathers. It's a long list, and before now she hasn't really had the time to start looking. Opening a bar is lot more work that she expected it to be. The two months since she arrived seems now like just two days.

But the bone changes everything.

Danni knows that she needs to find these things before anyone else does because they are proof that New Lulu is, in fact, a slave graveyard, and that's how it got its name and that's why it needs to be protected.

Turned over to the state.

At least, that's what Mr. P. told her. And although he didn't tell her where the graveyard was, that doesn't matter now. She has the femur. Proof.

Well, at least, a leg to stand on, she thinks. *Okay, just part of a leg. But there has to be more.*

And she believes with all her heart, despite the fact that during his lifetime Prescott told her many tall tales about yetis and snakes big enough to eat a car.

But that doesn't matter now. She believes it.

Of course, she still sort of believes in Santa, too.

Chapter Nineteen

According to *Byrne's Complete Book of Pool Shots,* "It's illegal to make the cue ball jump by golfing it off the cloth with a low hit."

Wilson has no idea what that means exactly, but when his father strikes with a downward blow and the cue ball is airborne, it arches over the huddle of blocking balls with a graceful trajectory. Lands gently back onto the felt with just a little backspin, just enough to place the four ball in the side pocket, which was Ray's intent, after all.

Wilson is breathless.

"And that's the music of the clack, Jack," Ray, beaming, says to Wilson.

Wilson and his father are on the deck of his condo. He looks out over the gulf. There seems to be some sort of storm brewing on the horizon. Dark clouds roll over each other, spark lightning.

But overhead, the sun is beating down, hot. It burns the skin. Makes Wilson squint. Makes his father's skin shimmer, as if he's made of flame.

This is so odd, Wilson thinks. *I don't remember how I got here.*

None of it makes sense. Somewhere in the back of Wilson's mind he knows he moved to the condo after his father's death. And yet Ray is here with him, playing pool on Wilson's new all-weather table.

Something's not right.

Ray smokes as he plays, as he always did. Half an inch of ash balances at the end of his Lucky Strike. He takes the five ball off the rail. The six is a frozen spot shot, the seven is right behind it—but both balls go easily and in the right order. The eight ball spins like a dying star.

The nine, the final ball, is an easy shot. Ray runs a hand through his Rat Pack hair and leans in. Gives it a wicked sidespin. The ball kisses all four sides of the table and then slips into the side pocket.

He is still leaning across the table, his back to Wilson, when he says, "I could feel the music in my bones, boy. You?"

Wilson could. For the first time in his life, he felt the shot as if he were the ball.

Fearless.

The ash falls from the cigarette onto the felt and Ray looks over his shoulder at his son. "Don't worry about me no more," he says gently. "No need."

And Wilson can hear the music of his father's voice, like the clack of the balls, in his bones. It calms him. *He's okay,* Wilson thinks. *He's good.*

Then the world goes dark.

"Clear!" the doctor shouts. Wilson's heart starts again.

Chapter Twenty

By the time the bread oven's bricks are finally dry and ready to be fired up for cooking, it's Friday morning, slightly past 2:00 a.m. Most of Laguna Key is asleep in their comfortable beds with bits of clay still stuck between their toes or underneath their nails. But Sòlas, Danni, and the crones are working through the night. If they don't, the bread will not be ready and the parade cannot begin.

Sòlas needs the parade to begin before dawn. He needs that very much.

By 3:00 a.m. the dough, made of saffron, eggs, raisins, butter, yeast, flour, and whole milk, is pushed and pulled until it becomes elastic and shiny. By 5:30 a.m. the final rise is over. Everything is nearly ready.

At 6:05 a.m. eastern standard time, the beach in front of the Bad Girl's Bar & Grill is filled with hundreds of candles perched in the sand and on banquet tables dragged over from the bar.

Bright yellow police tape waves unnoticed in the morning air— that was yesterday's sorrow.

Today, Laguna Key will celebrate the Feast of Santa Lucia—

whether it wants to or not. They will not only celebrate the life of the brave young girl from Syracuse, Italy, who became the patron saint of blindness, but also the lost Florida city that was founded on that saint's feast day. Most know the story of Santa Lucia the girl, but the odd and tangled tale of the town is mostly forgotten. And with good reason. Somewhere during the mid-1500s a band of mutineers stole a stockpile of food and dropped it off in a place they took the time to name Santa Lucia, but unfortunately forgot to mark on a map.

So no one ever found the food, or the town, again.

For Sòlas, Santa Lucia represents everything that is Floridian, including martyrdom at the hands of people from Syracuse and a missing town that could be the first in a long line of examples of the state's haphazard approach to development.

Plus, there are baked goods involved. The feast day is always celebrated by making saffron bread crowns and sweet rolls. And any holiday involving carbs is right up Sòlas's alley.

What's not to love, he thinks. "A little joy will do these people some good," he says.

"But isn't Santa Lucia in December?" Danni says. "Last time I looked, today was January twenty-first."

"You can't let the truth slow you down, love," Sòlas says, then hands her a costume. "Hurry up, now. Nearly showtime."

Danni really does have to hurry. In forty-nine minutes, the sun will rise. Darkness will ceremoniously be banished—Swedish-crone style—and breakfast will be served. There will be glogg, a mulled red wine and vodka punch spiced with cardamom, cloves, orange zest, cinnamon sticks, almonds, and raisins. Often, especially when the crones are serving, it is drunk with an aquavit chaser. And there will be warm saffron *Lussekatter,* or Lucia buns—tiny bits of fruited bread shaped like sleeping cats.

It is, Sòlas says, the breakfast of champions.

The crones are ready. They wear white lace dresses with red sashes and crowns of lingonberry twigs with blazing candles. Klara holds a basket filled with fragrant buns. Her twin, Marie, holds another basket bearing Mandy.

The shih tzu's bangs, tied with a lace ribbon and a few dangling tin stars, now form a topknot over her eyes. Her sweet chrysanthemum face—with those wise eyes, those tiny biting teeth—is exposed. It's uncanny how much she looks like Barry Manilow.

Sòlas is wearing his clan's kilt, but he is shirtless. His tiny wings are as unapologetic as an apostrophe. In the tradition of the celebration, he is the star boy—the elder brother, the protector. Three small tin stars are braided into his graying hair. But instead of the traditional staff, Sòlas carries a sword. Holds it high over his head like a beacon. He looks like a warrior angel, like the archangel Michael looking for a fight with anyone, including the demons of Macbeth within himself.

Six-ten a.m. Thirty-nine minutes until sunrise. The crones begin to sing.

> *Sankta Lucia, Sankta Lucia.*
> *Då i vårt mörka hus*
> *stiga med tända ljus*
> *Sankta Lucia, Sankta Lucia.*

The melody is like a waterfall: one word rolls off the other. Everything, and everyone, is ready—except Danni.

"I am not getting into a white dress and wearing a candelabra on my head," she says, pouty as a child.

Thirty-seven minutes to go, Sòlas thinks, and puts his pocket watch back into its sealskin pouch. This is not good. He has to get

Danni dressed and distracted. And quick. There's more at stake here than a celebration. He's planning to pay Wilson a visit. The security guard never made his rounds last night. Aunt Bee told Sòlas that Wilson's sliding glass door was broken and the police boarded it up.

Sòlas plans to find out what's going on, his way. Snoop around a bit without the inquisitive Ms. Danni Keene.

But she says, "You'll have to celebrate Saint Lucy without me. I just can't do this."

"And what are your reasons for this lovely mutiny?" he asks. The charm of his lilting voice would woo most women, but not the Slasher Queen; she knows that seduction and slaying both begin with smooth talk. She's been there before.

"I have three," she says. Petulant.

She and Sòlas and the crones have been up all night drying out the oven, and then making the bread. Danni is in caffeine overdrive, but takes another slug of coffee anyway. Words fly like a meteor shower.

"One," she says. "After three marriages, I have learned that white is not my color. Gives me hives.

"Two, I have used so many chemicals on my hair that my head is a toxic waste dump. You just don't want to put an open flame near it.

"Three. This is the Swedish interpretation of the celebration and I'm not Swedish. I once played a TransSwede stewardess in *Vampira: The Air Hostess of Horror*—which was, by the way, produced by the second cousin of Bela Lugosi. And as we all know, Lugosi himself was a Swede. But that's as close as I get."

Danni downs another slug of coffee, and Sòlas knows with absolute certainty that making that eighth pot might not have been a good idea.

"And as this Hellish Hostess," he interrupts, "what specifically did you learn about Santa Lucia?"

"Virginity," she says. Her words run together, maniacal. "I'm pretty sure you need to be a virgin to light your hair on fire on Santa Lucia."

"Ah."

It's true, of course, but Sòlas knows that the crones are also questionable in the virginity department. And he'd like to say this, but in his twenty-seven years of working in the theater, he's come to the understanding that logic often fails when trying to convince actresses to act. There are more effective tactics—flattery, for example.

He shines his flashlight on Danni like a spotlight.

"Well, Miss Slasher Queen," he says. "First of all, it's not December thirteenth, so I'm not sure the rules really apply to our particular performance."

"It's the principle of the thing . . ."

"Yes. Yes." Sòlas nods. "It's up to you, of course, but you know, Santa Lucia is the role of a lifetime for someone with a long and distinguished career such as yours."

Danni looks unfazed. Shrugs. Takes another sip of coffee, swallows hard. "I'm in retirement," she says.

This isn't going to be easy, Sòlas thinks, and looks at his watch. Thirty-four minutes to go. He can't afford to lose the cover of darkness. He'll be caught for sure. Desperate, he moves on to plan B—manipulation.

"I see," he says. "Of course, perhaps, the role is just too difficult for you."

"What?"

"Lucia was a saint. That might be a bit of a stretch."

Danni is red-faced. Huffing. "I'll have you know that the esteemed drive-in-movie critic Joe Bob Briggs recently presented me with a Drive-In Academy Award, or Hubbie, as it is known. During the ceremony at Paul's Lamplighter Lounge in Kokomo, Indiana, he announced to those assembled that it was for the entire body of my work—all one hundred twenty-three films. A distinguished career award."

And then she takes a deep breath. " 'Even when she's grenaded into bacon bits,' he said, 'Danni Keene never lets the plot get in the way of her close-up.' "

It is clear that Danni is very proud of this distinction. "So don't tell me about acting," she says, thumping Sòlas on the chest. "I know acting."

And pride goeth before the fall, Sòlas thinks. Now that he has Danni's attention, he says, "It is precisely because of your unique artistic sensibilities that I had envisioned you in this role. You see, Lucy was a lass who would not marry. They hitched her to a team of oxen. Dragged her around a bit. Put a dagger through her throat. Gouged her eyes out and put them on a gold plate—and still, no wedding bells. So they cut off her head."

"They gouged her eyes out?"

Danni is clearly inspired.

"Both of them," Sòlas says, which seals the deal.

Danni grabs the white dress that he pressed for her himself. "I will think of this as not white, but as the antiwhite," she says profoundly.

Not a shy woman, she strips down to her lace underwear. The sight of her dairy-cream skin in the torchlight makes Sòlas's heart beat faster. He commits the moment to memory. When she's dressed, he places the crown on her head and carefully lights the candles one by one.

"Beautiful," he says when he is finished, because she is.

And, like any good actress, Danni knows it. She laughs, clearly pleased.

Sòlas checks his watch. *Twenty-nine minutes.* It's just enough time to get to the end of Main Street, to the town houses, and back.

"You'll lead, love," he tells Danni. And she smiles what Sòlas can only imagine to be her perfect virginal martyr smile—all innocence, all determination, all waiting to have your eyes popped like peas from a pod.

Danni grabs a tray of saffron buns. "Showtime!" she says. Mandy yips. The crones shout, "Ta-da!" and begin the song of Lucia again.

Sòlas, as Star Boy, falls in behind. His sword cuts through the darkness as he walks.

Through the pristine streets they sing, they walk. Slowly. Their bare feet are a sign of humility. Their song is as soft as candlelight. As they pass under each streetlight, it goes off; one by one, they relinquish their own suns for the break of day.

Danni as Lucia is proud, graceful, and somehow otherworldly. The crones are wizened beauties, glowing like the shadow of far-off moons.

There's something about the sweetness of their song, and the sight of women bearing baked goods, that brings the citizens of Laguna Key to their windows and out their doors, into the thin salt air of morning. They follow.

The procession is so beautiful that Bill, unkempt and sleepless, breaks into tears at the sight. Closes his window. Locks it.

Damn clowns, he thinks.

When the parade passes the row of town houses where Sophie and Wilson live and makes that wide turn to travel back to the Bad Girl's Bar & Grill, Sòlas notices that the light is on at Wilson's. He must be home. Sòlas was hoping for that.

Sunrise is in eighteen minutes.

Sòlas slips away from the procession. He tries Wilson's door. It's unlocked. *The element of surprise is always good,* he thinks. Carefully, slowly, Sòlas opens the door. Holds his breath. Holds his sword close to his chest. Pauses.

Sòlas has never done anything like this before. Once he crosses the threshold, there's no going back. He'll be forever changed. The sound of the singing seems so far away. He watches the glow of the candles as most of the town makes its way around the corner and disappears into the ultramarine fog of morning. When it's clear that the procession has gone on without him, he enters.

The sight is shocking. The town house is in chaos. There's no furniture except for a big-screen TV and two overturned plastic chairs. Plywood covers the sliding glass door. Glass is everywhere. Blood, too.

There's a sound in the bedroom. It nearly stops Sòlas's heart.

"Wilson?"

The man who enters the room is clearly not Wilson. He is taller than most. Leathered skin. Thin, nearly elegant. He's wearing a bomber jacket and a long white silk scarf wrapped around his neck.

The Leatherneck Ghoul of World War I, Sòlas thinks, and hopes that he lives long enough to tell Danni that she is a very bad influence on the impressionable mind of a classically trained thespian like himself.

Unfortunately, getting out of this alive might prove to be the sticky bit.

The man has a Taser, otherwise known as Thomas A. Swift's Electric Rifle, in his hand. It's an M-26, the military version. Looks like a small machine gun, at least to Sòlas.

The man takes aim. His hand shakes. There's fear in his eyes, but all Sòlas can see is the gun.

"I'm just looking for—" Sòlas says.

"I heard."

The man who is called Mr. Whit, Whit Ashley Bissell V, keeps walking toward Sòlas. "You are on my property," he says. "Put the sword down."

Sòlas doesn't see that the man is as afraid as he is. It's all about survival. He offers the sword. "Fake. I've just come to talk to Wilson—"

"Most people knock."

The Taser snaps. Misses. Whit was just firing a warning shot, but the hiss of it means business—all electric current and hooks. The next time he might not miss.

But Sòlas, a trained clown, is quicker than most. Two somersaults, then a kick, and the Taser is jostled out of Mr. Whit's hand. It tumbles out the front door.

Before Whit can say a word, Sòlas's sword is against his neck. He's gently pressing the blade along the carotid artery, slowing the blood flowing from Whit's heart to his brain. If Sòlas presses hard enough, he can kill him. He knows that. Or maybe he should just slice the artery clean through. Whit'll bleed out in a matter of minutes.

He could be the one, Sòlas thinks. *He could have killed Peter.*

"You said the sword is fake," Whit whispers. The blade is pressing so hard that he can barely speak.

"I lied."

Whit frowns. He's clearly offended at the idea of being lied to. "That wasn't nice."

"Give me one good reason that I shouldn't kill you," Sòlas says. The darkness in his voice is ancient, unfamiliar. Scares him.

Suddenly, behind them, there's a cackle of a laugh. The sound startles Sòlas, and he relaxes his grip.

"Because evil won't die," Danni says.

Both men turn to see Danni Keene, Slasher Queen, standing in the doorway holding the Taser, looking a lot like Santa Lucia gone wrong. Her crown of candles tilts to the left. The flames spit.

"This guy's evil, you can trust me on that one, Star Boy," she says. "He's a real estate developer *and* a lawyer. He's the devil's spawn."

Then she grazes Whit's leg with the Taser and he screams.

"Nice pitch," she says. "B flat. A little girly, though. Next time, use your diaphragm."

The professional evaluation of his performance and the application of fifty thousand volts leave Whit writing in pain. Danni tosses the Taser back to him and grabs Sòlas by the hand.

"Let's go banish some darkness, baby," she says.

"That really hurt," Whit whines. "No fair."

But Sòlas and Danni can't hear him. They're running toward the Bad Girl's Bar & Grill. Her candles are throwing wax onto the pristine streets, onto her shoulders, and onto Sòlas's cheek.

Ten minutes till sunrise. They have to hurry.

Chapter Twenty-one

T*en minutes till sunrise,* Bill thinks. *Just ten minutes to go.*

He reminds himself that everything will work out fine. It's easy to make an effective pipe bomb—he read that on the Internet. The CNN website even had a diagram of how to build one. It's very easy. The bomb is simply a length of pipe capped at both ends and filled with an explosive.

Ammonium nitrate, one of the world's cheapest fertilizers, will certainly do.

Bill had plenty of that. Bought some last week in Cooper City, a small town known for its cricket grounds and dairy farms, just across the state. No questions asked. He also bought a box of latex gloves. The clerk at the farm and feed store suggested it.

"They're perfect for working with stuff like this."

And he was right. They were.

Thanks to the gloves, there are no fingerprints anywhere on the bombs. Bill dusted them with powder just to be sure.

As far as detonation goes, according to the Wikipedia website, a fuse can be inserted into the pipe with a lead running out through a hole in one of the capped ends. The fuse can either be electric, with wires leading to a timer, or a common wick, such as the ones used in fireworks bought at the grocery store. "All components are fairly easily obtainable," says the website.

And they were.

The Internet is indeed an amazing thing.

Next to the clear and concise illustration of the bomb, there was the statement "Pipe bombs are often packed with nails to heighten damage."

That's a nice tip, but human collateral is not what Bill is interested in.

Just fire—and plenty of it.

And so now, with the entire town busy parading down the street, it will be easy to plant the bombs under the Bad Girl's Bar & Grill.

Easy to set the timer, although his hand shakes when he does it. *Seven minutes.*

If you want something done right, you should do it yourself, he thinks. *This is easy.*

And it is.

There's only one problem: he has no idea that he's not alone.

Chapter Twenty-two

Ten minutes till sunrise and the old man—the Baptist turned Buddhist, the blues player—is dreaming of hurricanes again. Saving that blind gal on the beach triggered it. Vivid, the dream has no logic. It's just a collection of moments: the wide bend of the wind, the wall of water, the sirens, the gunfire, and the openmouthed wailing of those left living.

In the dream, as it was in real life, the television reporter asks him, "Why do you think there was so much destruction?"

The old man says, "The body is made of water. Maybe the water just wants us back." Then he picks up his suitcase and saxophone.

"Where you going?" the reporter asks.

"To find the answer to the problem of suffering," the old man says, because it is, of course, what Buddha had said.

And now he is deep in this dream when he hears the singing of the crones and the rest of the town of Laguna Key—a town he happened upon by chance, just a place to rest his bones for a while on his journey home.

At first, the sweet sound of the voices slips into his dream, becomes a part of it, but finally the song of Santa Lucia, with its lilting melody, wakes him.

For a moment, the old man is confused. He's not sure where he is exactly. Then he remembers that the boat he is sleeping on is not his. Nor are the mildewed blankets wrapped around his thinning body. It's just an abandoned boat, a place to take shelter, which he found in the mangroves. Then he remembers the dream again—and the hurricane—and he shakes. His skin is suddenly cold. His hands clammy.

But the sound of far-off voices is so beautiful and so pure it warms him. The first trace of soft morning light fills the rotting stateroom and makes him feel less lost, less alone.

Chapter Twenty-three

Within the last week, two men and a Hummer have lost their lives in the gated community of Laguna Key—but if you ask most of the residents, they would say that hurricane shutters are the real threat.

These shutters are not to be confused with the architecturally designed plantation-style shutter package that was offered as a $25,000 upgrade when the homes were first built.

These are aftermarkets. They are the kinds of shutters that anyone can order in home-improvement stores. Made of high-impact plastic and wavy like the bellows of an accordion, these shutters are designed to screw in over a window—any window, including glass block—and that is the root of the problem.

The shutters have brought a level of lawlessness to the community that many thought was impossible, and you just can't have lawlessness in a place like Laguna Key. But it is now rampant.

It's difficult for most residents to understand how things got so out of hand. It is quite clear that the Laguna Key Association does not allow these aftermarket shutters to be installed over glass block windows. It states that on page 522 of the bylaws: "The use of corrugated laminates, such as Lexan polycarbonate and Protexan clear panels, while they are Miami-Dade County approved (see ICC-ES legacy report number 2109 [TDI/SHU-90], in concordance with the state of Florida building code FL338), is, nonetheless, disallowed when said window can be measured with a per-unit ratio of 8 x 8 inches."

Couldn't be much clearer.

Still, Aunt Bee, as she likes to be called both in and out of her Mayberry costume, had them installed over the glass block windows in her garage.

"My contractor made a mistake," she told everyone. "He'll be back to take them down as soon as he can."

One week later, the shutters were still up and so papers were served. The association threatened to take her home—it was within their rights, after all. It's spelled out quite plainly in subprovision AA123, on page 654.

However, tragedy was averted. Two days ago, sometime after *Wheel of Fortune,* the shutters were stolen. Unscrewed and carted off.

Everyone in the association suspects Bill, even though he talks a hard line about rules and regulations. After discussing it among themselves over cocktails at secret parties, potlucks, and progressive dinners, the conclusion became inescapable.

First, he had the opportunity—he lives next door.

And then the motive—he's a lonely guy, a widower, with a soft spot for chocolate chip cookies, and Aunt Bee is a widow and a chronic baker.

And, perhaps most incriminating of all, Bill appears to be hiding something in his garage.

The Laguna Key Association CEO and de facto president of the Chamber of Commerce has been parking his car in the driveway overnight, which everyone, especially Bill, knows is an infraction of Code 1111.7.08, found on page 267 of the bylaws. And everyone knows he knows this because Bill and Whit wrote the bylaws—all 765 pages' worth.

So, since this is the case, why would Bill park his car in the driveway and risk penalty?

Ill-gotten hurricane shutters—there's just no other possible explanation.

Most wish this wasn't so. The implication of this unexpected turn of events is stunning. If Bill did steal those shutters, he broke the association rules, and everybody is pretty sure there's some sort of punishment for that. They just have to wade through 765 cross-referenced pages to figure out what it might be.

Of course, some argue that Bill did Aunt Bee a favor. Her house is prime property. Since the association rules were broken, and breaking them in such an egregious manner means forfeiture of one's home, Whit was planning to foreclose and resell it as soon as possible. She would have been on the street in a month. Even she knows that. And she's thankful—at least, somewhat thankful.

For his trouble, Aunt Bee plans to have Bill arrested. Favor or not, those were $495 shutters and Bill stole them.

Laws are laws.

But, at least for the moment, all that is forgotten.

It's seven minutes until sunrise.

Everyone in town seems to be on the beach. The glogg, the warm saffron buns, the sweet sound of the crones singing—most are lost in the moments before sunrise. The darkness is comforting, feels kind.

When Bill arrives, nobody notices. Not even Aunt Bee. Bill looks awful. He's still dressed in his Andy outfit, sweating bourbon, breathing hard.

"Damn town has no golf. If we would have had golf, we wouldn't have turned into a bunch of bleeding hippies," he says to himself, but is moved by the revelry just the same. It's like a scene from an Ingmar Bergman movie—Bill's wife used to make him watch those with her. The entire beach is candlelit. The crones, apple-cheeked and joyous with their crowns of candles, are standing on top of long covered tables singing. Some of the town has joined in. The small tawny dog named Mandy sits like a centerpiece. The light from the candles reflects in the stars tied to the dog's head, makes them seem real. Makes her seem like some sort of canine angel. The red tide has abated for the moment and the gulf smells clean.

"Damn it," Bill says. He's suddenly overwhelmed by the beauty of the moment. He reaches into his pocket to get a handkerchief and his garage door opener falls into the sand.

He's been walking around with the opener for days. It needs new batteries. The signal is weak. Useless, he thinks. His garage door is stuck open about a half foot. Just frozen. Won't move. He could unplug the system and try to roll it up by hand, but the door is too heavy. Bill needs those damn batteries, but he keeps forgetting to buy them. That's the kind of thing his wife always remembered and that makes him feel even worse. He picks up the opener and fingers it, like a worry stone. Looks at his watch.

Six minutes to go, he thinks. But Bill is having second thoughts. The plan seemed like a good idea—a half dozen evenly spaced bombs that would blow Danni's up, force her out. It seemed easy. Now he's not so sure. Somebody might get hurt.

Eloise, his wife, would never have let things get so out of hand. He begins to go back, wants to make it right, but suddenly there's a flash of red light. Blinding.

Too late, he thinks. Falls to his knees, covers his head, squeezes the garage door opener hard for no good reason at all, and then notices that there is no *boom.*

It's just sunrise. The storm clouds have broken away and the sky is now brilliant. The clouds are fat and pink.

On the beach, the crones shout, "Ta-da!"

The crowd cheers.

Darkness is banished.

Bill finds himself sobbing. Confused. Relieved.

Danni and Sòlas come up behind him, out of breath from running.

"What's wrong?" she says. Startles the old man.

Bill drops the garage door opener in the sand and runs.

Chapter Twenty-four

"I've read that the IRA uses these as detonators," Sòlas says. He's holding the garage door opener in his hand.

And so, while the town is eating, drinking, and singing Swedish folk songs, Sòlas and Danni climb under the caution tape and make a careful inspection of the bar, but find nothing amiss. On the beach side of the bar, back by the now-infamous Dumpster, it appears as if someone has dug a half dozen holes. They are evenly spaced under the foundation.

"Raccoons?" Sòlas asks.

Bones, Danni thinks. She imagines that Bill has discovered the slave graveyard and is in the process of removing the evidence. Desecrating it. The thought pains her. The six holes have a series of footprints, two different sizes, around them. *One set is probably Whit's.*

Sòlas holds the remote in his hand. "Maybe bombs. Six planted bombs. This could be some sort of a detonator."

"If there were bombs, wouldn't they still be here? Or blown up?" Danni says.

"If this wasn't a bomb site, why would he have this?" he says. "You just don't walk around with a garage door opener in your trousers."

Danni shrugs. "I don't know. Maybe he lost his house key."

She can see Bill's house from where they are standing, so she presses the button. Nothing happens. She opens the back of the remote, jiggles the batteries. Presses the button again.

The garage door opens. Bill suddenly pops his head out of the house. Danni presses the button again. The door closes. Apparently, it is just a garage door opener.

"Sorry," Sòlas says.

"That's okay," she says. "I'll take this over later."

And get my bones back, she thinks.

"I'd be careful, missy," Sòlas says. "He ran. He was afraid. That's odd."

She sighs. "Well, I have to go that way, anyway. I took some shutters down from Aunt Bee's house; only thing is, she doesn't know it yet. I did it as sort of a favor. They were in violation of the association's code. Bill and some of the guys were at the bar talking about it. She could have lost her house over it. So I just stopped by. It was late, so I stuck them in my wheelbarrow and carted them over here. I have to roll them back over quick. I don't want her to think they were stolen or anything."

"Who would steal shutters?"

Danni shrugs. "Who would murder Barry Manilow?"

Chapter Twenty-five

Later that day, when Danni delivers the shutters, Aunt Bee calls the sheriff. She's on the phone a long time, arguing. "Civil matter? Don't I pay you to come when I call? Isn't that what taxes are about?"

She huffs. Then slams the receiver back in its cradle.

"I guess I'll have to sue you," she says.

"I was hoping for a cookie," Danni says. There's a plate of fresh-baked chocolate chip cookies on the kitchen counter. "They look great." She leans over to pick one up.

Aunt Bee slaps her hand.

"Law is law."

Aunt Bee, however, does not say this with her usual all-knowing chipper lilt. It's clear she's disappointed that Bill is not her lawless hero.

"You know," Danni says, "you could just tell everyone it was Bill. Sue him. I wouldn't say a word."

This suggestion seems to perk Aunt Bee up. "Thank you, my dear," she says. "I will give that some consideration."

"Could I have a cookie, then?"

"May I?" Aunt Bee corrects.

Danni blushes like a toddler. "May I have a cookie, then?"

Aunt Bee smiles. Offers the plate. The chocolate is slightly shiny. They're still warm. Danni reaches out for the biggest one. It's the size of a saucer.

She slaps Danni's hand again.

"Law is law. You stole my shutters, after all. It wouldn't be right to reward you with a cookie. You need to learn your lesson."

The day just doesn't seem to be going as well as Danni had hoped.

Next door, she rings and rings the doorbell but Bill won't answer. "I can hear you breathing on the other side of the door," she tells him.

"This is private property," he shouts, because the best defense is a strong offense. To him, the facts are clear: nothing exploded.

It is as if the incident did not happen. He has no idea why it didn't happen, or where the bombs actually are, but he knows his rights.

"Look," Danni says. "We need to talk. This is childish."

Childish? he thinks. The word infuriates him. "This is all your fault," he says. "You're the one being childish. You know you can't make that bar work. We'll close you down. Take the property."

Danni has had enough. "Give me my damn bones back," she says.

She has tried to be nice. Tried to understand his position—he's just a lonely sad guy, after all. But it is also clear to her that Bill has her bones, and coupled with the fact that somebody is killing people and burning her Hummer and just not being very nice in general, Danni Keene has had enough.

"I want my damn bones."

"I have no idea what you're talking about," Bill says, because he doesn't.

Danni is confused. Behind his locked door, Bill sounds honestly confused. The sense of befuddlement in his voice is breathtaking. Give this guy an Oscar, she thinks and decides to rise to the challenge.

"Don't mess with me," she says. "Because *I Know What You Did Last Summer.*"

And she says this as if she's a fisherman in a slicker with a hook in hand ready to exact bloody justice. She means it as a metaphor— she says it a lot, actually. She loved that script, wanted the role badly. *No longer ingénue material my ass,* she thought, thinks it now. The way she just delivered that line is proof that on a good day, in a bright light, with just a minimum amount of soft focus and an oil-based full-coverage foundation two shades lighter than her own skin color, she can still play a high-school senior with questionable driving skills.

I still got it, she thinks.

Bill, on the other hand, is not thinking this. What he's thinking is—*She knows.*

Not just about pipe bombs. About everything. He can tell by the tone of her voice. How she knows is at question, but it is clear to Bill that Ms. Keene is more aware of what's been going on than he suspected.

He keeps the door locked. "So how much do you want?" he says. His voice shakes. "To keep quiet?"

The fear in his voice bothers Danni, makes him seem more human and frail.

"I'm just trying to do the right thing," she says gently. "I just want you to understand that. Call a truce."

This confuses Bill. "You have no evidence?"

"I didn't see you, but . . ."

Bill is clearly pleased. "Then get off my property."

Danni places the garage door opener in the mailbox. *"I Still Know What You Did Last Summer,"* she says, sadly, although she's never been much for sequels.

The problem is that Bill knows, too. He knows exactly what he did last summer. Can't forget the look of surprise on Prescott's face as he fell hard, dropped like a stone.

"It was an accident," he whispers, but Danni is long gone.

Chapter Twenty-six

The sight of a three-pound slab of baby back ribs being slid into a bus through a window can create an ethical problem for a small dog who is just trying to get some sleep. On one hand, a piece of raw pork that weighs nearly as much as you do does provide a tasty treat.

On the other, even Mandy knows that pork doesn't slide through an open bus window on its own. But there it is. Followed by another. And another. They are piling up on the floor.

Danni is curled around the small dog, unaware of the sudden bonanza of meat and snoring hard. She's been asleep in Sòlas's hammock on his bus since shortly after dusk. Sòlas is bunking with the crones. "Until our wedding day," he joked.

Danni threw a plate at him.

She's usually an night owl, and a light sleeper, too. But after the shock of finding Buddy, two sleepless nights, tossing Bill into mud, building an oven, baking bread, cleaning up after a pseudo–Santa Lucia celebration, Tasering a guy, and drinking too much glogg, Danni is sleeping that deep innocent sleep of a child. Drooling, too.

And now, at daybreak, deep in that hard sleep, she pulls the covers over her head and the hammock swings slightly. Another slab of meat is pitched and lands on the hammock, by her feet, but it doesn't wake her.

Mandy, on the other hand, is deliriously alert. She sniffs at the pork and another slab nearly hits her. She yips with joy.

The world has suddenly become a veritable raw-meat wonderland.

As an intelligent dog, Mandy knows that although in the known universe many unusual things fall from the heavens—including parts from Sputnik, pigeons with coronary conditions, and former American presidents celebrating their eightieth birthdays—something airborne that is USDA inspected is fairly rare. Given her Tibetan watchdog lineage, she should be concerned. Bark, at least.

But it is, after all, meat. And she wants it. And she'll have it. Why not? She has everything else. Mandy has an entire wardrobe of doggy clothes, including a black sequined ensemble that Buddy would change her into when he opened the second set with "Copacabana."

She also goes about in a knockoff Louis Vuitton Sac Chien.

Wears a Swarovski crystal dog collar.

In her presence, the word *no* is never uttered.

Fetch? *Please.* There is no "fetching" in Mandy's world. Unless you're referring to the tiny pink bows on her head—which are very fetching, indeed.

And so, instead of worrying about the implications of a world suddenly raining protein, Mandy just starts rolling around in the pork—licking and laughing.

When the final slab is thrown onto the hammock, and the Kryptonite bike lock is snapped shut around the outer doors of the old pink school bus, Danni, deeply asleep, says, "Sh. Be a good girl.

It's Saturday morning; let's sleep in," and reaches out her hand to pet what she thinks is the small tawny dog that bears a striking resemblance to Barry Manilow but, instead, is six pounds of the finest baby back ribs that SYSCO food services offers. And it's sticky.

"Stop licking yourself," she says. Yawns.

That's when the hissing begins.

"Yikes."

Danni bolts up. Mandy stops rolling.

Both are quite surprised to see a rather large vulture in the bus with them. It is standing with its iridescent wings high over its head, poised in a V-shaped position. Ready to eat.

"You're not a dream, are you?" Danni says.

The angry bird spits a wad of undigested pork in her face.

"The word *no* would have been fine," she says. Wipes it off.

The bird begins to hiss again. It clearly wants the stack of meat at her feet and is willing to fight for it.

Danni doesn't break eye contact. She slowly pulls the pillowcase off the pillow. There's some duct tape on the bus seat next to the hammock. She reaches down carefully. No quick moves.

At this moment, Danni is beyond fear, working off adrenaline and her previous training. She has had some experience with birds of prey. Hawks, mostly. But all birds of prey are essentially the same. Pillowcases are essential. She stuffs it into her jeans and tapes the pillow onto her arm. The heavy tape pulls at her flesh. That's when she remembers reading that some scientists have recently reclassified vultures, like this one, as Ciconiiformes—in the same order as storks. And storks are untrainable.

Hopefully, this bad boy doesn't know that, she thinks.

Danni looks out the bus window. The sun is rising, which, unfortunately, illuminates the dozens of vultures surrounding the bus and feeding on pork ribs. Her pork ribs. Cases of them.

Hundreds of dollars, Danni thinks.

The vulture perched on the back of the driver's seat cocks its bald red head, gives Danni a questioning look. She's wondering if it remembers her from that fire extinguisher incident the other night.

"You know, when I called you a chicken," she says, "I meant that in a good way."

The huge bird begins to furiously flap its wings.

Great, she thinks. It remembers.

The bird will not calm down.

Mandy is now growling, barking, jumping up and down on Danni's stomach. It's an obvious attempt to protect her, to frighten the vulture, but instead it starts the hammock swinging. The bird is unfazed.

The rocking combined with the smell of blood and meat makes Danni feel seasick. The large bird doesn't break eye contact, seems to be evaluating his chances. Danni is, too. The bus has an emergency door, right behind her, but Sòlas has placed boxes and boxes of old china, clay, paints—everything he needs—in front of that door. It's blocked. The front door is the only way out.

Unfortunately, the vulture is perched on the driver's seat between Danni and the exit.

The tiny Mandy is now snarling. Suddenly, without warning, the large bird swoops down on the dog, talons out. Mandy screams, bleeding. Danni grabs for her, falls off the hammock, ribs tumbling onto her head. The confusion startles the bird. It rears back. Frantic, it bangs itself against window after window trying to get out of the bus. Screeching.

Danni's heart is beating so fast it nearly loses its rhythm. She's under the hammock, Mandy is whimpering in her arms. Danni takes the pillowcase from her pants and swabs up the blood.

"It's not bad," she tells Mandy. It looks like a flesh wound, but it's tough to be sure. Danni's shaking so hard she can hardly see. The vulture is still flailing against the glass. Hissing and spitting.

Danni wants to scream, but knows that would make matters worse.

What would Broderick Crawford do?

In *The Vulture,* an atomic experiment gone wrong pits Crawford against a giant vulture with the face of a man.

At least, that's what the promo said.

The key to the problem was something about neutrons, she thinks. Unfortunately, she left her nuclear reactor in the bar.

"Stay," she says to Mandy. The small dog curls into a ball. She is shaking, apprehensive. "It's okay," Danni says, and places the blanket over her. Then she grabs a rack of ribs and throws it into the air. The vulture swoops down on the meat. Danni rolls toward the bus doors. She kicks with both feet, as she did in the critically acclaimed *Cheerleading Werewolves of Iowa State.*

Unfortunately, she didn't see that someone had locked it from the outside. The bike lock holds. Hurts like hell.

I hate civilian life, she thinks.

The vulture rips and gnaws at the meat with a single-minded fierceness.

Danni, watching, remembers what they taught her about hawks. She takes the pillowcase in one hand. *No fast moves,* she thinks, and pulls the ribs closer to her. Bit by bit. The vulture doesn't notice until Danni pulls the rack away and slaps the pillowcase over its head.

"If you wanna eat, you play by my rules," she says.

As with hawks, the pillowcase focuses the bird. It stops hissing. Danni slips her pillowed arm underneath it, like a perch. It works. Calms the bird and Danni, too. She stands ever so still holding the bird. Examining it. It appears as if it hurt a wing. The left one quivers oddly. There's a little blood. Looks painful.

"I think I'll call you Poe," she says, and feels uneasy. Danni knows once a bird is tamed it can never be returned to the wild. But it isn't like she had a lot of choice.

Mandy pops her head out from under the blanket.

"Mandy, meet your new brother," Danni says.

Mandy, not terribly pleased, whimpers.

Chapter Twenty-seven

When Wilson and Sophie arrive back in Laguna Key, it's clear that he is fired. There's a Realtor's lockbox on the front door.

"I'll fix it," Sophie says.

"No," he says. "I'll fix it."

But Wilson isn't sure he wants it fixed. What he is sure of is that it appears as if someone nearly killed him in Sophie's hospital room with a Taser. He can't help but wonder if it was one of those that Bill bought on the Internet for the neighborhood watch program. The program consisted of Bill and Whit, and Bill said he lost his "piece," as he put it, last summer.

So it could have been Whit—even though it really doesn't make sense. Wilson couldn't imagine Whit trying to kill anyone, even by accident, other than boring them to death with his convoluted theories about how biofuels will turn America into a Marxist society.

Still, he thinks, *Whit is nuts.* So maybe the zap was just Whit's little way of evaluating Wilson's job performance.

Rich folk have no sense.

Tasers are supposed to be safe, that's why so many law enforcement groups use them. At Quantico, cadets are told that for healthy people the Taser is statistically harmless, unless modified.

"Statistically" is the key word in that sentence, Wilson thinks. He still feels weak.

Sophie puts the kettle on for tea. "Let me talk to him."

Wilson sighs deeply. He doesn't want to have this conversation—not sober, at least. He checks his watch. *5:40. Saturday night. Happy hour.* "I'm going down to Danni's for a drink first and then I'll give him a call," he says.

Sophie looks worried. "Look," she says. "You checked yourself out against doctor's orders—"

And that reminds Wilson why he left Quantico—authority issues. So he changes the subject.

"Don't you think you should be lying down?"

"I'm fine," she says, but looks miserable. Her foot is still swollen, bandaged. She's pale. Thinner. Her dress is torn. Her hair is knotted. Even her dark glasses lean to one side.

He reaches over and straightens them, a brotherly gesture. "You look like an extra in *Les Misérables.*"

"Nice," she says.

The two stand quietly. There's nothing more to say. She still won't tell him how she ended up on his pool table. Why she went outside after dark alone. Wilson suddenly feels pissed off.

I'm fired, he thinks. *So I'm out of here.*

He hands her back the ocean of a scarf that he found wrapped around her shoulders. "You might need this."

"I was just thinking," she says. "That homeless guy in the Dumpster—he could have been Tasered, too . . ."

"Don't even think it," Wilson says.

"Maybe it's connected."

"By Whit?" he says.

Sophie turns away slightly. She's obviously worried about that, or something worse. "You know how he feels about those kind of people," she says. "They wreck his perfect Laguna Key."

"So you think he killed that guy. And then tried to kill me?"

She shrugs. Sheepish. That really sets Wilson off.

"Jeez, even I know that's impossible," he says. "And it makes me sad that you don't. He's your father, for God's sake."

For the first time in a long time, a song is not running through Wilson's head. Makes him feel lonely. Old.

"I was just trying to rule him out."

"Trust me, you have to be some sort of adrenaline junkie to walk into a hospital and purposely try to kill a man point-blank like that with everyone around. At the academy, they called them 'pathological narcissists'—that's not Whit. It sounds a lot like Whit, but it is not Whit."

Wilson's trying to make a joke, lighten the moment, but Sophie is unreadable. Thinking.

"Look," he says. "We don't even know how that guy died yet. They think it was a heart attack, but it hasn't even been a week; the autopsy results aren't back yet."

"But the doctor did say that Tasers can sometimes kill people. So it's possible."

Wilson can feel his blood pressure rise. "Okay. Your father may have come across that homeless guy and threatened him for trespassing. May have even zapped him. But throwing his body in the trash is so meanly poetic and not Whit's style—the man doesn't have an ounce of poetry in him.

"And another thing," Wilson says. He is now officially ranting.

"If that homeless guy died because of being Tasered, do you really think if Whit zapped him, he would have come into your room and zapped me? Your father would know that he was running the risk of killing me. And he has no reason to kill me. So he wouldn't take the chance."

"Why are you so quick to defend him?"

"Why aren't you?"

Sophie's hand goes to slap Wilson, but he catches it. Holds it in his. It's small and delicate, trembling. Makes him understand how fragile she is. He blows on her hand to warm it. "You could chill beer with this," he says.

Wilson has no idea why this discussion is making him so angry. Maybe it's that he's tired. Maybe it's that he feels guilty. He blamed a lot of things on his old man and never really had the chance to make it up to him.

She pulls her hand away. Stuffs it in the pocket of her sweatpants.

"Sophie," he says gently. "Only a pathological narcissist would exhibit this sort of behavior. Trust me on this."

"What does that mean exactly?"

"It means crazy bastards. Eventually, things escalate and they start killing for the rush of it."

Sophie is clearly alarmed. "But what if—"

"Listen to me," Wilson says, and puts his hands on her shoulders. "Don't go there. Your father is nuts, but not freakin' insane. I'll talk to him. If he did zap me because he was pissed, it wasn't that he was trying to kill me. It was an accident that I got hurt. And if he did do this, he'll either have to pay me off or adopt me. And it might be cheaper to adopt me."

Sophie says nothing. Wilson is confused. He was hoping that the mention of extorting money from her old man would at least bring a smile to Sophie's face. It usually does. But she's stone quiet.

She's hiding something, he thinks. "I got to go," he says.

"Fine," she says. Shakes him off. But Wilson is big. Sophie trips on her shawl, falls into him. That's when he kisses her. It happens before he realizes what he's done, realizes that he's never kissed her before.

What an idiot I am, he thinks.

It's moments like this when he's glad Sophie is blind. Wilson knows he's not a handsome man. Right now, he's flushed, sweating, and hulking. She would have cringed. He's sure of it.

"Sorry," he says, and is still holding her when she kisses him back. It's short, sweet, nearly sisterly, and quite astonishing.

For a moment or two, Wilson is speechless. On one hand, he's worried that she's fallen in love with him. At the same time he's worried that she hasn't.

"I'm sorry you got hurt because of me," Sophie says quietly. "I really am."

And she sounds sorry—just sorry—but nothing more.

Wilson clears his throat. "Okay, then," he says, and pats her on the back. "Sounds good. See ya later." Slams the door behind him.

See ya later?

Smooth, he thinks. *Real smooth.*

Chapter Twenty-eight

Whit can't decide if his daughter's phone call makes him furious or sad, but he feels exhausted by it. He sinks back into his leather chair while she accuses him of all manner of things. She's worse than that FBI agent going on and on about that actress's Hummer. He has no idea why his own daughter is annoying him about what clearly is a personnel issue between him and an employee—now a former employee.

So he stopped listening shortly after she began.

Whit is a man who has done well for himself. Over the last decade, parcel by parcel, his Laguna Key Development Corporation bought the unsightly, insipid Tiki Gardens and razed it. Redesigned it. Re-created it, actually. Now there are streets filled with rows of perfectly white wedding-cake houses that "begin in the millions" and look out onto the gulf. Town houses, a steal at $850,000, are stacked one on top of the other like tiny meringues. Even the post office seems to be spun from sugar.

Laguna Key is a town where everything is beautiful. Safe. There is no chaos. It is, in fact, perfect. It's close enough to Naples, which offers shopping, nightlife, and endless doctors. And it's far enough away so that it's not affected by Naples's riffraff.

It is a community with hometown values and picket fences— and the inconvenience of a few dead bodies, but that's just a small glitch. At least, that's the way Whit sees it.

"Did you do it?" Sophie asks.

Whit has no idea what his daughter is going on about. His doctor called him and told him she'd been injured. She was all right— probably not interested in seeing him, but all right. So, sure, he fired Wilson for letting Sophie get hurt and not telling anyone and leaving behind a bloody apartment, but at this moment, Whit's going to slide right over that. He has to. If Sophie thinks he doesn't like Wilson, she'll assume he hates Wilson and therefore she'll want to marry him as soon as her divorce is final.

If he were brain-dead, she would have married him already.

"I asked you if you did it," Sophie says. "Are you going to answer me or not?"

"Um," Whit says. "Would you feel better if I said I did it?"

"Yes," she says, "because if somebody else did it, that would be even worse. That would be worse for us all, because that would be crazy, and not crazy like you, but real crazy. And that would mean that things we thought were an accident weren't and there'd be an escalation." Then she takes a deep breath and says, "You know what I mean?"

Whit doesn't have a clue. "Sure," he says.

"So it was an accident?"

"Sure."

"Your hand was sweating and slipped?"

"Okay."

"And you ran away because you were startled?"

"*Startled?*"

"Daddy?"

"Sure."

Whit really wishes that he'd been listening. This just doesn't sound good. But Sophie seems very pleased with his answer. That's all that matters.

"Great," she says. "I mean, not really great. It was an awful thing to do, even by accident," she corrects. "But great that you felt that you could confess to me. I'll tell Wilson not to worry. It was an accident and you are deeply sorry."

Whit doesn't like the sound of this at all, but it's clear that the moment of clarification has passed. Still, he's a little worried that because of his confession he might be spending every Thanksgiving for the rest of his life with Wilson and his double chin and his surf music.

"Okay," he says, just because it feels as if he should respond. Sophie, unfortunately, continues to prattle on about Beach Boy.

Not good, Whit thinks. Time to nip this in the bud.

"You know," he says. "I really like Wilson. Real pal. Great guy. Stand-up sort of Joe. Son I never had."

"He is?"

"You bet."

"Oh."

Sophie sounds really confused.

Great, Whit thinks. *Now I won't have to fight for a drumstick with the Incredible Hulk.*

"Wilson is a prince among men," Whit says, and wishes that he and Sophie could be more like other families. No deception. No manipulation. No guilt. He could just forbid her to marry the help, and she would obey.

But he knows that's a lost cause. Sophie is always doing things to spite him. Last month, she used her brand-new voice-activated computer software and Braille keyboard to crack his PIN and drain his online bank account. And while he was proud of her ruthlessness, in the end she disappointed him. Again.

Instead of transferring the stolen money to an offshore account, as he would have done, Sophie gave it to some charity group so that they could send "a gift of sustainable agriculture"—some fourteen thousand pigs—to the Dominican Republic.

"And I had them all named after you," she said.

At least it was tax-deductible.

But a marriage misfire is not. No matter how many times Whit explains it to her, Sophie has no understanding of the sanctity of marriage.

"It is the only financial union in America that strengthens the gene pool and doesn't always need a shell company to misdirect liability," he tells her. But she just doesn't understand.

This makes him very sad. Sophie has no sense of history or lineage. He often finds it amazing that she's his daughter.

Mr. Whit Ashley Bissell V—the name is so rich in history that it gives his life purpose. From plantation owners to Prohibition moonshiners to used-car magnates to real estate developers, a long line of Whits has amassed fortunes based on the twin principles of supply-side morality and inventive bookkeeping.

"The Whits of this world are the very foundation of American society," he tells his Sophie, but she doesn't care.

And now, thanks to her bad choices, the chances of having grandchildren, a little Whit VI and possibly VII, to continue this legacy are slim to none.

Maybe I can buy a couple, he thinks. *Those Marxists always need a few bucks.*

"Are you listening?" Sophie says.

"Of course," he says, and remembers how sweet Sophie was as a toddler. Always hugging him around the neck when he came home. She smelled of baby powder for such a long time. And so did he. He often wonders what it would have been like if Sophie's mother had lived. Easier, maybe, but it's difficult to tell.

"I don't think you're listening," Sophie says.

"Yes, I am. I just have a headache."

"Are you going to tell me why you did this to him?"

We're back on the firing issue again, he thinks. "Would you believe me if I told you the truth?" he says.

"I'll try," Sophie says.

"Well, there's some comfort in that."

"Well?"

"He let you get hurt."

"That's it?"

"That's it."

There's a long pause, then Sophie says, "That's what Wilson said, but I'm not sure if I can believe you."

Whit runs a hand though his hair; a few fall onto his lap. He turns on his desk lamp. Studies them. Wonders when he got so gray. He turns off the lamp and it occurs to him that Sophie wants him to say something more.

"I understand," he says, although he doesn't. He has no idea how his daughter can mistrust him so greatly. "I understand and respect your decision not to believe me," he says, because with daughters appeasement is everything.

The phrase works. She softens. "So how are you going to make it up to him?"

About now, Whit wishes she'd just send a memo about her grievance, like everyone else. Still, "What do you think I should do?" he asks, and tries to sound interested.

This question is apparently what Sophie has been waiting for. She begins to list a number of ways for Whit to make it up to Wilson, including having those Heifer International charity people send some water buffalo in Wilson's name to northern India. "Sustainable agriculture is the gift that keeps on giving," she says, but Whit, again, is not really paying attention. He can't. If he listened it would spoil the moment. It's sunset, his favorite time of day. The sky is streaked with paint-chip colors like mango and sage and plum and a midnight shade of blue that Whit never tires of.

But he can't tell Sophie that because her blindness changes everything. Whit has to be careful about what he talks about and how. Her blindness makes it so difficult. Not like they talked a lot before, but still. At least they talked. Now he's worried he'll say something to remind her of what she's missing in the world. And that would hurt her. And he doesn't want that, so he tries not to say too much.

It's odd that things turned out this way. When Whit first heard about the accident, he had this strange moment of happiness. Sophie finally needed him again. It was like she was three years old with her arms around his neck. But that didn't last. She just turned angry, so he hired somebody to watch over her and now he doesn't see her very much. It's just too painful.

She's all he has left, but she's damaged. Not perfect. Makes him feel helpless.

"You have to hire him back, too. With a huge raise."

The idea makes Whit uneasy. "He let you get hurt," he says.

"How do I know that you're not going to slip away and kill yourself next time?"

"Because I don't need a babysitter," she says. Angry. Hangs up the phone.

Damn, Whit thinks. *That didn't go well.*

Chapter Twenty-nine

When Wilson arrives, Sòlas and Danni have peeled back the crime scene tape and are sitting at the bar. There's a bottle of good single-malt Scotch between them and Sòlas's laptop. An old coat of Danni's, an Yves Saint-Laurent faux black Russian sable with an embroidered red silk lining and silver chinchilla-tail trim that was once worth nearly ten thousand dollars, is balled up on the end of the bar. Mandy, wearing a rather large Band-Aid, is curled into it.

It was just a flesh wound, but the small dog is making the most of it. Earlier, she turned up her nose at her dry food and made her way through most of Danni's strip steak, medium rare, and a baked potato. And now she's snoring.

The sight of her makes Wilson laugh. "You do know that's just a rat with good hair," he says, and startles them. Mandy yips. Danni jumps.

"Jeez. You look awful," she says.

Then Wilson sees the vulture. "What the hell is this?" he says. The huge black bird is leashed and sitting on a barstool next to

Danni. It's wearing a rufter hood that the crones fashioned from bits of old leather, velvet, and tin stars.

"Poe," Danni says. Takes off the hood for a proper introduction.

The cold dead eyes, the bloodred head—the bird gives Wilson a chill. "Shit. Last time I saw one of these he was eating lunch."

Peter, Sòlas thinks. Cringes. Danni can't help but notice, puts her arm around him.

"Wilson, sit down," she says. "We have to talk."

She grabs a glass for him. Pours some Scotch. Wilson doesn't take it. Won't sit. The bird is making him twitch. "What's the deal with that thing?"

"I think he's a gift from Bill," Danni says. "But he didn't leave a note, so it's hard to tell."

"Scary bastard."

"It's okay," Danni says. "Poe banged up his wing, so he's our guest for a while. He's pretty tame. I've been working with him."

Wilson still looks uneasy.

"It *is* okay," Danni says. "Sit down."

The tone of her voice makes it clear that there's something very wrong. Wilson takes the stool that's the farthest away from Poe and notices a wad of police caution tape on the floor. "Why is it so quiet around here? Saturday night. Happy hour. Where's that Manilow guy?"

Sòlas clears his throat. Danni shrugs. "Found him out back," she says plainly.

It takes Wilson a moment to understand what Danni is saying. It doesn't seem possible that there's another death. "Dumpster?"

Danni nods. "Thursday morning, though he looked like he'd been there awhile."

"Oh man," Wilson says. He feels guilty. When he did his rounds Wednesday night, he didn't go near the bar or the Dumpster. Convinced himself that nobody would be out there. Waste of time. But the truth was, he was scared. *No wonder Whit fired me.*

"What did Whit have to say about this?" he says.

"Nothing," Danni says. "Last time we saw him he was at your place and wasn't in the mood for a chat."

"He was looking for you," Sòlas says. "We were all looking for you."

"He came at Sòlas with one of those electric guns," Danni says.

Wilson's heart sinks. *Maybe it was Whit in the hospital.* "When was this?" His voice is sharp.

"Friday morning. Why?"

"Damn."

"Where have you been?" Sòlas asks.

"Dead."

It's clear Wilson isn't kidding. *"Really?"* Danni asks.

"Sophie had an accident. I took her to the hospital. Next thing I know, some SOB is Tasering me."

"Whit?" Danni says.

"I don't know. Didn't see. It was late Thursday night. Could have been Whit, but it doesn't really make sense. Why would he do that? He's not that nuts. Do they know how that what's-his-name died?" Wilson says.

"Buddy," Danni offers. "Hard to tell."

"Vultures?"

She nods. Closes her eyes. It's clear that this is difficult for her, as it is for him. Wilson raises his glass. "To Buddy and that homeless guy." Then he drinks the Scotch in one swallow, coughs. No one else touches theirs.

"His name was Peter," Sòlas says, his voice cracking. "I'd prefer you call him that. He was my brother."

At this moment, Wilson believes that it's impossible for him to feel any worse. "Sorry, man," he says and knows just how lame that is. He grabs the bottle of Scotch and pours himself another. Tops off their glasses, too.

"To Peter," Wilson says. The three raise their glasses. Sòlas would like to say the traditional Scottish toast for the departed, *"Cha bhithidh a leithid ami riamh"*—"His equal will never be among us again."

But he can't. He never really knew Peter; it seems false to say.

"Slàinte," he says. A wish for good health. Hardly appropriate but he says it anyway. And they drink. Then sit for a moment in the darkened bar.

The small dog is back asleep. The vulture is calm. It's an odd moment, because the three are all thinking the same thing: *Whit. It has to be Whit.* Although Danni and Wilson just aren't that sure.

"So what do we do?" Danni says.

"I think the better question is, what do we know?" Wilson says. "At least one of those deaths could have been from natural causes."

Sòlas says, "Before you came, we were looking for clues on my brother's website." He moves his laptop around so that Wilson can see it.

On the site, there's a journal entry with only one line of text. "Play me," it reads. Wilson leans across and hits PLAY.

It's some sort of homemade video. Peter appears wearing a Santa cap. The white beard and round-rim glasses make him look like a Santa at an upscale shopping mall. It's disconcerting.

"The nuns at the shelter lent me the hat," he says. "It just goes to show what a radical group of chicks they are."

His voice is manic, cocktail party pitched. The camera shakes and laughter is heard. *Probably a nun,* Wilson thinks.

Peter straightens the red cap and begins to paw at his beard, as if to brush something out of it. It's a nervous twitch. "Here's what your local homeless guy wants for Christmas," he says.

He keeps pawing at his beard. It's difficult to watch. Peter reads off a list that includes socks, batteries, old computers, and gift certificates to Starbucks. "The shelters put us out by 6:00 a.m., before sunrise, coldest part of the day. Gift certificates get us inside and feed us. Coffee's good, too."

Sòlas turns it off. It's too much to bear.

"That's just spooky," Wilson says. "Why'd he come here?"

Sòlas shrugs. "I was hoping you knew."

Wilson shakes his head. "He wasn't saying much when I found him." Sòlas pales. Wilson shrugs. "Sorry."

Danni is about to propose that the three of them should work together to solve these murders, because the major reason why the babysitter always gets decapitated by the guy carrying the chain saw is that she's going it alone, but before she can say a word, Bill walks in, red-faced, shaking, clutching flyers in his fists.

"When pigs fly!" he shouts. "Workshops! Parade! Circus! You are not going to turn this place into some damn hippie enclave."

Then Bill leans into Danni. "I thought you learned your lesson," he says. Doesn't notice the vulture.

Poe hisses. Spits at Bill.

"I don't think Poe likes you," Danni says.

"Do you have a license to engage in falconry?" he screams.

"Matter of fact," Danni says. "I do. I apprenticed with a falconer from Disney in 1999."

Then she smiles. Her Hollywood teeth glow. She only apprenticed for two weeks, but it doesn't matter. She's an actress, after all. Her plan is to act as if she knows what she's doing.

Bill throws the flyers in Sòlas's face. Storms out.

Mandy the dog looks up from the ten-thousand-dollar pile of faux fur and yawns, rolls over. Starts snoring.

Poe's eyes close again.

Wilson picks up a flyer.

Danni goes to the window. Outside, in the parking lot, Bill begins screeching at the Swedish crones. "When pigs fly!" he screams over and over again, pounding on their bus. The women open the door, laughing. They nod while Bill rants. They are still wearing their Santa Lucia outfits: the white lace dresses with red sashes. They still have laurel leaves braided in their long pigtails and are wearing their red-striped stockings and red clown shoes. They look like elderly angels: bemused, oddly innocent, and stranded on Earth. Bill shakes as he shouts.

"Maybe we should go out there," Danni says to Sòlas. "He's screaming at the crones."

"God help him, then," Sòlas says.

Danni watches the crones turn their backs to the screaming man and in unison, bend over, lift up their white ruffled dresses, and show him their knickers, as Danni's Grammy Keene would have said.

Then, in a feat of limber supremacy, they defy gravity—and probably nature, too—duck their heads between their legs, and stick out their tongues at him.

Danni doesn't need to be Swedish to understand the gesture. And neither does Bill. "When pigs fly!" he shouts again and storms away. The crones throw their arms around each other, laughing.

"Tough crowd," Danni says. Sòlas shrugs.

Wilson is studying the flyer. "Circus?"

"Sounds like fun, doesn't it?" Danni says. Enthusiastic. "You make a few masks, build a few life-size puppets, beat a drum, walk around on stilts—what's not to like? Sure, it's a little on the neo-pagan side, but so is Halloween, which is nearly a national holiday and my personal favorite. Besides, Sòlas promised that there would be fresh bread, and lots of it. Good bread is impossible to find in Florida. So I'm in."

Then she takes a breath. "You?"

Despite the lure of a well-formed crust, Wilson is apparently not enthused. He has a worried-about-the-neo-paganism-element look on his former-FBI face.

Danni would like to reassure him. "Hey, what's a little ritualistic behavior between friends?" she wants to say, but doesn't. She once said that in *The Lust of the Vampire Cheerleaders* and things did not go well—not well at all.

"Creating a circus together builds community," Sòlas says.

"Sounds goofy."

"The circus is a serious art form that dates back to Roman times."

"Forgive me," Wilson says, "but you wear a skirt and drive a pink bus with little hearts on it. I know goofy when I see it. I majored in badass at Quantico."

And minored in bullshit, Danni thinks.

Wilson leans over and pats Sòlas on the arm. "It's goofy, bud. Trust me."

"I like it," Danni says.

Wilson smirks. "See? Women love goofy stuff." Then he leans in. "Look," he says. "I'm guessing you came to Laguna Key to get some answers. That's what I'd do if I were you. But you can't get information from people using arts and crafts. It's just not a technique recognized by the Geneva Convention."

"What do you suggest?" Sòlas says. "The authorities seem to be no help in this."

"First," he says, "we need to sort out the facts."

"I hadn't spoken to my brother in twenty years."

"The last time I saw him," Danni says, "he was using our wireless system and was plugged into an outlet beachside. He was drinking that well water out there. Stuff is awful."

"What time was that?"

"Midnight. I opened the back door and asked if he wanted a cup of coffee and a blanket. Told him he could sleep in the kitchen if he wanted to, but he didn't say a word, just waved."

Wilson shakes his head. "Or waved you off."

"What you mean?" Sòlas says.

"I don't think he was alone," Wilson says. "When I found him, there wasn't a camera or a laptop anywhere. Seems odd. Somebody must have taken it."

"Maybe there's something in his blog," Danni says.

They all lean in. Read. The more they read, the more they drink.

Outside, an airplane flies low over the beach. The Piper Tri-Pacer. Again. It spits and rattles. Its four different sets of radios, none of which works consistently, screech and pop.

It flies low over the condos. Circles back, its engine groaning. Then returns. It's not Monday or Wednesday, but it is definitely him, Sophie thinks and is dizzy. Angry. Glad Wilson is not around. She feels her way to the telephone and picks it up. Her father had a voice-activated dialer installed on her phone. "Who would you like to speak to?" the computerized voice asks. It's a woman's voice, midwestern, pleasant, expectant. Mr. Whit programmed in forty-three numbers for Sophie to use; forty-three numbers he felt she needed. She had Wilson program in one more.

She hesitates.

"I'm sorry?" the voice says. "I'm afraid I didn't catch the name."

The voice sounds so hopeful and kind. And all Sophie has to do is say who she wants to call, and the computer will dial the number.

"I'm sorry. I'm having a hard time hearing you."

The Piper Tri-Pacer circles again and its engine stalls a bit. Sophie holds her breath, prays. A moment passes and the engine recovers. Sounds strong. She's relieved. But still, the plane is so low that she can feel its rattle as if it were the beat of her own heart.

Damn him.

"Would you like to try again later?" the voice asks.

"No," Sophie says.

"Okay." The voice sounds so bright. "Then who is it that you'd like to call?"

The Piper Tri-Pacer takes another low turn.

The name is said. The number is dialed. Sophie has no choice. It's what he wants, after all. As usual, he won't give up until she gives in.

Chapter Thirty

He is waiting for her on the beach, as promised.

She is naked, as promised. Her long black raincoat and the endless blue-water scarf lay at her feet.

"Chère, you have forgotten your sunglasses. Let me give you mine," he says. His voice is still filled with the music of the Deep South, its sloe-eyed beauty and wrought-iron grace.

"You said to come naked," she says. Angry. "So I did."

Without her sunglasses, it's clear that Sophie is blind. Her eyes wander independently. The left favors the extreme right. The other seems to be searching for something in the night sky.

He can't bear to see her like this. She's turned into some sort of creature, not the woman he knew. Ruins everything. He reaches into his shirt pocket and pulls out his Ray-Bans. Puts them on over her straying, unseeing eyes.

"Now you look like a movie star," he says, and pulls her into his arms.

Sophie knocks the glasses onto the sand. "You said naked and here I am."

He picks the sunglasses up, shakes them off, and puts them back on Sophie. Then kisses her passionately before she can knock them off again.

"I have missed you," he whispers. Bites her lip, her neck, the small pink lobe of her perfect ear. "I have so missed you."

He's so convincing, he nearly believes it himself.

How stupid do you think I am? Sophie thinks.

Chapter Thirty-one

They've been going over Peter's blogs for most of the night and Wilson has had enough. And enough Scotch. He leans over to the coffee and holds the pot in his hand.

"Anybody else?"

"I'm fine," Sòlas says, but he doesn't sound fine. He grows sadder and smaller with each entry.

Peter's blogs are painful to read. One had a link to a recent news segment from a Fort Lauderdale television station. Peter is begging in front of a storefront café on trendy Las Olas Boulevard. The chalkboard next to him lists the specials of the day, including a grilled Caribbean spiny lobster with jicama, crispy yucca, and passion fruit–vanilla bean vinaigrette. He looks as if he's starving to death. He hisses at the well-dressed tourists who pass by quickly and leave nothing in his cup.

The café owner is nearby. Tall. Balding. An Austrian. He has a kind face and that Arnold Schwarzenegger accent. Tells the reporter, "I come to this country to build my dream, to cook. If the city does nothing, I will soon be like him."

The next shot is Peter struggling with police. Then pepper spray. The reporter says, "It's a complicated issue."

Danni couldn't help but cry.

Just before he died, Peter began to document murders of the homeless. In January alone, he listed three in Fort Lauderdale, one in Sarasota, two in Destin, and three, each taking place one hour apart, in a middle-class neighborhood in Saint Petersburg.

Wilson shakes his head. "Just last week, a gang of teenagers killed a man in Orlando. He'd only been homeless a month. They hunted him down, kicked him to death."

"It's just all too sad," Danni says. Sòlas is stone silent.

"The key is in this blog somewhere," Wilson says. "I think it's weird that he never mentions that he has a brother, don't you think? He knew how to get hold of you, but he never mentions you."

"We left on bad terms," Sòlas says.

Wilson shakes his head, feels his brain rattle. *Man, am I tired,* he thinks. *That booze didn't help.*

"But he would have written about that. He wrote about getting beaten. But no mention of you or why he came to Laguna Key. It's really strange. It's like he had a reason to leave it out."

"There's one more post," says Danni. "About a job."

"I'm tired," Sòlas says.

"Peter was a guide. In the Keys," she says.

"Diving, right?" Sòlas says. "I read that. Ends badly. Some accident."

"Oh my," Danni says. Then reads aloud, "The woman was beautiful, long black hair rolling down her back. Stubborn, too."

"Let me see that," Wilson says, and it suddenly becomes clear that Peter came to Laguna Key because of Sophie. Things are finally making sense. He reads the entry quickly, his head and heart pounding.

Danni says, "The entry ends with this line from *Macbeth.* 'The Thane of Fife had a wife: where is she now?' "

Sòlas nods. "Dead. In *Macbeth,* the wife of the thane was murdered."

"Gotta go," Wilson says. The words slur, just a little. *Damn Scotch,* he thinks.

"You okay?" Danni asks.

"I think I got this figured out, Scottie," Wilson says. Then he pats Sòlas on the top of his head as if the Scot were a small black dog.

"Man, I am drunk," Wilson says. Then jumps into his little yellow golf cart and drives back to the condos. Weaves along on the deserted streets. When he arrives, he rings the bell repeatedly.

It is, of course, two o'clock in the morning.

When Sophie finally opens the door, Wilson says, "We have to talk," and means to be all business, but is suddenly overcome with a prickly sensation.

It's been a long time, but he's pretty sure that it's desire.

"You are going to have such a hangover," she says gently.

Sophie is backlit by the moonlight streaming in through her sliding glass doors. Her skin has a seashell sheen. She doesn't seem quite real. She smells of baby shampoo and soap.

And she's naked. Well. Nearly.

Sophie is actually wearing a large white terrycloth towel and a pair of Ray-Ban sunglasses that Wilson has never seen before. But she's still naked underneath it, he thinks. And a little damp.

And you just don't answer the door in a getup like that for nothing.

He breaks into a cold sweat because it's clear that for some amazing, unfathomable, happy, inexplicable, unbelievable reason, she wants him.

Wilson's hands sweat. "This is how," he says, and takes a deep breath, "you answer the door?"

"I took a shower."

"You don't have a bathrobe?"

She shakes her head. "No. But I looked through the peephole."

"Funny."

"True." Sophie shrugs. "Some habits are harder to break than others."

Sorry, he thinks. "Let me get you some clothes," he says. "We need to talk. You have any booze? I don't need any, but you might."

Wilson flips a light switch, but the room remains dark. Probably burned out. He feels his way into the bedroom.

"Wine okay?" Sophie says.

"Great," Wilson says, and turns the bedroom light on. The room is such a mess that it's shocking. There are no sheets on the bed. The mattress has huge tea stains on it. Half-eaten plates of food and moldy cups are stacked on the nightstand and on the top of the dresser. Last month, the physical therapist suggested that Sophie get rid of her maid so she could begin to learn how to become self-reliant. So she did. Now the closet is empty and clothes are piled in heaps on the floor.

"Are you subleasing to frat boys?" he says, and picks up the long black raincoat that Sophie left wadded up on the floor near the sweats. Weird, he thinks. It's wet. Sandy. Smells like dead fish.

She's been out. Again. That's why the shower.

Sophie stands in the bedroom doorway, holding a couple

of jelly jars filled with wine. He tosses the raincoat back on the floor.

"It's Opus One," she says before he can ask. "I paid the maid to steal a case from Whit before she left."

"Is that a felony?"

She thinks about it a minute. "It's the 1977 Proprietary Red. What's that? About five hundred bucks per bottle and we have twelve?" She does the math. "Could be. Want some ice? I like it with lots of ice."

"Remind me never to piss you off," Wilson says. Takes a slug. The wine is bitter. Despite the fact that he could be a murderer, Wilson still feels a little sorry for Whit. After all, a man's wine is sacred. Even a beer guy like Wilson knows that.

He hands back the glass. Carefully picks up the raincoat again. He can't help himself. He has a sudden driving need to know why it's wet, and he's a little afraid to ask considering what happened to Whit's 1977 Special Reserve Opus One. Sophie's a little high-strung.

"There's sweats at the foot of the bed," she says. "Did you find them?"

"Hang on," Wilson says. "I'm limping my way through this jungle." He roots around in the pockets of the raincoat. There's something in the left one. It's sandy. At first he thinks it's a shell, then he pulls it out—a woman's wedding band. The sight of it makes him feel queasy. It's small, like Sophie, and channel-set with at least a dozen diamonds.

"What are you doing?" she says.

There's some sort of inscription, but it's difficult to make it out in the dim light. Wilson puts the ring in his pocket for later. He's come too far. He has to know what it says.

"What pile is clean?" he asks.

"The one to your right. Sniff to make sure."

"Sniff? Sniff them yourself," he says, and hands her a set of sweats from the top of the huge pile. "I'm turning around now."

And he turns, but Sophie just stands there with the clothes in her hands. Weighing the moment. "My coat's on the floor, probably by your feet," she says, her voice odd. "Will you pick it up?"

She knows.

"Okay," he says. "I'll hang it in the closet."

"Fine," she says. She definitely knows. It's clear by her tone.

Wilson turns on the closet light. The ring is caked in sand. He licks it clean. Holds it up to the light. Shit, he thinks. He spits the grit onto his sleeve. Total weight is about eight carats, maybe more. Blue-white and clear. Maybe flawless. And you've got to believe it's not set in silver, either, he thinks. *This is worth some serious change.*

"Do you like it?"

Wilson's face goes hot. "It's a nice closet," he says. "It would be nicer if you had clothes hanging in it."

That's when he realizes that the inscription is in Braille. That's why he couldn't figure it out. The ring must be new.

"You finished?" she says. He takes a quick look. She's still in the towel, clothes in her hands.

The ring unnerves him. He has a horrible need to know what it says. So Wilson puts it back in his pocket. He'll check the Braille later. Tells himself he'll be able to put it back before she notices. But, of course, that's impossible. She knows he has it. She must.

"Say something," she says.

The airplane, he thinks. He suddenly remembers hearing that airplane again tonight. And it's Saturday night. That's odd. Not a Monday or a Wednesday.

"Do me a favor and put some clothes on," he says, and is saddened by the coolness in his voice.

"Sure," she says. Couldn't be icier.

Wilson turns back around and can hear her yank and struggle. Embarrassed, he looks around the room at the piles and suddenly realizes that all her clothes are sweats.

Man, he thinks. *That's a bitch.*

He's seen pictures of Sophie before the accident; Whit has an entire wall of them. There's Sophie in an emerald sequined evening gown on the night of her high school prom, Sophie fresh-faced in her red-and-white cheerleading uniform, Sophie wearing a traditional African robe in the Peace Corps, and Sophie wearing a white-and-gold Japanese kimono on her wedding day, standing next to an old airplane with tin cans tied to it.

Wilson can't believe that he didn't put this together earlier.

The airplane.

The husband is back.

"Safe now," she says.

He feels as if he's been kicked in the stomach. He wants to hold those visions of Sophie in his head for a moment more—the Sophie who is bright and vibrant, the Sophie without a returning husband, the Sophie not wearing gray sweats.

"Wilson?"

There's a slight edge of panic in her voice and so he turns and can see that despite everything, she is still the Sophie he knows. Beautiful. Vibrant. Nothing can dampen her spirit. Not even blindness.

No wonder he wants her back, he thinks. *I'd never let her go.*

He returns the ring back to the pocket of her raincoat. It's suddenly clear that it's none of his business what it says. It's a personal matter between married people, he thinks. Hopes he doesn't regret that later.

"Right here," he says, and takes her hand. It's clammy. He blows on it to warm it. "Jeez, you *still* could chill beer with this."

"My pants are on backward," she says.

And they are, so he laughs.

They sit down on the edge of the unmade bed. It feels good to sit. "Look," he says. "There's been another death."

"You're kidding?"

"Wish I was. Danni found that new singer of hers in the Dumpster, same place I found that guy."

"That's sick. My father couldn't have done that."

Wilson doesn't want to talk about Whit right now, it's too complicated. "The thing is," Wilson says. "That guy I found in the Dumpster might have something to do with your accident." Sophie stiffens, but doesn't say a word. "I think he was your tour guide."

"That's not possible."

"Well—"

"No," she says. "The tour guide was a kid. Teenager. He knew some spots where the tourists don't go, dangerous places. Derek thought it would be fun."

Wilson has never heard the husband's name before. *Derek.* Makes him uneasy. "Was this boy with an older man?"

"No."

"You sure?"

She nods. "Yes. He came up to our boat. Had his own gear. There was nobody else. Just the three of us."

"Nobody trailing you? Maybe another boat?"

"No way. It's a Cigarette, a real one. No knockoff. Forty-six-footer. Two supercharged nine-hundred-horsepower Mercury nine-hundred-SC V-8s. It's what's called a go-fast."

Even though her sweatpants are on backward, the sight of Sophie talking engines is the sexiest thing Wilson has ever seen. "I am so sorry that you weren't naked when you said that," he says, and laughs.

She's smiling again and Wilson now realizes that he's flirting with another man's wife. "Sorry. Out of line."

"No, that was sweet."

Sophie pats his hand kindly, just like someone else's wife would do.

"It was just an accident," she says. "My blindness. Derek had nothing to do with it. Really." She doesn't exactly sound convinced.

The two are quiet for a moment and then Sophie says, "I made up the couch for you, clean sheets and everything."

It's then that Wilson realizes that he has no place else to go.

"He says he's sorry," she says. For a moment, Wilson thinks she's speaking about the husband. He coughs, uncomfortable. Then she clarifies. "Whit. He's sorry he fired you. He wants you to stay. Big raise and everything. Maybe even a few water buffalo thrown in to sweeten the pot."

It's clear that Sophie talked to Whit, even though Wilson asked her not to. Nobody seems to care what he wants. "And the Taser. Is he sorry for that, too?" he says.

Sophie hesitates. She knows Whit did confess, or sort of confessed—at least agreed to a confession—but Wilson is angry. Might misunderstand. Might think he killed those other guys, too. It just looks bad.

Her silence makes matters worse. *This is just some sort of game to them,* he thinks. *The rich are all alike. I'm out of here.*

Then Wilson thinks of Peter, thrown in the Dumpster like some bag of trash. He was Sòlas's brother. *And that singer probably has family, too.*

"Stay for me," Sophie says. "Out of friendship." She reaches out for his hand. "Don't go."

Wilson moves away. He knows it's the blindness talking. It has to be. Don't go *right now* is what she really means. *Not until Whit and my husband make nice again.*

Wilson's not stupid. He knows that, even blind, Sophie's not in his league. But he did promise Danni and Sòlas that he'd help them get some answers. They deserve answers, he thinks.

"Do you remember his name?" he says.

"Who?"

"The one who took you diving."

"Poor kid."

"What do you mean?"

"He's dead."

Chapter Thirty-two

"Looking for this?"

This is not good.

As soon as Danni hears Sòlas's voice, she knows that he has found the bone she was looking for. He doesn't need to tap her on the shoulder with it, but does. It feels cold against her skin. Gives her a chill. She turns, and much to her surprise, Sòlas is bare-chested, barefoot, wearing only his kilt, and holding the bone across his chest like a sword.

"I was hoping, actually, that I made a mistake," he says. "I thought I saw you try to hide it—"

"I thought you went to bed," Danni says. "This doesn't involve you."

Over their heads, the incandescent moon makes Sòlas look as savage as any relative of Macbeth could be. His shoulders are broad. His hair is a wild tangle. His violet eyes are that smoky shade of far-off fires.

She reaches out to take the bone from him. *Bill has probably destroyed the rest,* she thinks sadly. *Sorry, Prescott. Gave it my best shot.*

Still, she plans to send the femur to a guy she knows, a forensics expert. One bone is better than nothing.

Sòlas turns away from her slightly. "Ah, Danni," he says with such sorrow, such mistrust.

His small wings make him seem even more earthbound. She reaches out to touch them again. This time, she thinks, it will not be a mistake. She's not sure why, but she wants to hold them gently in her hands. Wants to hold him, but he moves away.

"You know, I tried to make an angel once," he says. "For a parade. No matter what I did, I couldn't get the face right—"

Then he stops.

This time of night, this time of the year, the beach is often filled with bats. Hundreds of them, diving low in flocks.

And so they arrive. Now. Unannounced.

The moment is startling. Bats are suddenly everywhere. Sòlas and Danni hold their breath, afraid to move. Bats fly by them, around them, between them. Their wings are silver in the moonlight, like mercury. Molten. Their mouths are open—all claws and teeth. Fox eyes. Their shrill calls bounce off Danni's hand, Sòlas's cheek, and the bone of the dead slave buried long ago.

Radar, Danni thinks.

It only makes sense. They fly so close, so fast, that the speed of their beating wings turns the night air cold.

Then it's over—just like that—as quickly as it began.

Danni watches the flock bank up and away toward the gulf, toward the mangrove forest and safety.

"I'm sure this reminds me of a movie," she says, and falls to her knees into the soft sand. "But I'm too tired to think which one."

The tide is high, the water rough. Waves break around her. For a moment, she wants to be pulled into it, wants to be taken away from this place. Sòlas places the bone on the deck. Kneels down beside her. "Danni—"

"Do you know why horror films are important?" she says. Doesn't wait for an answer. "Terror. We need terror to appreciate joy."

And so Sòlas kisses her.

And there is heat, tenderness. And terror.

And Danni pulls Sòlas down into the surf with her. Their kisses are salt. The sand feels cold. The water is even colder. The smell of dying fish is everywhere. She runs her lips down his spine. The wings flutter for a moment. They seem smaller than she remembered.

He pulls her away from them, uncomfortable.

"They're beautiful," she says. And he kisses her again. Waves crash around them.

The moment is iconic. Danni knows it. *From Here to Eternity,* she thinks.

But Sòlas is not Burt Lancaster. And she is not Deborah Kerr.

Even though Sòlas wants her, he can't stop thinking about his brother. On this beach. Alone. Waiting for something, or someone. Then being thrown away. The Dumpster is directly behind them. The caution tape waves in the wind.

"I'm sorry," Sòlas says and kisses her again—this time gently. The taste of salt in her mouth is his tears.

He walks away—not like the archangel Michael, the warrior figure, but like a man who cannot find his way home.

For the second time that night, Danni finds herself crying.

Chapter Thirty-three

The next day's forecast is chilly by Florida standards. The National Weather Service reports that conditions are overcast. At 8:47 a.m., the air temperature is 49 degrees. Dewpoint is 39 percent. The "feels like" temperature is 24. The gulf is a cool 56. Winds are out of the north at 15 to 25 knots. There are freeze warnings posted for early evening.

Despite the weather, a handful of people are standing on the beach. Watching. Their morning walks are forgotten. Some are on their cell phones calling others to join them.

The crones are windsurfing in their bikinis.

The women are strong and lean. Ageless. And yes, the bikinis are itsy-bitsy and have yellow polka dots. That is, of course, to be expected. Their short boards also have yellow polka dots on them, as do their sails. In windsurfing, style is important. They've even woven yellow ribbons into their long gray braids. The only nod to their circus training is their bright red surf shoes.

Wilson leans over to Danni and says, "Isn't that kind of cold?"

"They're from Sweden," she says. "They invented cold."

Wilson looks as if he hasn't slept all night. And he hasn't. He needs a computer, and Sophie's talks to him. That freaks him out. The Braille keyboard is weird, too.

It's difficult not to gawk as the crones take the waves. They're sailing, steering, planing, jibing, tacking, and jumping. And making it look easy.

The whole town is watching.

"We could use a few bars of 'Surfin' Safari' right about now," Danni says to Wilson.

Wilson shrugs. He hasn't thought of a Beach Boys tune since they jump-started his heart in the hospital. "Not in the mood," he says.

"You okay?"

"I guess," he says, but doesn't sound okay.

Danni gives him a sisterly hug. "Girl trouble?"

"Speaking of . . . where's your boyfriend?" he asks.

Danni slugs him in the arm as if she's fourteen years old. "He's back in the parking lot. In his bus, doing bus things. I don't know."

"Danni has a boyfriend," Wilson whispers in a singsong tease. The crowd around them cheers, but not for Danni.

The crones, who are members of the Swedish Windsurfing Organization, Stockholm branch, are now doing figure eights in the slate-blue water. Graceful as kites, and all in yellow, they are like ribbons of sunlight slashing through the damp fog.

They wave at the crowd. The crowd waves back. Even Wilson.

Everyone seems to be having fun and that makes Danni nervous. "Where's Bill?" she says. "Bill isn't here." She looks at her watch; it's nearly 9:00 a.m. "Neither is Whit. This isn't good."

That's when the shouting begins.

Chapter Thirty-four

While everyone was at the beach that morning watching the crones, Bill was very busy. A few early phone calls and a couple of faxes later, and there are three transport trucks, one extremely large sheriff, and two deputies removing the wildly pink Rose and Puppet buses from Danni's parking lot.

Bill was surprised that he didn't think of this earlier. In the banking business he had things repossessed all the time. You don't even need to own things to have them repossessed. You just need convincing paperwork. It's easy.

So now, he's in his front yard watching the drama unfold across the street. "A brilliant plan," he says. But no one hears him. They're all in the bar parking lot milling around. The buses are perched on top of the transport trucks. Sòlas and Danni are looking for answers.

Windsurfing is over.

"But I have the registrations," Sòlas says and waves the papers at the sheriff. "The buses are legally mine."

"Uh-huh," the sheriff says again. He is perfectly square and has the molasses drawl of a man from the real South, not Florida.

Maybe Georgia, Danni thinks. *Or North Carolina.*

It's a little difficult to tell. His southern drawl—the diphthongization or triphthongization of the traditional short vowels—is indeed evident. And the phrase "right here" is pronounced "righ'tchere," but his syllabic emphasis in general is often misplaced.

When Danni thinks like this, it makes her head hurt—but she's used to it. It's an occupational hazard of being an actor.

The sheriff continues, "All I know is that some northern lawyer sent these papers righ'tchere down to serve on you," he says, "and I'm repossessing these vehicles."

He also pronounces the word *vehicles* with an unfortunate emphasis on the "hick" of it.

Wasn't he in The Debutant Bloodsuckers of Beauford County? Danni thinks. *Victim Number One?*

"This parking lot is private property," she says. "My private property. I'm not sure this is legal."

The sheriff clears his throat. "Miss, that is a technicality and I do not deal in technicalities. All I know is that there's a lien against these vehicles and all the contents of these vehicles," he says. Then he furrows his unibrow.

If these were the old days, Danni thinks, *this is the point in the plot where the debutante bloodsuckers pull out a chain saw and make the guy into coleslaw.*

Danni is feeling wistful again. Real life is just one ongoing disappointment.

"This is not possible," Sòlas says. "How is this possible?"

The sheriff shrugs. "The name of the lawyer is on the papers. You can contact him. He'll explain it."

Danni steps up. "But it's clear that this man owns these things."

"You'll have to take it up in court."

"But—"

"It's perfectly legal, miss."

"May I ask you where you were born?" she asks. Just can't help herself; she needs to know. Professional curiosity.

"Rhinelander, Wisconsin, miss," he says. "I find that it's more effective if I talk this way."

Then he turns his bulk back to Sòlas. "Sir, I have noticed you are not an American. Do you have a passport from your native land and a green card?"

Sòlas looks as if he's about to pop.

Luckily, while this is happening, the crones have opened the emergency doors on the back of their buses. They pass down their suitcases, Sòlas's sword and bagpipes, the computer equipment, and anything else they can get their hands on to some of the townspeople gathered around.

"This just doesn't seem fair," one woman whispers.

"I love their bikinis," says another.

Bill is standing off to the side, watching it all.

Danni pulls out her cell phone and speed-dials her lawyer in LA. The sun hasn't even risen there yet. The phone rings, unanswered.

"Why can't there be a chain-saw-wielding psycho around when you need one?" she says to no one in particular.

As if on cue, Whit pulls up on his silver Vespa. The long silk scarf waves as he drives by Danni. She'd like to give it a yank, just for fun.

Wilson whispers, "As crazy as this sounds, I don't like him for the murders."

"He's awfully trigger-happy with that Taser."

The mention of the word gives Wilson a chill. "But both men

were strangers to Whit," he says. "I've thought about it over and over again. Only a psycho kills a stranger."

"Hmm," Danni says, and watches as Whit circles the crowd on his shiny Vespa. He does seem more like a used-car salesman running for Congress. Ballot tampering is plausible—expected, even. Murder—not so much.

This launches Danni into a detailed analysis of the psycho film genre as an existential albeit self-conscious metaphor for the anticonsumerist, identity-crisis-ridden American-style form of capitalism. When she begins to illuminate and annotate the several decapitation scenes in *Trauma* and elucidate how the famed director Dario Argento hacked off people's heads and put them in hatboxes as a profound statement of rage against shopping malls, Danni makes the mistake of taking a breath. Then says, "Amazing, you know?"

Wilson does. He knows. He knows he has to leave. Right now. Before his head explodes. "Fascinating," he says. "Hate to leave but I got to talk to Whitless. He owes me some workers' comp."

Across the street, Whit pulls up alongside Bill. "What's going on?" he asks.

"Housecleaning," Bill whispers. Then laughs.

Whit is pretty sure that's more information than he wants to know.

The last pink bus is loaded onto the transport, and the crones vault from the side windows, land on the soft sand of the parking lot, and shout, "Ta-da!" Whit notices that Wilson is in the crowd trying to pull himself away from Danni.

Outta here, Whit thinks. "Great, then," he says to Bill, and starts to pull away. Bill grabs his arm.

"We need to talk about phase two," he says with great portent.

Phase two? Whit thinks. *Not that damn shopping center thing again.* Wilson starts to make his way across the tangle of people toward him. Whit slips out of Bill's grasp and drives away, waving. "Call me!" he shouts.

This is his doing, Danni thinks as she watches Whit make his way down the whitewashed street. His long white silk scarf trails after him like a jet stream. "Bastard," she says under her breath. *"Adieu, mes amis. Je vais à la gloire!"* she shouts after him. Shaking her fist.

Wilson is back, laughing. "And that would mean?" he asks.

It's the last thing the actress Isadora Duncan said before her long scarf wrapped around the wheel of a sports car and snapped her neck.

"Good-bye, my friends, I am off to glory!" Danni says. "It's kind of a curse."

But it doesn't work. Whit safely zips up the hill to the end of the road and speeds out of sight.

"Why couldn't he just Duncan it?" Danni sighs.

"Yeah," Wilson says. "Dunkin' would be excellent about right now. Maybe jelly-filled or chocolate custard. Maybe a couple with sprinkles."

Chapter Thirty-five

When Bill's doorbell rings, he expects it to be Whit. Most everyone else in town left after the sheriff and those damn buses. So he doesn't even look through the peephole. "Welcome to phase two," he says as he opens the door.

Unfortunately, it's not Whit.

The man is a stranger, but Bill's seen him before. Titanium racing helmet, black with a dark face shield—it's hard to forget somebody like that. The fact that he's standing at Bill's door is a bad sign.

He knows who I am, where I live, Bill thinks.

The fact that the man is wearing latex gloves—the same kind that Bill bought last week in Cooper City at the farm and feed store, maybe even the same pair—is even worse.

Even though it's 10:30 in the morning, and any minute now a postman or a delivery person or a neighbor could walk by and see, the stranger reaches in the pocket of his padded leather jacket and pulls out a length of pipe capped at both ends. He fingers the long, slightly charred wick.

He must have been watching me the other morning, Bill thinks. *That's why the bombs didn't explode.*

"I'll be in contact," he says, and hands Bill's pipe bomb back to him. Bill is dizzy, speechless—afraid, most of all, afraid. The man turns and begins to walk down the sidewalk. Then stops. Turns back.

"I almost forgot," he says, and reaches into his other pocket. "Catch."

Thomas A. Swift's Electric Rifle, the M-26, the military version, spins through the air for just a moment, then clatters to the ground at Bill's feet.

"You lost this," the man says. "I hope you don't mind, but I tinkered with it. Juiced it up." Then he turns and walks slowly down the street. Laughing.

Chapter Thirty-six

The article is dated November 28. The second sentence makes Wilson slightly queasy.

"The only witness, Jason MacKay, eighteen, was killed by a hit-and-run driver."

Peter had a kid, he thinks.

Danni left Wilson in charge of the bar and her newly acquired menagerie of toy dog and bird of prey while she, Sòlas, and the crones took a taxi to the sheriff's office to see about the buses.

"Don't worry, I walked them both," she told Wilson as everyone climbed in. A tight fit.

"Walked them?"

Danni shrugged. "They have leashes."

A vulture and a shih tzu. Wilson wished he'd been around to see that.

"If you could," she said, "try to take that feather and stroke Poe's feet, just lightly. We need to get him used to being touched so he doesn't attack. If you could walk him around, that would be great."

"Maybe take him for an ice cream?"

She shook her head. "I think he's lactose intolerant."

"You know I'm not going to do any of that, don't you?"

"A girl can hope."

While Danni's gone, Wilson uses her computer to do an Internet search on Sophie's accident. The bandaged Mandy supervises. Poe, safely tied to his perch, sleeps.

Surprisingly, there are several articles to choose from, but the first one catches his eye. "Heiress Vacation Tragedy Unsolved." It's from Wilson's hometown paper, the Fort Lauderdale *Sun-Sentinel,* and there are lots of details about Sophie's being the only heir to Whit's fortune, which is considerable and includes properties both in the United States and the Bahamas.

"Apparently, she's quite the catch," Wilson says to Mandy, who yips.

Despite Sophie's assurances, the article clearly says that her accident didn't seem to be an accident. Not only was the witness dead, but the husband, their boat, and the diving equipment could not be found.

The emergency room doctor is quoted saying "something seemed to pop" in Sophie's brain. Which Whit had already told Wilson, but the rest of the paragraph gave him pause. "But there was an alarming amount of digitalis in her system."

The reporter went on to explain that the drug, originally derived from the poisonous foxglove plant, is most commonly used to restore adequate circulation in patients with congestive heart failure and also can slow the rate of ventricular contraction in patients with atrial fibrillation or flutter.

It was something that she had no prescription for.

Sophie, apparently, refused to cooperate with police. Whit had no comment.

Wilson does a quick Internet search on the drug. Doesn't like what he finds. Taken in large doses, digitalis will cause hallucinations, then death. An entry under "interactions" nearly makes his heart stop.

"Ginseng. Can cause blindness."

Every morning, Sophie wakes at 6:30 a.m. and makes tea. Wilson, just back from his rounds, hears the kettle's whistle cut the quiet of darkness. Furious. Insistent. He hears her walk to the stove. Sometimes, she knocks into something. A table falls over. A cup crashes to the floor. This always makes Wilson's chest go tight. Only when the kettle's whistle deflates can he relax. A few minutes later, he'll hear her open the sliding glass door and hear the creak of her rocker as she finally sits, facing the ocean, and knits.

Then he falls back asleep. Somewhat.

"Can't you drink coffee?" he asked her. "It's quieter."

"Ginseng makes you live longer."

Unless your husband spikes it with digitalis.

Wilson wants to grab the dog and the big bird and tool over to Sophie's, but he knows that all this is just conjecture and maybe—probably, most certainly—a huge amount of jealousy on his part. He has to be sure.

The newspaper ran a sidebar about the boy. Jason wasn't a certified diver. There was a mention of a mother, Suny. Said she was a waitress at the Floridian Diner in Fort Lauderdale.

Wilson knows the Floridian well. Its banana split, which the menu asserts features bananas "gently peeled" by a "banana expert," is one of the many reasons why Wilson spent his youth shopping in the husky boys department of JCPenney.

"Time for breakfast, dog," he says.

Chapter Thirty-seven

Gayle Hennessey, that redhead Wilson sat behind at Quantico, the one who came when the Hummer exploded, is standing at Whit's door. He watches her through the peephole, suspects she's wearing that same cheap suit she wore last time. It's shiny. Hangs funny. Her legs are an unattractive shade of navy. *Probably bought those nylons at the grocery store,* Whit thinks. Even though there's a chill in the air, he can see a bead of sweat across her top lip.

She rings the bell for the third time.

"I've got something on the stove," he says. "Could you come back later?"

"No."

Whit opens the door. The suit is, indeed, the same one she wore last time. The polyester glints in the sun. "Come in," he says. "I'm frying some candy bars."

She cocks her head, as if she didn't hear him correctly.

"I'm trying to pair them with a wine," he says.

The countertops of his vast Euro-style stainless-steel kitchen are covered with every permutation of snack food known to man. They are arranged in alphabetical order, from Almond Joy bars to Zapp's potato chips, and include several types of fried pork rinds, ranging from mild, regular, and hot to megahot, blazing hot, atomic hot, and meltdown.

Even though it's not yet noon, he pours a large glass of Saint-Émilion. Holds it up to the light. Examines its ruby tones. Sniffs.

"If I can find the perfect wine to go with something most people eat—let's say Cheetos—then I can sell a whole new lifestyle to middle America." He takes a long sip. Gargles it. Spits it out in the sink.

Hennessey opens her notebook. "I just have a couple of questions."

"I would like my lawyer present." The last time she had questions it was about that homeless guy and his son. Didn't go well.

"These are just housekeeping items."

Whit holds up a perfectly fried chocolate bar. The batter has a tempura texture, looks light. Golden. There's a slight hint of caramel goodness in the air. Hennessey leans in a bit.

"Do the FBI eat?" Whit asks.

"Do you know a Florence Heaney?"

Whit takes a bite; a bit of caramel drips onto his chin.

"He also went by the name of Buddy," she says.

Whit's face colors. It's clear these are not "housekeeping questions."

"If you leave your questions," he says, "my lawyer will issue a statement."

Whit tosses a handful of tiny peanut butter cups into the tempura batter, and then in the oil. Smoke covers him like a cloud.

"We now believe he was the one who set fire to the Hummer."

Whit opens up a drawer, takes out a business card. Writes the number. "Here's my lawyer's cell. Just give him a call."

Hennessey flips the card over and writes down a time and date. "This is when I will see you in my office," she says. Leaves a card of her own.

I'm screwed, Whit thinks, and stuffs another fried peanut butter cup in his mouth. Takes a slug of the Saint-Émilion. Then brightens.

Fried peanut butter and Saint-Émilion are perfect together.

"I'll let myself out."

"Sure," Whit says. Drops another handful of peanut butter cups into the batter, just to be sure.

Chapter Thirty-eight

Wilson grew up in Fort Lauderdale. Buried his old man there. It's about an hour across Alligator Alley from Laguna Key, but the state troopers aren't out, so he makes it in less. The city's welcome sign gives him a sinking feeling. He parks his GTO in the municipal parking lot. Plucks Mandy from his lap. "Come on, dog," he says. "Hop in the girly bag. We got some snooping to do."

Mandy is so happy that she licks him on the lips.

"Dog, do not *ever* do that again. *Never* again."

Mandy whimpers. It appears as if the small dog has a bit of a crush.

Wilson suspects that being kissed by the near-rat, as he thinks of her, will be the high point of his day. Being back in Fort Lauderdale makes him itch. Once on the street, Wilson knows why.

Urban renewal sucks, he thinks as he walks down Las Olas Boulevard, the trendy section of Fort Lauderdale. The Chamber of Commerce calls it "a shopping and dining district." Wilson calls it annoying. The whole place reeks of potpourri.

He tells Mandy, "Urban renewal is the pansy-fi-cation of a culture," and the small dog cocks her tawny head to one side.

Wilson is sweaty, wrinkled, unwashed, and unshaven. He carries Mandy in her knockoff Louis Vuitton Sac Chien. It's a very good knockoff—the original retails for about fourteen hundred dollars with a monogram, and so all the fashionable women think he must be European. They stick their well-manicured fingers into the Sac and see the Swarovski crystal dog collar they knew would be there. They ooh and aah.

"So cute," they say in faux Continental accents.

It's slow going until one sees the Band-Aid on Mandy and says in a tinny high voice, the kind of voice that makes the considerable amount of hair on Wilson's neck stand on end, "Does the baby have a boo-boo?"

Wilson has been waiting for this moment. "Yeah," he says. "My pet vulture, Poe, thought she was a Dorito."

The woman's screams could be heard two blocks away.

When Wilson and Mandy come to the Riverside Hotel, he says, "See here, dog? Back when my old man was a kid, this used to be called Hotel Champ Carr. Couple of rich brothers loved deep-sea fishing. Bought the hotel. Put their fishing guide, Champ Carr, in charge.

"And you know why?" He figures the dog doesn't have a clue, so he doesn't wait for an answer. "Because Champ was a manly guy who could tell a good story and he didn't even know how to spell potpourri."

Mandy gives an approving howl.

"Yep," Wilson says. "That's what I think, too."

At the end of the "district" is the Floridian Diner. Across the street, Wilson notices the café Peter was arrested in front of from the news video on his blog.

Cozy, he thinks. He crosses the street. Looks in the window of the café. The Austrian is there, sweeping. Wilson taps on the glass.

The man opens the door, points back down the street at the Riverside, and says, *"Il y a un bon restaurant à l' hôtel."*

"I am *not* French," Wilson says.

"Sorry," the man says. "Still, I am not open yet and the hotel does have a good breakfast."

"Look, I just want to know about that homeless guy who usually is here." The man is suspicious. He eyes the Louis Vuitton Sac Chien.

"I am busy," he says but doesn't move. Wilson opens up his wallet, palms him a ten. The Austrian's suddenly chatty.

"I have not seen he or his friend, in over a week."

"Friend?"

"Another man. Homeless. I think he had TB, very ill. He coughs all over my sidewalk customers until I would pay him to stay away."

The Austrian closes the door. Locks it. Goes back to his sweeping.

"Dog," Wilson says, "this town just isn't as friendly as it used to be."

Chapter Thirty-nine

Wilson's note read, "Dog and me gone a-hunting," and Danni knows that Mandy is in good hands. Well, maybe not so good hands, but the small tawny dog that bears a striking resemblance to Barry Manilow is, at least, not lost. Still, she misses her. The trip to the sheriff's department seemed to depress Sòlas even more.

"You can always replace the buses," Danni said as they waited for a rental car.

"My puppets," he said quietly.

Danni looked at the buses locked behind the chain-link fence. The puppets seemed so real. Trapped. Their gentle faces were as innocent as children's. At the back of the bus named WATCHFULNESS, the two puppets that Sòlas named Sorrow and Joy were still posed as if lovers locked in an embrace.

"You can make more," she said, but she knew that wasn't really true.

Sòlas's eyes were the color of bruised plums. "Peter once told me that I made these puppets in the likeness of our parents," he said.

"But I don't remember what they look like anymore. Not really. I'm afraid if I lose them, I lose my heart."

It was a quiet cab ride back to Laguna Key.

And so now Danni is missing Mandy. She tries to feed Poe. Passes the last of her baby-back ribs over the bird's feet. She knows that's how it's done, but the vulture does not take the meat.

"I'm sorry," Danni says to the bird. "We've made a mess of you, haven't we?"

And it's true. The building of Laguna Key destroyed a good deal of the vultures' natural habitat. They're not sleeping at night. They're eating the upholstery from everyone's golf carts. And now, in the case of Poe, they're not eating at all.

Sòlas and the crones are meeting at the other end of the bar.

"I'm going for a walk," Danni says. Then she offers her arm as a perch, which Poe takes, she hopes, for the very last time.

Chapter Forty

The Floridian is more than sixty-five years old and open twenty-four hours a day. It features blaring oldies music, teetering chandeliers, creaking floors, and memorabilia splayed across its fluorescent-colored walls. It's one of the finest examples of the Tourist Trap School of Interior Design that Fort Lauderdale offers. It's always full.

When Wilson opens the door, he remembers the last time he was here. It was with his father, not too long ago. Ray had just finished the last round of his chemo. They sat by the Richard Nixon wall. Wilson ordered him the Fat Cat Breakfast, a New York strip steak with two eggs, grits, biscuits, and a bottle of Dom Pérignon—$229.99.

"You got to think lucky," he told his father, but Ray was too weak to eat or drink. He called the waitress. Canceled the order. Asked for water.

Wilson takes a table by the wall containing a homage to Marilyn Monroe. "Is this Suny's station?" he asks the waitress who comes to the table bearing coffee and a bowl of water for Mandy.

"We can swap," she says. Pours the coffee without asking.

Wilson looks over the menu. The sausage gravy with biscuits makes his stomach growl. Mandy, inside her Sac, paws at the bowl.

"You thirsty?" he asks. Opens the case.

"You asked for me?"

Wilson looks up. It's Suny—it says that right on her name tag, but she's not at all what Wilson expected. Too tan and tall. Pretty. Silver rings on all her fingers. She hardly seems old enough to have lost an eighteen-year-old son.

Instead of taking his order, she sits down across from him.

"Nobody ever asks for me," she says. "I took a break. Figure you brought a check." Before Wilson can say a thing, she adds, "You know, you're a lot fatter than I thought you'd be."

"I'm not sure what to say."

"And I didn't expect you to be walking in with a dog in your purse," she says. "But that could explain why you never married."

Mandy growls.

"Do you have a problem with me?" Suny asks the dog. " 'Cause if you have a problem with me, you can go outside where you belong."

Mandy's hackles rise. Makes her looks like a giant bouffant hairdo. Wilson puts her back in the Sac.

"Can we start from the beginning?" he says.

"You know, if you would have just given him the money, he wouldn't have had to live like an animal. And die like one. You should be ashamed. Borderline personality disorder, that's what the doctors always said. You know what causes that? Harmful experiences. They were his parents. He had a right to half. Made him crazy. Man, he hated you."

Peter, Wilson thinks. *She thinks I'm Sòlas.*

"Of course, your parents were a piece of work, with all that crap about Macbeth. That screws up people, too."

"Look, I'm not—"

Suny leans across the table. "You better have the money. Peter always said he'd make you pay up. Used to talk about it all the time. Went crazy when he saw on your website that somebody *gave* you even more. Genius award, my ass. You had all that money, how could you not help him? What is wrong with you?"

Wilson looks around, uncomfortable. He thinks of the vultures, their feeding frenzy. It was bad enough when their dinner suddenly had a name, not just "some homeless guy." But now it's somebody's brother, somebody's father. The guy had a real life, tough as it was, and people loved him and still are willing to fight for him.

The music is so loud, Wilson feels as if he should shout, but doesn't.

"I'm the one who found him," Wilson says. Hopes she doesn't ask for details. "I'm not his brother."

It takes a moment for this information to register. "Oh," Suny says. She suddenly seems smaller. Tired. "The brother . . . ?"

"He knows. Police called him as soon as the body was found. Didn't they tell you that?"

She shakes her head. "I had to fill out a missing person report. Peter was dead three days before I even knew."

Wilson doesn't know what to say, but feels the need to say something, give some sort of comfort. "I'm not sure they knew about you. Peter had an old ID and Sòlas's number on a slip of paper when I found him. What was he doing in Laguna Key?"

"Police just found the van that killed our boy. Registered to the

Laguna Key Development Corporation. It was in the newspaper. Don't you read the papers?"

Wilson doesn't read the papers. Or watch the news. It's depressing. He hates to be depressed. And when he did the Internet search, he only read the top article, nothing more. *Damn sloppy.*

"Did he go alone?" he asks.

"Naw. He and Choo-Choo went."

"Choo-Choo?"

"He's from Chattanooga. Choo-Choo, get it? Like the song? I don't know what his real name is. Has a stack of white hair. 'Like smoke from a steam engine,' he used to say. He smoked like a steam engine, too. Has emphysema or something like that. Could hardly breathe sometimes. Haven't seen him since. I figure that's where my car is."

Then she seems to remember something. "Hey, you're the rent-a-cop, aren't you? Cops told me a rent-a-cop found him."

Thanks, he thinks. *Thanks a lot.*

He corrects her. "The security guard, yes."

She shrugs. "Well, whatever. Like I told that redhead from the FBI, the whole van thing really set Peter off again. He stopped taking his pills altogether. He said they slowed them down. He had this idea of himself as a warrior: the whole Clan MacKay gig."

"He was violent sometimes?"

"I never said that," she says. It seems for a moment like she's going to cry, but she doesn't.

A waitress walks by with a cheese omelet, a side of bacon, and toast on a tray. Wilson's stomach growls; Mandy's ears perk up.

"You got to order if you sit here," she says.

"I'll be gone in a minute," Wilson says but realizes that he hasn't eaten in a while. His stomach growls even louder. "What was Jason doing in Key West?"

"Why do you care so much about this?"

That's a good question.

Sophie, he thinks out of reflex and maybe it's still true, but it's more than that. "I know the agent in charge of the case," he says. "She's okay, but for her it's just her job. I found Peter. It's personal."

Suny hesitates, and then leans in. "They went to Key West a lot but never hurt anybody," she whispers. "During tourist season, they'd go down. Find a mark, usually a couple, at the docks—big boat, lots of money. You know . . . ," she says, and shrugs.

Some sort of scam, he thinks. Doesn't want to press. "What happened this last time?"

She shrugs.

It's clear that even if Suny knew, she wasn't going to tell Wilson. "Look," Wilson says, "here's my cell. Call me if you need something." He writes the number down on a napkin and gives it to her. "I'll talk to Sòlas; he didn't know Peter was married—"

She shakes her head. "It just never worked out that way for us," she says, and stuffs the napkin in her pocket. Then goes into the kitchen without another word. Wilson takes a couple of twenty-dollar bills from his wallet and leaves them on the table. It's not much, but it's the best he can do.

On the way home, he calls Hennessey and tells her about his talk with Suny.

"That's an old lead," she says. "We checked the DNA on the boy and Peter MacKay. There were no markers in common."

"Jason *wasn't* his son?

"Not by blood, although the woman claims otherwise. But as we all know, facts never lie."

"What about that Choo-Choo guy?"

"I ran the alias but no priors. How do you find a guy named after a train?"

"And the van? You think Whit did it?"

"What did he tell you?"

"Nothing. This is the first I've heard about any of this."

"Obviously, your employer is working on a need-to-know basis and this isn't the kind of information a security guard needs to know," Hennessey says. "Unless, of course, he picks up a newspaper and reads it."

Bitch, Wilson thinks, but knows she's right. He's just a glorified babysitter and these aren't the kind of people who confide in the help. Or even gossip with them.

She takes a deep breath. "Brian," she says, and he hates the tone of her voice already. "I know you're trying to help, but this is a very complicated case."

Wilson hangs up. "Dog," he says. "This is going to give me an aneurysm."

Chapter Forty-one

Threatening a man is one thing, but when Danni leaves the Bad Girl's Bar & Grill walking a hooded vulture on a pink dog leash, Bill has had enough. She's got to go.

And this is such an inconvenience, he thinks. *I'm out of fertilizer.*

As Danni walks across the street, she can see Aunt Bee in full Mayberry regalia. She appears to be pulling weeds in her front yard. Unfortunately, there are no weeds to pull. The lawn people come every Tuesday. Still, she's there sitting on the cold cobblestone walkway staring at Bill's car, which, despite association rules, is still parked in the driveway.

There's a single weed in her white-gloved hand.

"Be glad you're a bird," Danni tells Poe.

The gigantic vulture flaps its wings; this catches Aunt Bee's attention and she runs screaming into the house. The weed is left behind.

"There's probably a rule against that, too," Danni says. She notices that the hurricane shutters are still leaning against the side of Aunt Bee's house, where she left them. And Bill's garage door is open a bit. She has an idea, but it will have to wait.

When Danni gets to the edge of the mangrove forest, she takes the hood off Poe. The vulture looks at her with those tiny jet eyes, curious. Cocks its shiny bald head. Up close, the bird is truly beautiful. The head is the color of a beating heart. Its huge wings catch the light and shine with a dark iridescence.

She gently strokes his carrion-picking beak. "I read on the Internet that scientists just discovered that you're a stork," she says. "Not a bird of prey at all. So technically, when I let you go you should be able to go back to your pals. Got it?"

She touches Poe's wing where it was bruised. He doesn't react. The wound is no longer bleeding.

"You're okay now," she says. "Time to go."

The bird tilts his chin to one side, striking a pose. Then growls. It's not a threatening growl, but the kind of low dark growl that most males make during mating season.

"Stop that," she says. "Trust me. I'm no good for you."

Slowly, Danni removes the pink leash. In a grand sweeping gesture, she raises her arm, and the bird, to the heavens.

Once released, Poe does not hesitate. He catches a thermal and circles. His elegant wings tip this way and that. He seems happy to be free.

As soon as Danni lets the bird go, she regrets it. She regrets it nearly as much as she did when she released those three husbands and the countless other males who tried to pluck out her eyes and growled when they wanted something—usually sex.

She doesn't regret it for long.

As she walks away, Poe circles back, lands on her head. The force of it slams her into the sand.

"Men," she says. "They're all alike."

Chapter Forty-two

"Don't make me pick you up and carry you in," Wilson says to Sophie. Even though they're outside the Bad Girl's Bar & Grill, the music is cranked up so loud that he has to shout over the blue-velvet voice of Ella Fitzgerald scatting her way through "Hawaiian War Chant."

The song does indeed have, as Ms. Fitzgerald promises, "a sunny little funny little melody."

"The hula hula maidens starting swinging it," Ella sings.

A funny little gay Hawaiian war chant? Wilson thinks. *Tiki music will make you insane.*

He'd like a second opinion on that but Mandy is sacked out in her Sac. It's been a long day for the small dog; it's exhausting work being both pretty and good.

"It's either Danni's," Wilson says to Sophie, "or I'm dropping you off at Whit's."

"I don't understand what the issue is," she says.

Sophie's been saying this ever since Wilson stuffed a grocery bag with her underwear, toothbrush, and one of the endless pairs of gray sweats. It's clear she's lying. There's not much conviction in her tone.

"Nobody would think to look for you here," Wilson says.

She shrugs. "I don't know. I just can't do this. Feels weird. She and Whit are always fighting—"

"Don't worry about it," Wilson says. "I called ahead. It's okay." And he opens the door to the Bad Girl's Bar & Grill. Then pauses. Wonders if he might go blind himself.

Sòlas is shouting into Danni's cell phone. "The number I dialed *is* in service. It's the number for the barrister who has my buses . . ."

But this is not what Wilson finds disturbing.

On top of the long pecky-cypress bar are Danni and the crones hula dancing, or performing some odd version of the hula. It's difficult to tell. Wilson can't get past the fact that all three of them are wearing coconut-shell bras.

And the crones look pretty good for women of an ancient yet undetermined age.

Perky, even, Wilson thinks, and for a moment is afraid that God will strike him dead.

"What's happening?" Sophie whispers.

"I'd describe it to you, but then you'd want me to kill you."

Poe hisses.

"What's that sound?" Sophie says, clearly alarmed.

Poe is flapping to the tiki beat.

"Let's just say it's a parakeet," Wilson says. "But don't make any quick moves."

For a moment, no one except Poe realizes that Sophie and Wilson are there.

"Now let's do the Coconut Tree!" Danni shouts as she dances.

"I did this in *Blood and Bongos,* an ultra-high-concept slasher film designed for the art-house circuit!"

And the crones shout, "Bongos!"

They have no idea what Danni is talking about. But then, of course, neither does Wilson.

"Bongos!" they all shout again.

Wilson turns off Ella.

"Hey there," Danni says, and jumps down off the bar. "Just working off a ton of negative energy."

Mandy starts barking at the sound of her voice. Wilson opens the Sac. The small dog runs, jumps on Danni, and licks her face so frantically that Wilson feels guilty he's taken so long to get back.

Sòlas slams Danni's cell phone shut. "Gone," he says. "The phone number on the legal papers is a phony. And someone has towed the buses away from the lot. Everything is gone."

There's no need to translate this into Swedish. Sòlas walks out of the bar onto the beach. The crones, who are softly weeping, follow.

"We'll figure this out," Danni says as the door slams behind them.

Mandy starts to whimper. Danni kisses her on the top of her tawny head. "It's okay, he'll be back," she says.

"This isn't a good time," Sophie whispers.

"It's okay," Danni says, but doesn't sound completely convinced. She takes a close look at Sophie in her baggy sweat clothes. Scowls. *A beautiful woman shouldn't look like that,* she thinks.

"It's happy hour," Danni says. "Let's find you something in a nice gold lamé."

Danni takes Sophie by the hand and Sophie lets her and that

confuses Wilson. Suddenly Sophie wants to play dress up. *Got to be something about the husband.*

He reminds himself that he's not jealous. *Not at all.*

Poe squawks. His coal eyes are mistrusting.

"Don't look at me like that, bird," Wilson says, but the vulture keeps staring.

"Okay, maybe just a little jealous."

Chapter Forty-three

The fact that Thursday is Tongo-rific Mai Tai Night haunts them.

Danni wrote that in fluorescent pink chalk on the "Specials Board" over the bar and, for some reason, it can't be fully erased. So it lingers. Wilson writes around it, carefully listing all the facts of the case as he, Sophie, Danni, and Sòlas know them. There aren't many.

1. Two dead.
2. One barbecued Hummer.
3. Somebody zapped me.
4. Whit's stolen van killed Jason.
5. Jason was the only living witness to Sophie's accident.

"I don't like four and five," Sophie says. "They have nothing to do with one and two."

"Personally, I'm not that keen about three, but they are the facts," Wilson says.

The list has become a point of contention, but glamour is in the air. Sophie didn't choose the gold lamé—the short, snappy dress Danni wore in *Chainsawing Mr. Goodbar.*

"What else do you have?" she said. Then accidentally bumped against Danni's jewelry armoire. It was as big as Sophie.

"Careful," Danni said. "That's not so much a jewelry box as an archaeological dig through my love life." Then she opened a middle drawer. "This is Marriage Number Two: The Cubic Zirconia Years."

Danni turned away from the armoire and back to the closet. She pulled out dress after dress and described them in detail and told the story of each while Sophie tried on rings and necklaces. It was clear to Danni that she was going for a certain look. Not just any dress but something spectacular and sexy.

The husband, Danni thought. *It has to be.* She's seen pictures of him at Whit's. Model perfect. It's tough to kick a guy like that out of your heart.

"So where are you meeting him?"

"I'm not—"

Danni sighed. "You know, Wilson told me that you were okay and that you might be in some danger. And I said I'd help you out. But you got to be straight with me—"

"He's my husband—"

"Trust me, there's plenty more where he came from."

"I know what I'm doing."

Danni wasn't so sure. To her, Sophie seemed young, spoiled, and hardheaded. Maybe a little too bruised. Certainly too trusting.

"Just be careful," Danni said.

The dress Sophie finally chose was a knockoff of Rita Hayworth's gown in *Gilda*—black satin and strapless. Danni bought it just in case she was ever nominated for an Oscar, so the tags were still on it.

"Gilda was the role that made Hayworth," Danni said. "It's a story about a woman who married an evil man—"

"It's perfect," Sophie said and shook the dust off the dress and began to wiggle into it.

Danni was afraid of that. It's been her experience that irony never works in real life. So she rambled through the plot of the movie that Hayworth once said both made and ruined her—"Every man I've ever known has fallen in love with Gilda and awakened with me."

But when Sophie finally zipped up, Danni wolf-whistled. The dress fit like a mile of river road. Sophie's seashell skin set off the satin of the black dress, the satin of her hair, the dark sunglasses. The transformation was complete.

Gilda, Danni thought, and was worried because she couldn't remember how the movie ended.

So now, it's a little difficult for Wilson to concentrate. It's not just Sophie in that dress. It's Danni, too. She's still wearing that coconut-shell bra. And this is serious business.

"I didn't even know Peter had a child," Sòlas says. His voice cracks. That pains Danni. It was difficult enough to convince him to come back into the bar to do this, but she did. Now she's not so sure it was a good idea.

Sòlas is growing more and more upset with each fact written on the board. "Why didn't the FBI woman say that? She didn't even mention it."

"They ran the DNA. No markers in common."

"So it *wasn't* his son?" Sòlas says.

"Technically, no. Which is probably why Agent Hennessey didn't mention it."

And while that's accurate, there's something about this that nags at Wilson. It doesn't seem possible that the child wasn't Peter's. But facts never lie, as Hennessey says. Or do they?

Sòlas is having a difficult time with all this. "Now the boy's gone, too?" he says, but it's more of a lament than a question.

Sophie, uneasy, doesn't say a word.

"Suny, the mother, seems pretty close to homeless herself," Wilson says. "Your parents left an inheritance?"

Sòlas colors, clearly ashamed, and then tells the story of the last time he saw his brother.

It's okay, Scottie, Wilson thinks. *Everybody makes mistakes.* Then writes the number six and the name *Derek.*

"Oh," Danni says. *Must be the husband,* she thinks.

"What did you write?" Sophie says, but she knows exactly what he wrote.

"That tea you drink, the ginseng?" Wilson says.

"I have it blended in Naples."

"Because you ran out of the blend Derek gave you?"

Sophie doesn't say a word, but it seems very clear to Wilson that she knows exactly what he's talking about—and that she still loves Derek.

"I need some air," he says, and slams the kitchen door behind him. It was just an accident. It slipped out of his hands; he didn't mean it, but the effect is the same.

"Fine," Sophie says, and stands up in all her Rita Hayworth fury, but doesn't know where to go.

She is so painfully beautiful, so helpless, that Sòlas takes her hand. "Would you like a bit of a walk?" he asks. She nods, takes his arm. "Danni?" he says.

"I have to feed Mandy and Poe." Danni knows that Sophie needs to let off some steam and Sòlas is a good listener.

Out back, Wilson is skipping rocks off the top of the Dumpster. Nobody's thrown anything away in there since Buddy was found. Trash piles up in black plastic bags, rots in the sun. A group of wild parakeets screeches and chatters on the telephone wire above him. A couple of pelicans dive in the gulf for a mouthful of fish.

One eats. The other doesn't.

Like Sòlas, he thinks. *And Peter.*

The sun is starting to set. There's a chill in the air. Wilson knows everything revolves around Sophie but isn't sure how the pieces fit. And Buddy's death seems inconsistent with the pattern. None of it seems to fit together.

Pool, Wilson thinks. *I need to hear the perfect music of the clack, Jack.*

Just then, there's the rumble of a Harley. *Damn it.* Something in Wilson's gut tells him the husband is back. By the time he runs out to the street, it's too late. Sophie, in all her Rita Hayworth finery, is perched on the back of the bike. The long black dress, her long black hair: she speeds away from him.

"Sophie!" he shouts, but she doesn't turn around. The bike picks up speed.

"I'm sure she'll be back," Sòlas says.

"Why didn't you stop her? What the hell's wrong with you?"

Sòlas looks stricken. "She said it was her husband."

Wilson is red-faced and huffing. "The husband who blended some digitalis into her ginseng tea. The same guy who probably killed your brother and nephew."

Sòlas is stunned. "How was I to know? You didn't write it on the board. This is the first I've heard of it. I would have killed him with my bare hands had I known."

Wilson suddenly realizes that Sòlas is right. He only wrote the word *Derek.* "Damn it," he shouts. "Details will bite your ass."

Chapter Forty-four

As Wilson leans across the pool table to take the last shot, he thinks of his father. Runs a hand through his thinning hair and leans in. Gives it a wicked sidespin. The ball kisses all four sides of the table and then slips into the pocket.

It's his father's shot. He feels its music in his bones.

He turns to watch the sunset. A flock of bats skims over the gulf, banks high to the right, and disappears into the mangrove forest.

That's when he hears the Piper Tri-Pacer barreling though the sky. His heart is pounding. *Sophie,* he thinks. *Gone for good.*

His face goes hot. They told him at Quantico to count to ten, but it doesn't work. He picks up the cue ball and flings it at the new sliding glass doors that Whit just had installed. He expects the ball to bounce back. After all, it's hurricane glass, and that's what it's supposed to do with small objects. And *Byrne's Complete Book of Pool Shots* states that a regulation billiard ball weighs between five and a half and six ounces and has a diameter of two and a quarter inches, plus or minus five-thousandths of an inch—which would be a small object.

Useless information like this I remember, he thinks, *but identifying the bad guys slips my mind.*

But when the cue ball hits, there's no bounce. The door explodes. Glass is everywhere, again.

"Damn it!" Wilson shouts. The Tri-Pacer buzzes low overhead. Wilson tosses the nine ball at it. He wants to grab the plane's wing and yank it down from the sky and then jump into his GTO and drive through Whit's front door and then over him and crush his worthless sack of Miami-Dade-Hurricane-Building-Code-averse bones.

But suddenly he thinks of the shot again, the music of it: his father's music.

The nine ball in the side pocket is easy, he thinks. *Direct. Ray only made it seem complicated.*

With all the distractions, Wilson had forgotten what he'd learned at Quantico. The reasons most people murder are simple—money or lust.

"Money," he says. Then starts to rethink the problem from there.

Chapter Forty-five

Sophie knew. She always knew. She tried to deny it. Even when Wilson's heart was stopped, she told herself it couldn't be Derek. That would be evil. He couldn't be evil. He had the kind of face that haunted Michelangelo: biblical in its beauty.

But the ring made it clear. The reason why Derek insisted they take that scuba-diving trip, a second honeymoon just six months after the first, was because she knew. He really thought she knew. The ring is proof.

Money is all he really wanted, and she could see that now. His interest in her father's holdings, especially Laguna Key and its planned expansion, consumed him. He spent his days on the property.

"Dirt biking," he told her.

But you don't off-road a thirty-thousand-dollar customized Harley-Davidson Fat Boy—even she knew that. And there were so many fires and so much vandalism around town that Prescott started to sell bits and pieces of his beloved Tiki Gardens. Whit seemed pleased but confused. She finally asked Derek about it.

"Old men scare easy," he told her. Then Prescott died.

At first, she thought it was just a coincidence. It was, after all, a heart attack on the beach. But when the doctor found digitalis in her system . . . she had no idea how Derek did it, but she knew he did. She just couldn't admit it.

Now he's back and people are dying again.

She has to stop him.

"You look beautiful," he says, and helps her down from the back of the Harley. He adjusts her dark glasses so that they don't slip off her nose.

Sophie's not quite sure where they are, but she knows they didn't go far. *Must still be in Laguna Key.* The smell of the gulf is strong. She can hear the surf. Her knees are shaking. She puts her hand on the bike seat to steady herself. It's too late to go back now.

He takes her small hand in his, kisses it. "But you do not have my ring on?"

"No."

"You do not like it? Each diamond is perfect. As you are."

Sophie takes a deep breath. "I put it someplace safe," she says. Like Danni's massive jewelry box.

"Did you read the Braille?"

She did. It took her awhile to figure it out. She's not fluent. There was only one word inscribed on the inside—*Digitalis.*

That's when she knew for sure and knew it had to end.

"To me," he says, "that word means 'forever.' " Then he laughs that rich deep laugh and she remembers why she fell in love with him in the first place. It was his voice, the danger in it.

Heartless bastard.

"To me," she says, "it means 'evidence.' "

He laughs again. "Cher, the ring is just a reminder that we are in this together. A love token."

"Because the digitalis didn't kill me?"

He kisses her gently. "I've done this all for you—all of it. If the authorities ask, I will tell them that and they will believe it. How can they not? My devotion to you is clear. Even though your father tried to tear us apart."

He runs his finger along her breasts, the soft line of her shoulder. She pushes away, nearly loses her balance, but he doesn't seem to care.

"Have you noticed that there is a large trail of evidence in all the mishaps of Laguna Key?" he says. "Things that point to your father and that old fool of a partner he has?"

"But I have the ring," she says. "And it says 'Digitalis.' "

"And I can say that the word is a celebration that you survived your suicide attempt. That's what I told the jeweler. She was very sympathetic."

Sophie tries to slap him, but he moves away.

"If I had a murderous father," he says, "I would want to kill myself, too."

A flock of gulls flies toward the gulf. Their shrill cries make Sophie jump.

"You'll never get any money. I'll divorce you," she says.

"But you haven't already."

It's true. The papers are still on her kitchen table. Unsigned.

He opens the black leather saddlebag on his bike. Takes out a pair of latex gloves, slips them on. Removes a large bottle of digitalis wrapped in a plastic bag. "You still love me," he says. "That is the way everyone sees it. You still love me. And now I am back."

Then he places the bottle in her hands.

"What's this?" she says. Holds it.

He takes it from her gently. Puts it back in the plastic bag. "You know the funny thing about fingerprints? You really can't tell when they're made. I could say that you gave me this bottle to poison the well water and since your fingerprints were on it, people would believe me."

She spits at him, misses.

"Poor little blind girl. If you divorce me, I will have to connect the dots for the authorities, and your father and his old fool of a partner will spend the rest of their lives in jail. And you will be blind and alone."

"No one would believe it."

"Your choices are clear. If we live in wedded bliss, no one gets hurt. Everything continues on as it is, except that I will be rich again."

He gets on his bike, starts it up.

"Till death us do part?" she says, and is surprised how bitter those words can sound.

"Unfortunately, our prenup does not allow for any other choice," he says.

"Then drop dead."

"Then walk back," he shouts over the ragged roar of the engine. "It's not far; you just go across the mangroves and your daddy's house is right there. But I'd be careful in there. I have spent a good deal of time in that swamp. There are gators. And snakes. And the American crocodile, which they thought was extinct, but is now back. I would watch for them. They are mean and fast and will attack without warning."

Then he speeds away.

When the rumble of the engine finally fades, it's quiet. Clouds of mosquitoes buzz around her bare shoulders. Bite her face.

In the distance, there's a violent whirlwind of noise: the screeching of wild dogs, or maybe bobcats, and then a hopeless howling that is unmistakable. It is the one sound that all animals, even humans, understand. Whatever was being stalked has fallen. The rawness of the sound, the agony, is remarkable. The pack yips and growls around the fallen creature, shreds its flesh.

There is no mercy, just that horrible, hollow sound.

Sophie starts to shake uncontrollably. She grabs the bottom of her dress and begins to run. She's not sure where she's running, just that it's away from the swamp. Suddenly, behind her, there's the sound of something coming through brush. Branches snap. Whatever it is picks up speed.

Bobcat. Cougar. Panther. Bear. She thinks of all the things that Whit has told her he's seen near the mangroves.

"Leave me alone," she screams. "Go away."

Then Sophie hears a familiar voice.

"Darling, if you don't mind my saying, you have odd choices in beachwear, but I like your style."

She stops.

The old man, the Buddhist blues player, sets down his crab trap and saxophone. Takes her hand. "You okay, darling?"

She nods. "Just stupid."

"We are all stupid," he says. "Especially in the matter of love."

Then he sings as if he's Fats Domino himself: "Please let me walk you home . . ."

Sophie doesn't know the words to the song, but it doesn't matter. She says, "You know, I never thanked you for saving my life."

"Your beauty is like the lotus, pure and fragrant, and that is thanks enough."

He hands her the crab trap. Slings his saxophone over his back. "But—"

"Sh, darling," he says. "In the words of the almighty Buddha, it's all good."

And then he takes her hand and begins the song again as they walk into the mangroves toward home. "I want to walk you home." And even though she can't carry a tune, Sophie sings along. And that makes Jimmy Ray smile.

Chapter Forty-six

Wilson is on his hands and knees on the beach searching for the nine ball when he realizes that she's standing there in that dress, which is now sandy and torn. The sun is setting behind her. He can hear the Tri-Pacer off in the distance. She is holding the yellow-and-white ball in her hand.

"I stepped on it," she says.

Wilson looks farther down the beach and sees an old man in a suit with a saxophone and crab trap. The man waves and Wilson waves back. *Great,* he thinks, *more clowns.*

"I'm sorry," she says.

He takes the ball from her and starts to walk away.

"Will you help me back to Danni's?"

He doesn't even turn around.

"Don't—"

Wilson is so furious that he's squeezing the nine ball in his hand; his knuckles are white. The sound of the Tri-Pacer in the distance doesn't help matters.

"Don't what?" he says, and he's about to list all the reasons he has to be furious but instead he just says, "Tell me why you left with him."

"Please, I would just like to go to Danni's."

"Tell me what happened."

"I left something at Danni's I need."

"Then call a taxi."

Sophie might have said something after that, but it's difficult to tell. The whine of the Tri-Pacer buzzing overhead is deafening.

Chapter Forty-seven

Outside the window, the red sun slits into the Gulf of Mexico—
his gulf. Whit owns miles and miles of it. Not just shoreline, but also
stock in the oil companies that use the pipeline just a few miles out.

The gulf is a place of predictable chaos, and he likes that. Not
the chaos but the predictable nature of it. Hurricanes come and go
in their season, as do the visitors. It's all very orderly. No surprises.

Whit's house is shaped like the letter *v;* it's more aerodynamic
that way, with huge walls of windows that come to a point over
the gulf. Dwarf him. The structure is protected for winds up to
165 miles per hour and surges up to sixteen feet. It's the same archi-
tecture the National Weather Service uses in Key West. Same plans,
in fact. It's amazing what money will buy.

Every night, Whit sits and watches the sun set. Drinks his fine
wine. The closer the sun gets to the gulf, the redder it becomes. Like
a huge fireball, it seems to spread across the water, and everything
looks as if it will be destroyed. But it isn't. The moment passes.
Everything's fine.

Not like life.

He picks up the envelope that he found under his front door. No postage. No return address. Just his name written with black grease pencil in large block letters. MR. WHIT BISSELL V.

Probably another complaint from a resident, he thinks. The association keeps putting up suggestion boxes at the sales office. Whit keeps taking them down.

He throws the letter in the trash and flips through his collection of CDs that are designed, as the boxes state, "to create your own tranquil acoustic environment." He listens to each one for a moment, trying to decide. He has the complete set: *Rain, Summer Night, Stream* (although he doesn't like that one because it makes him have to pee all the time), *Wind, Silence* (he thinks he might have gotten ripped off with this one), and *Ocean Surf.*

He often plays one all night long, on a continuous loop. Makes him feel at one with nature.

Tonight, it's *Ocean Surf.* It's his favorite. It sounds much more real than the gulf ever could. Each wave always has the same tempo and tone. And there's none of that incessant squawking of seagulls. Just perfect waves crashing perfectly on a perfect shore. Wilson's golf cart can putter by on its rounds, and that nasty airplane that recently has taken to buzzing the beach can buzz away—but Whit can't hear them.

All he hears is his perfect ocean.

He sits back in his wing chair and lets the sound wash over him. *Money is good,* he thinks. *Wonderful, in fact.*

The last moments of sunset are streaking across the sky when something catches his eye. He stands up and looks out the window. Squints. There's someone walking on the beach—his beach. It's a man. A stranger. Regal yet shabby, dressed in a three-piece suit and a shirt with French cuffs. His dark face is lined with living, rutted. His shoes are in one hand, a crab trap is in the other. There's a battered saxophone strapped across his back.

Whit clicks off *Ocean Surf* and opens the window to shout at the old man, get him off his property. But before he can say anything, the sun touches the horizon. It appears to set the water aflame, and the man, too. The burning man puts down his shoes and trap. He moves his sax to his lips and begins to play the old song "When the Saints Go Marching In." But he plays it slowly, mournfully, as a funeral dirge. He lingers on each note.

The effect is truly eerie. Beautiful. The fire and the song seem to consume the old man. The night goes black. The notes remain.

Whit has never seen anything like this before, especially on his beach, in front of his gulf, on his property.

He opens the desk and takes out his Taser, the M-26, the military version. It looks like a small machine gun in his hand.

"Beautiful," he says. He tosses his long silk scarf around his neck and heads out onto the beach—his private beach. *And it's going to stay that way,* he thinks.

Chapter Forty-eight

Recently, things have not gone well for Mr. Whit. His only daughter is angry with him for protecting her, a rather badly dressed FBI person is pestering him, and clowns have invaded his beloved Laguna Key. And now he's lying on the wet sand with the tide creeping up his linen pants. Sand fleas are crawling into his Italian loafers.

The last thing Whit remembers is trying to teach a lesson to some bum on his beach. Currently, the man is shining a flashlight in Whit's face. A gnarled foot is on Whit's chest, pinning him down.

"What happened?" Whit asks.

"Bowlers bowl," the man says.

This is not good, Whit thinks.

"It's a Zen thing," the man says.

Even worse.

Whit can see that the man is aristocratic. Seems shipwrecked on this beach, as if from another time. He is spinning Whit's Thomas A. Swift's Electric Rifle in his hand like a six-shooter. Whit tries to sit up, but the old man has leverage. Leans a little harder. Whit can't budge.

"Let me up."

"Are you going to play nice?"

"Just give back my Taser," he says. "And I won't have you arrested for assault."

"That's exactly what I thought you'd say," he says. Unbuttons his double-breasted jacket and stuffs the military-issue stun gun into his black pin-striped pants. Makes him look like a gangster.

"That's mine," Whit says.

"You'll like the new ones. I read in the *Wall Street Journal* that they're like cell phones. Can't fire until you do an online background check on your target—and you can't tamper with them."

"But I paid a lot for that."

"It's not very stylish. The new ones come in this pearly white. It'll match your scarf."

Then, like an old-school magician, Jimmy Ray pulls the long silk scarf out of his French-cuffed sleeve with a grand gesture. "Silk?" he says.

Whit nods.

"I'd get it to a dry cleaner, then. The salt spray will eat right through it."

He drops the scarf in a bundle on Whit's face. Snaps off the flashlight and walks away in the dark, down the beach, as if nothing had happened.

The light blinded him; it takes Whit's eyes awhile to adjust to the darkness. His arm hurts. His head hurts. His chest hurts where Jimmy Ray was standing on it. He sits up slowly. "Where do you think you're going?" he shouts, not sure where the old man went. "I could have you arrested."

He can hear a chuckle.

"Wait a minute," Whit shouts.

Jimmy Ray keeps walking.

Whit runs after him in the dark like an ill-tempered child. Arms flailing. "This is private property," he shouts, although it isn't his private property. It's Danni's. It's the remains of mangrove forest that Prescott wouldn't sell. If he would have sold it, Laguna Key would be big enough to have its own zip code by now.

"You're trespassing," Whit shouts.

But Jimmy Ray turns into the mangrove forest. Whit, limping, tries to follow behind, but it's very dense and very dark. An owl hoots and he jumps.

Whit's never been in the forest before. He knows that Prescott had some sort of backwater place there where he used to sit and wait for yetis. *Probably snake-infested by now,* he thinks. He wonders if the old man has taken up residence there. Wonders if that's where they're going.

It is.

Beached along the swamp, in a thicket of live oaks, is an old shrimp trawler. It's impossible to see from the road or the gulf. Like most trawlers, it's wide-bodied. A good boat to live on, plenty of cabin room below. For some ironic reason, someone—probably Prescott—painted USS MINNOW on its side. The boat has been here some time. The paint is peeling. Spanish moss hangs from it like rotting lace. There's a gaping hole where the engine once was; an alligator uses it as a nest. Tiny gators swarm the hull. When Jimmy Ray reaches the boat, he stops. Out of his suit pocket, he takes a loaf of bread that somebody had thrown in the sand. Jimmy Ray brushes it off, pulls off a chunk. Tosses it into the water.

"There you go, children," he says. The tiny creatures rip and gnaw.

Whit doesn't see this. He's too far behind. But he can hear Jimmy Ray's voice off in the distance and wonders who he's talking to. It's frustrating not to know what's up ahead. For a moment Whit wonders what it would be like to be blind. Thinks of Sophie. He tries to push back the thought; it's too painful to bear. Her beautiful eyes, unfocused, unseeing: it's the one thing he can't replace for her. It is the one unperfect thing that money cannot perfect.

At least she's still alive, he thinks, and for a moment his chest goes tight. Makes it difficult to breathe.

Up ahead, Jimmy Ray opens the trawler's cabin door and enters the elegant but weathered salon. He strikes a match and lights the gas lamps that hang on the walls. Places the crab trap in the sink.

"Home," he says. It's a word he's come to cherish. He carefully takes his saxophone off and puts it back in its mildewed case. Steps into the formerly lush stateroom and opens a small closet next to the head. Hangs up his coat, slips his shoes into their shoe bags, and takes out his purple velvet smoking jacket with matching slippers. He catches a look at himself in the long thin mirror attached to the back of the door.

He might be in his seventies, and might have been through some tough times recently, but he looks amazingly good these days. Healthy. Strong. As a Buddhist, he knows he's supposed to ignore the physical trappings of the body. Live in one's mind. But still, he says, "I'm looking fine," under his breath. He whistles and runs a comb through his brilliantined hair.

When Whit finally reaches the trawler, he is surprised. He had no idea this old boat was in here. Tucked away. "What's going on here?" he says.

Jimmy Ray is still dressing. "I hope you find the place to your liking," he says over his shoulder. "You notice the teak? You don't see trawlers with such nice teak. I think this was once a working shrimp boat, too. But now it has real brass. Look at this."

He picks a lamp off its hook on the wall and shows it to Whit. It doesn't have a glass shade, but it is beautiful. Looks like an antique.

"Cleaned up nice, didn't it?" Jimmy Ray says. "Found some polish in the galley. Did the trick."

Then he puts the lamp back. Straightens it just so. Then he returns to the stateroom to finish his dressing. To Jimmy Ray, civility is essential. Not wanting to be rude—Whit is a guest, after all—he keeps on chatting.

Whit is wondering if this is some odd dream; maybe all that junk food has finally taken its toll. He keeps on thinking about how beautiful this place is, and that worries him.

Jimmy Ray keeps on talking. "The hull's got some serious damage, and it's a little musty, but somebody's fixed it up real nice. A little hideaway."

He enters the room resplendent in his velvet smoking jacket, and fragrant as crushed violets. He takes a pot from the stovetop and fills it with water.

"I'm hungry. You hungry? There's crab I caught today and some already cooked in the icebox. And I found me a gator pear tree; can you believe that? Wild avocados in the middle of this forest, tons of them.

"And you would not believe how many edible greens there are in a swamp like this. And shrimp! That's why the flamingos are pink, you know, from eating all that shrimp."

He puts the pot on the stove. Turns up a burner. "Have a seat," Jimmy Ray says. "Clean. I promise."

Whit looks at his hands and they're sandy.

Jimmy Ray opens the door to the tiny bathroom. "Cleaned the tank if you need to use the facilities."

Whit gets up and washes his hands, brushes off his sandy pants. "What are you doing here?"

"I'm on what our Australian brothers call a walkabout. You go into the wilderness for six months as a rite of passage. Do some heroic deeds. I am a spiritual warrior."

"Well, I'm a Republican."

Jimmy Ray shakes his hand. "It's very nice to meet you, sir."

The water boils. Jimmy Ray takes the crab trap out of the sink. He apologizes to the crabs. "I am so sorry to be eating you," he says, and then closes his eyes. Prays a minute. Tosses them into the boiling water.

Next to Whit, there's a shelf filled with books. He runs his finger along the spines. Many of them are by Hemingway; there are two copies of *The Old Man and the Sea*. There's also a copy of *The Odyssey* and Plato's *Republic*. At the end of the row, there's a small worn paperback; the title is rubbed away. Whit pulls it out. It's a collection of letters from the painter Paul Gauguin to his wife. There's a bookmark in it. He reads aloud, " 'May the day come— and perhaps soon—when I can flee to the woods on a South Sea island and live there in ecstasy, in peace and for art.' "

"That's so Buddhist," Jimmy Ray says. He takes the crabs out of the pot. "You notice that the books all have a name in them?"

Whit opens to the front cover: EX LIBRIS GORDON PRESCOTT. It's what he thought, that this is the old yeti-hunting shack, but to see the old man's name in print like that makes him uneasy. As does this place. It's not primitive, as Whit had imagined. It's more like something he himself would do.

"Do you know the fella?" Jimmy Ray says. He's assembling a salad of dandelion greens with wild green avocados. "Do you think he's coming back?"

Whit takes a deep breath and says, "No."

The way he says this tells Jimmy Ray all he needs to know. "Sorry." He sits down across from Whit, crosses his legs elegantly. "We'll let the crab cool a bit," he says.

Whit takes another book from the shelf and places it on the table between them. It's a leather-bound journal. "In Search of the Florida Skunk Ape" is written in florid script on the title page. A flat purple ribbon marks the beginning of the last entry. It's not even an entry—it's just a collection of words written across page after page, including *graveyard, bones,* and then Danni's name written over and over again. Some of the words don't even seem to be real words, just letters placed together. None of it makes sense. He closes the book. *Poor crazy son of a bitch,* he thinks.

"Sh. Listen," Jimmy Ray says.

For a moment, the two men sit quietly.

"I have an entire CD of this," Whit says.

"Hush."

There's a rusty squawk and then another, a call-and-response, like an old-time spiritual.

"That'll drive you nuts," Whit says.

Jimmy Ray looks transformed, blissful. "Music," he says. "It's everywhere out here."

"Sounds like frogs."

"Heron."

"Still sounds like frogs," Whit says. His stomach growls.

"Let's eat," Jimmy Ray says. Whit watches as he divides the crabs between a couple of cheap white paper plates. Arranges the salad of wild greens and avocado off to the side.

It is an amazing meal. The most amazing part to Whit is that he doesn't have to pay for it.

Then he thinks for a moment. "Hey, how do you have electricity?"

"I think it's yours," Jimmy Ray says. "Best I can figure is that somebody was pulling power off your line."

Before Whit says anything, Jimmy Ray places the plate before him. "Eat your crab," he says. Sits. Picks up a thin crab leg and cracks it in his teeth. Sucks out the meat. "It's sweet."

Whit hesitates. The crab his housekeeper buys and leaves for him is pasteurized and sealed in cans. He likes his food served in ways that do not remind him that there is a food chain and he's on it. Still, he is hungry. He picks at the shell, stuffs a bit in his mouth. It is sweet.

Jimmy Ray smiles, pleased.

At that moment, there's the sound of an old airplane flying low over the beach.

"Who is that guy?" Whit asks. "He always flies at night. Hard to get a good look."

"Let me take a look," Jimmy Ray says, and opens the cabin door. He steps out onto the deck. The lights of the plane seem small, far away. It sounds as if he's gaining altitude. The night is cloudy. It's difficult to see.

"It's that same fella who's been out here before. Looks like he's going straight up."

Jimmy Ray suddenly has an odd feeling of being watched. Not by a bobcat or a vulture or a bat, but by a person. He can smell the acid of sweat on skin. There's somebody out there. Close.

He keeps watching the plane. *No quick moves,* he thinks. "You got yourself some of that Château Lafite Rothschild up at your fine house? I bet a house like that has a massive wine cellar. Maybe the Pauillac?" he says. "I could use me some fine juice, couldn't you?"

Whit looks up from his plate of crabs, confused. Bits of shell stick to his chin. Jimmy Ray keeps talking.

"I hear the 1982 vintage is still youthful and quite spectacular, and not as controversial as the '98," he continues on, but slowly. Gives each word emphasis. "I could use me a solid *grand vin* right about now, something heavy enough to knock a man to his knees, something with a dark hardness that lingers in the shadows, if you know what I mean," he says.

He then gives Whit a knowing look, slides his eyes ever so slightly off to the right, where he thinks he now sees an outline of a man in the shadows.

"Something lingering in the shadows, big and heavy. You know what I mean?" Jimmy Rays says with great portent.

Whit is up to his elbows in crab but, miraculously, he understands.

"Like a Florida skunk ape?"

"Indeed, a wine like a big old Florida skunk ape lingering in the shadows would be perfect."

Praise Buddha for the paranoid mind, Jimmy Ray thinks. Whit's obviously been waiting for this moment for years.

"I have a Château Haut-Brion '95," he says, wiping his mouth as bits of crab shell tumble onto his linen pants. "It's all about the surprise." Then he winks. Picks up Jimmy Ray's sax by the throat and nods. "The element of surprise is everything. If you know what I mean."

"That won't do," Jimmy Ray says. "We'll need something with

a bit more authority. Powerful, like a Margaux '98—something that will knock you flat with a zap o' fruit. A big crackling zap." And Jimmy Ray grabs his own arm, right at the spot where he grazed Whit with the Taser.

"Wrap up that crab," he says.

Whit raises an eyebrow. He'd forgotten all about the Taser. Doesn't know where it is. Cocks his head in question.

"Put it in the *icebox*," Jimmy Ray says.

Of course, the refrigerator, Whit thinks. And there it is, although its submachine-gun styling looks a tad out of place. He takes out the Taser and puts in all the crab. *No sense letting that go to waste.*

Jimmy Ray takes his velvet slippers off, one by one. Slowly. And then his elegant smoking jacket. *No sense ruining these,* he thinks. When he takes a step toward the cabin to put them away, the man in the bushes moves toward him.

"Son, you okay?" Jimmy Ray says to him directly. Calm. Reassuring. "Why don't you come in and join us. We are gonna have some fine juice, boy."

Suddenly, the horrible sound of a Piper Tri-Pacer's engine straining overhead makes Jimmy Ray stop. Turn around.

The man runs.

Chapter Forty-nine

As the Piper Tri-Pacer begins its steep decline and planned rapid descent into the Gulf of Mexico, Derek decides that perhaps this part of his plan was not as well thought out as the rest. Sure, when he accuses Whit of tampering with his plane—"I knew too much," he plans to tell the police—they will believe him. No one crashes a plane on purpose.

But what if my face is scarred?

That, of course, would not be good. Derek knows that looks are not everything, but they do mean a lot. Luckily, he's attractive in a careless sort of way. He spends a good deal of time and money cultivating that look. Shaves his beard just so. Trims his hair on the shaggy side. Wears expensive silk blends that he knows will crease in all the right places.

Still, what woos them is his brain. It's big. "I am tragically intelligent," he tells the ladies. And they believe him. When Derek speaks at great length about existentialism and the writer Albert Camus as the real founder of rock and roll, women nearly swoon. Especially because he doesn't pronounce the *t* in Albert, just rolls that *r* as hard as dice.

"He lived in Paris," Derek always explains. "The city of my birth."

Gets them every time.

Unfortunately, Derek was born in Parris *Island* in South Carolina. That's Parris with two *r*'s—not one. Makes a difference. Parris Island is home to the U.S. Marine Corps training facility. Sixteen thousand Marines pass through the boot camp every year.

He's a military brat. Derek's father was a drill instructor from Louisiana, which later worked out well for Derek since a Creole accent is nearly French—if you're careful. And Derek tries to be careful. Tries to never let a "ga-lee look at de size o' dat gator!" or an "I tink dat's right" pass through his lips. The word *cher,* however, is a tic he finds hard to break.

Still, the tragic truth of the matter is that Derek is undeniably intelligent. His IQ is 165; he is a card-carrying member of Mensa. He spent most of his early years in gifted and talented programs in Beaufort County banging his head against the school walls.

He wasn't autistic, although some of the other kids were; he just felt like banging his head against the wall every now and then. Just to see what it was like. "If your father was a drill instructor, you'd understand," he'd tell the counselors who would call his baffled parents in for intervention meetings and prescribe sedatives and weekly therapy sessions, none of which Derek's father would agree to.

Eventually, Derek discovered that banging your head is boring, like most things. Once you get past the shock value, it just leaves you with a headache.

Like this plane-crash thing—which was really getting on his nerves.

Maybe if I screamed, it would be more fun, he thinks.

"Oohhhweee!"

No. That didn't seem to work, either. He just sounded like his uncle Ramón back in the parish.

Do they scream in Paris? he wonders. *Probably not.*

Derek knew he would miss his plane, but he also knew that crashing on the shore in front of Whit's house was the final sign that he was serious. Whit and that partner of his could no longer ignore his demands.

It's a perfect plan. And he knows that Sophie, even if she finds her way home safely, will be no bother to him. Once he destroys the plane, he knows she will also understand he's serious, even if he has to break his own nose to prove it.

Still, as the engine screams, he sighs, disappointed. Again, another of life's mysteries that didn't live up to its press. He thought there would be flames and the world would spin by in slow motion. Time would somehow elongate. Scenes from his youth would stretch out before him like "ze lanky languorous snake on ze summer day," as Uncle Ramón would probably say.

Derek was looking forward to all that. He'd read a lot about airplane crashes, and everyone said it was just like that. Exactly. Time slowed, the past flashed by, blah, blah, blah.

But it was, in fact, a lot like being in a blender, with the sky and the sea swirling around. You're dizzy. Your hands sweat. Your brain pushes up against your skull.

It's not really that much fun, he thinks. *Too bad, too.* Right before he went into the tailspin, it seemed like such a good idea. *Nearly perfect.*

But the explosion will be immense—Derek comforts himself

with that. Lighting up the sky. A grand gesture, even grander than the rose petals. Which, in retrospect, given the fact that Sophie was blind, might have been a little insensitive.

But this will work. It had better. He's bored to death of all of this lurking in the swamp. If he wanted to do that, he'd go visit Uncle Ramón.

"I will miss you," he says to the airplane and kisses the windshield, which is the only part of the plane he can kiss, because he's in a vertical spin and his face is pressing down hard on it.

"Je regrette," he says. But he is not sorry.

Derek has wanted to crash the plane for a very long time. Ever since he was told it was nearly indestructible, the challenge was set in place. That was back before he met Sophie, back when he was running coke for the Colombians—that long ago. Six years. That's a long time to want to do something. He even used to dream of it. He wanted to beat the plane. Wanted to destroy that which could not be destroyed.

Everybody's got to have a goal, he told himself.

If he survived, cool. If not, oh well.

The problem was, again, he was bored. Derek has issues with boredom. As glamorous as smuggling sounded, it was as boring as being a newspaper delivery boy. All you had to do was make it to Cayo Confites, a speck of a place on the northern coast of Cuba. Thanks to the U.S. embargo, the Cubans had little in the way of drug enforcement back then, just an aging Soviet-era patrol boat, a British radar system with a six-mile range, fifteen soldiers, and a rather large mural of Che Guevara proclaiming the inlet the "last defense against imperialism."

You dropped the payload, a boat picked it up and took it to

another boat, and ninety miles later the coke was being sold up and down South Beach and a check was direct-deposited into your account.

It was a lot like work, which he has always tried to avoid.

So sometimes, just for fun, he'd drop the load and circle toward the patrol boat. He'd take it head-on. Then, just as he passed, he'd flip the plane over and buzz the deck upside down just to watch the Cubans dive into the water.

But that got old after a while, too.

The problem is that the Tri-Pacer is a beauty to spin. And if you get lost, you can fly it so low that you can read the name of a town off its water tower. If you're landing in a storm, a very strong cross-wind will flip you, but most of the time, the damn thing is nearly indestructible.

So he'll destroy it and they will pay up. How can they not? They owe him.

Besides, Sophie will feel so guilty. She told him to drop dead, and so, like an obedient husband, he said he's giving it his best shot.

So sad, he thinks. They had a perfect thing going. Sophie hated Whit and Whit hated Derek and Sophie liked that. Best of all, Sophie is rich. Derek likes money. And he's nearly out.

How was he supposed to know that seven million dollars' worth of shares in Laguna Key isn't worth the pink slips it's traded on?

I'm a genius, not a stockbroker, he thinks, and with great effort, takes out his gold cigar lighter and sets his copy of *Conversational French* aflame. Holds his breath. Pushes against the g-force and jumps out the cockpit window. Pulls the rip cord. Clears the plane.

Can't risk scarring the face, he thinks. Blacks out.

Chapter Fifty

Bill is not sleeping or eating. He's drinking—a lot. In fact, he's drinking so much that he's stopped taking his Xanax because it conflicts with alcohol; if something happens to him, he doesn't want it to look like a suicide. That would be no way for the Laguna Key Association CEO and de facto president of the Chamber of Commerce to die. He's invested his retirement savings into a vision of developing this swamp into an unrelentingly wholesome, antiseptic, and safe subtropical community.

He wants to be remembered fondly. He thinks he has a good chance at it. If it weren't for the hordes of vultures, bats, stingrays, alligators, rats, sharks, jellyfish, fire ants, hissing roaches, poisonous spiders, and several kinds of snakes (both poisonous and nonpoisonous), and if it weren't for the seasonal onslaught of red tide, floods, hurricanes, tornadoes, and the occasional earthquake, this place would be absolutely perfect. Except for the rampant mildew and rust. And humidity. And summer heat, which can fry an egg on a white-washed sidewalk in seventeen seconds.

Other than that, it's perfection in stucco.

And so Bill wants to be remembered in the same breath as Sir Edmund Hillary, conqueror of Mount Everest, the New Zealander who went from being a lowly beekeeper to "King of the World."

Bill understands that there'll have to be a few slight modifications when people tell his story. Still, not that many. Not really.

But now there's the problem of the letter. It complicates things.

It was slipped under his front door. No postage. No return address. Just his name written in large block letters with black grease pencil: WILHELM WARREN BRYON. It's his legal name. That was odd, too.

There was only one demand: "Liquidate Laguna Key."

What the hell does that mean?

Bill still can't figure it out, and he spent all his life in banking. He knows what "liquidate" means, but it's impossible to liquidate a development because the developers only own the land rights to it. Each house belongs to the home owner.

You can't liquidate other people's property, he thinks, although he likes the idea. You could make a lot of money if you could figure out how to liquidate things that didn't belong to you.

Still, that's off-topic.

Bill's pretty sure that Danni is behind this. She knows. The guy this morning was probably just some extra from a movie or something.

Actresses are so stupid, he thinks, and pulls back the curtains of his great room to take a look at the bar across the street. Maybe get a clue to what she's doing now, but, unfortunately, all he can see are pigs.

They are Swedish Landrace swine, to be exact. Bill's a man

who knows his pigs. Made a small fortune on pork futures in the late 1970s.

Still, pigs are the last things that Bill expects to see, especially pigs flying in the pale moonlight. But there they are. He said he'd let the circus perform when pigs fly, and now they are everywhere. Every window he looks out of—there are pigs. And they are flying. And white. Some are tiny piglets. Some appear to be hundred-pound sows. And all have wings, heavy drooping ears, and a high proportion of lean meat.

Upstairs, downstairs—even outside of the cupola windows—there are swine. If he would look closely, he'd see that they are marionettes suspended on fishing wire. But Bill doesn't look closely. For a banker, he was never very detail-oriented. And he is drunk.

So when the Tri-Pacer hits the gulf waters hard and explodes, Bill is running aimlessly through his house watching pigs fly. He doesn't even notice the ancient crones as they jump off the roof of his four-million-dollar homage to Mayberry R.F.D. and race down the beach toward the flames.

It's not surprising that they are running. They are, after all, trained in first aid.

Chapter Fifty-one

It is as if a huge thunderstorm tumbled in with the tide. Churning. Billowing. No lightning—just fire. Apocalyptic. Dreamlike.

At the center is the not-exactly-FAA-approved Tri-Pacer. Well, what's left of it, anyway—the canvas went quickly. All it is now is a crumble of melting tubes. Its four sets of radios, none that worked consistently, are tumbling down deep into the gulf waters—past the dolphins, past the stingrays, past the unseeing starfish—and wedging, stubbornly, into the sand.

Jimmy Ray is in the water before Whit even reaches the shore.

"I got me a fella," he calls out, coughing. The words come hard. "Parachute. Pulling us under."

Smoke is everywhere. And heat. Whit feels as if he's in a volcano. "I'm here," he says and jumps in. The water is so cold it's shocking. The smell of gas is overwhelming. His heart is pounding. For the first time since Sophie went blind, he feels afraid.

"Where are you?"

"Here."

But "here" is in the middle of darkness. Smoke. Fog. Clouds. There is no moonlight. "Talk. I'll follow your voice," Whit says.

Jimmy Ray coughs, sounds weak. Whit panics. He's not sure why. Two hours ago, he tried to Taser this guy. But now he doesn't want him to drown.

"Say something," he shouts. "Just make some noise."

And so, out of the darkness, a disembodied voice filled with smoke and sorrow croons, "Let the Midnight Special shine her light on me."

This is not Creedence Clearwater Revival's version, studio-based and pitch-perfect, but a rough-hewn jangle of backwater blues that Huddie Ledbetter, better known as Leadbelly, intended. Breathy. Dangerous. It's the song the way it was meant to be sung, with the right pitch of wanting.

"Great!" Whit shouts and follows the trail. As he makes his way though the cold gulf water, chunks of airplane, seaweed, and dead fish bang up against him. He steps on God knows what, but still follows the voice. It's a song he knows. Or at least knows the chorus to. So he joins in: "Shine her ever-lovin' light on me."

Makes him feel less afraid.

For a moment, the smoke shifts and he can see Jimmy Ray: his pure white teeth, his brilliantined hair catching the light from what's left of the burning plane. He's holding a floating man, trying hard to keep his head above water. The parachute has twisted around them both and they are being rocked back and forth by the waves.

"I can see you," Whit shouts. "Don't stop singing."

The smoke rises again. He is gone.

Whit has no idea how to save this man. He wants to turn back. *I don't owe him anything,* he thinks. *I'm no hero. I'm not a brave person. This is too much.*

Then suddenly he hears voices behind him singing, *"Låt special midnatt skin her någonsin lovin lätt på mig . . ."*

And then a chorus joins in. "Shine her light on me."

People are everywhere. They push by Whit. Follow the sound of Jimmy Ray's voice. Then disappear back into the darkness.

To save him, he thinks. *To save a complete stranger.*

For some reason, the thought overwhelms Whit. He chokes. Tears roll down his face. But before he can wipe them away, that man, that Scot, that clown, appears out of a dark cloud of smoke, pats him gently on the back.

"The heart never ceases to amaze," he whispers.

The crowd cheers.

The men are saved.

Chapter Fifty-two

The 1966 Château la Mission Haut-Brion is everything that *Wine Spectator* magazine promised it would be. Despite the fact that mice had nibbled at the cork and the label is slightly torn, it is perfect. Although not quite as resonant as the 1964, it is still beautifully made, with an elegant leather overtone, a medium fruity bouquet, a cedar nose, and a long—almost unendurably long—velvety finish.

"Pass those Pringles," Jimmy Ray says, and grabs at the can. Whit is hogging them again. "So, this fella I fished up is your son-in-law?"

"Technically," Whit says. Doesn't sound very happy about it.

The two men are sitting in the dark in Whit's office. The gas fireplace is cranked up high. Both have changed out of their wet clothes and are wearing silk pajamas. Jimmy Ray chose the navy. Whit opted for black. Over each pocket is a large white embroidered *W*. Matching silk robes, again with a *W* monogram, ward off the night chill.

"I have a little girl myself," Jimmy Ray says. "Little older than

Sophie. Such sweet misery girls are; they break your heart with just a look."

"Sophie is blind," Whit says flatly.

Jimmy Ray shrugs. "I know. I have recently had the pleasure of meeting her on two separate occasions. You're a lucky man. She has a remarkable kindness about her—and a stubborn streak." Jimmy Ray laughs. "My Dagmar is just like that: beautiful and stubborn as the day is long."

Whit looks at Sophie's wedding picture on the wall: the white Japanese kimono and the Piper Tri-Pacer on a better day. "She'll never see again."

"You think the husband had something to do with it?" Jimmy Ray asks.

Whit carefully pours the last of the vintage in their glasses. "I think there's a good chance."

"But they're still married?"

Whit nods.

Jimmy Ray swirls his glass gently. The wine is a deep shade of mulberry. "Then one must embrace the improbable."

"Buddha?"

"Bumper sticker."

The two men are lost in thought. They drink their wine in silence. Whit takes a Pringle from the can and dips it in the wine, as if it's a cookie in milk.

Jimmy Ray slowly chews. Then inhales the wine deeply. "The play of fruit against the salt edge is perfection," he says.

Whit is still thinking about the bumper sticker. " 'Embrace the improbable.' I'm not sure what that means in this case."

Jimmy Ray closes his eyes for a moment and lets the fruit of the wine develop on his tongue. "It's improbable that somebody would hurt a rich wife, abandon her, and then come back. Unless you paid him off and he ran through the money."

Whit shrugs, guilty as charged.

"And so now, I think this son-in-law of yours just upped the price. I mean, why would he crash such a beautiful plane?"

"Crazy?"

"Greedy. Since she didn't divorce him right away, he's pretty sure she still loves him and now he wants your money. All of it. And he'll get it as Miss Sophie's legal husband."

"But that would be impossible."

"Not if you were in jail. Or dead."

The thought gives Whit a chill. "I thought you were all about finding Buddha's heart in people. Looking for goodness."

Jimmy Ray takes the last sip; even the dregs of it give him pleasure. "I am," he says, "but I also know that the looking is one thing. The finding is another. As the wise man says, some men are just bad to the bone."

Chapter Fifty-three

Bill knows that Danni has to be stopped—it is clear. The list of her offenses is long, and it includes blackmail—that letter obviously came from Miss "I Know What You Did Last Summer"—harboring clowns, and the flying Swedish Landrace swine incident. She probably even had something to do with that airplane crash. She is clearly out of control.

Luckily, it's easy to make a nuclear bomb—Bill read that on the Internet. And convenient, too. Although it is slightly expensive. At most chemical suppliers, commercial-grade uranium runs about forty dollars a pound, but it's only 3 percent to 20 percent enriched. So you have to buy about fifty pounds, which runs about two thousand dollars, plus overnight shipping.

There are incidental expenses, too. You can't just use store-bought uranium. If you could, everybody would be doing it. You have to purify it using hydrofluoric acid, fluorine gas, rubber tubing, six feet of rope, a case of calcium supplements from the vitamin store, a few old milk gallons, six buckets, and a bicycle pump. And Bill doesn't even own a bicycle, so all these things add up.

But it would be worth it, Bill reasoned. And, given the circumstances, it would also be tax-deductible. It's a business expense, after all.

The instructions were a little tricky, however. Once you use the bicycle pump to add air into the uranium hexafluoride, you have to place it in a bucket and swing it over your head for forty-five minutes. That was a little tiring. But, as promised, the enriched liquid uranium did rise to the top of the bucket like cream.

In the end, it was well worth the effort.

Bill had paid special attention to the safety note: "Don't put all your enriched uranium hexafluoride in one bucket. This will prevent the premature buildup of a critical mass." So he used three buckets in three separate corners of the room, as it was the preferred method.

The rest was really easy. To convert the liquid uranium back into metal, you just toss some of those calcium supplements in the buckets.

By the time the sheriff's department arrives at Bill's, he's just about to do that.

"A turkey vulture on a pink leash," he explains.

Backup is called.

As the crowd gathers, FBI agent Gayle Hennessey helps Bill into the back of her car. "Watch your head," she says.

Aunt Bee waves. "Have a nice day," she says, and feels a little bad that she called the sheriff. But Bill did, after all, finally steal her hurricane shutters. And everyone could see that because they were sticking out of his garage. Law is indeed law.

"Have a nice day," Bill says back. Friendly. That is, after all, the way he wants to be remembered.

Chapter Fifty-four

The residents of Laguna Key were right. Despite the fact that within the span of three weeks, two men and a Hummer have lost their collective lives in the gated community, the hurricane shutters were the real threat to their way of life.

After Bill's arrest, nothing is the same.

Aunt Bee bakes cookies and takes them down to the edge of the mangrove forest and tosses them to the vultures one by one. They swoop and squawk: grateful. Vanna spins the Wheel of Fortune alone.

Whit feels somewhat responsible. When he first approached Bill about investing in Laguna Key, a publicly traded company, he forgot to mention the pink-slips thing.

Due diligence, he tells himself now. Bill was a banker. Every banker knows to do due diligence.

Still.

The morning after Bill's arrest, Whit calls Sophie, but the phone rings unanswered. When he hangs up, Wilson calls.

"Hennessey's been trying to reach you," he says, sounding all business. "Derek ripped out his IV, took some clothes from the doctors' lounge, and walked right out the front door of the hospital."

Whit doesn't know what to say. He isn't even sure if Wilson is still working for him.

"Sophie's okay," Wilson says. "She's at her place."

Just to be sure, Wilson sticks his head though the gaping framework that was once his sliding glass doors. He can still hear the clicking of her knitting needles. She's been at it since dawn.

"She's all I have," Whit says plainly.

"She's fine," Wilson says, but he knows that isn't true. She's not speaking to anyone. Danni dropped off something earlier and it's been quiet over there ever since.

"So what happens now?" Whit says.

"Don't go anywhere, okay?"

"You're staying on, then?"

"Just get my damn doors fixed," Wilson says and hangs up. It's time to pay Miss Sophie a visit.

Whit calls the glass company, orders the new doors. "Miami-Dade code," he says this time. Then he goes into the kitchen and turns on the deep-fat fryer. The safflower oil bubbles to life.

He eyes a package of Fig Newtons and wonders what they would taste like fried, without batter but individually wrapped with a strip of beef jerky—sort of like rumaki. That could stand up against the 1995 Pomerol he's been trying to off-load.

He opens the package, but doesn't have the heart for it. The silence of his house is impossible. He turns off the fat, grabs the cookies, and heads out the door and back to the trawler to find Jimmy Ray.

The day is clear, dry. Gentle. The sun is warm against his skin as he walks along the beach. Charred bits of plane are everywhere. The FAA investigators have been tagging and logging pieces of the Piper Tri-Pacer all night long. Right now, they seem to be on a lunch break. A couple of guys in white jumpsuits sit on the sand watching the water, eating hamburgers from a sack. They wave. Whit waves back.

"Dinner and a show," one of them shouts, and points toward the gulf.

In the dark green water there's a pair of fins. They arch and weave. Dolphins. Whit wonders if they mate for life; he can't remember.

Must be easier for them, he thinks.

In the daylight, the beach looks very different. He can't quite remember where the path was that leads to the trawler. Finally, he sees some bent saw grass and a large tree that looks as if it's blooming orchids. That looks somehow familiar. He gives it a try. The mangrove trees are beautiful. Their branches weave into each other like a canopy. Their roots are above ground, silver and leggy.

The boat is farther away than he thought and difficult to see. It's painted a mottled green, like camouflage. Once onboard, he knocks.

"It's your turn to make dinner," Jimmy Ray says.

Whit offers the bag of Fig Newtons. "I'm here to get some Buddha stuff. I think I could use some."

Jimmy Ray pops a cookie into his mouth, slowly chews, thinking. "That's a serious request."

"It's in English, right?"

"I'll trade you for some of that Saint-Émilion. I've had a powerful craving for deep-fried peanut butter cups all day long."

"Let's juice," Whit says.

When Whit and Jimmy Ray arrive back at Whit's house, there's a card from FBI agent Hennessey stuck in the door with a note, "Call me." Whit tosses it on the counter. Jimmy Ray pops the *Loving-Kindness* CD into the stereo. The CD contains Buddha's teachings on loving-kindness, including an explanation of its practice, the basic technique, and a guided meditation given by the Venerable Heart, an Australian monk and founder of Buddha.com. Loving-kindness is a meditation practice taught by Buddha to develop the mental habit of selfless, or altruistic, love.

As the Venerable says, "Hatred cannot coexist with loving-kindness; it dissipates it." His Australian accent is grating.

After forty-three minutes of loving-kindness, Whit wants to kill someone—anyone—maybe all of Australia. Certainly all the Australian Buddhist monks he can find. Maybe he could get lucky and snag Mr. Buddha Dot Com himself.

It's certainly worth a try, he thinks. "How do you listen to this?" he asks.

"I don't," Jimmy Ray says. "My little girl gave it to me and I haven't the heart to toss it."

Whit looks disappointed. Jimmy Ray pats him on the back and says, "To be a Buddhist is simple. Just fling your heart into the world like a Frisbee."

"Did Buddha say that?"

"Nope."

"Just fling your heart into the world like a Frisbee," Whit repeats. "That's catchy, I like that."

So he says it over and over again. The more he says it, the more he likes it. Finally, he loves it. T-shirts, bumper stickers, and an entire line of greeting cards: by the time the telephone rings Whit has created a merchandising plan, which, even after he takes his

12.5 percent licensing fee, will make Jimmy Ray a rich man. "We'll get the Wal-Mart people to be the exclusive distributors. Four thousand stores in the United States and more than twenty-nine hundred throughout the rest of the world," he says, excited. "Cha-ching."

Whit picks up the phone without thinking. Doesn't look at the caller ID, doesn't see that it's a blocked call, which can mean only one thing.

"What the hell do you want?" he says, suddenly angry. Jimmy Ray stops laughing.

Chapter Fifty-five

The options Derek laid out before Whit were not good.

"You can't liquidate a development," Whit says over and over again. As he explains the fine points of the development business to his still son-in-law, Jimmy Ray is looking for Agent Hennessey's card. When he finally finds it underneath a bag of "atomic" pork rinds, the phone call is over.

"For an insane megalomaniac," Whit says, "my son-in-law is quite a thorough little planner."

"What are you going to do?"

"Well, I can sign the Laguna Key project over to him. Or I can pay him forty-seven million dollars."

Whit sinks back in his chair. Jimmy Ray hands him the bag of pork rinds, which he opens, then pops a piece of atomic fried fat in his mouth. Chews, unfazed.

"Why would you do either?" Jimmy Ray says.

"Sophie."

"Ah."

"It's the only way to keep her safe."

"I wouldn't be that hasty," Jimmy Ray says, and takes a handful of rinds, puts them in his mouth. "I have a plan." And he would like to explain the details, but, unfortunately, his head suddenly feels as if it's on fire. He coughs wildly.

"I better open up some more juice," Whit says.

Chapter Fifty-six

Wilson breaks the rack. It's a good strong break. The one ball goes into the side pocket, along with the four and five. The nine sits at a bad angle, though.

"I never figured your father to be a murderer," Wilson says. Squints. The sun is in his eyes. He gets down low to shoot. "But all the evidence leads to him and even Hennessey thinks that's an interesting turn of events."

Wilson is sweating hard, although it's not that warm. It's a nervous twitch of his. He always sweats when he's bluffing. That's why he never plays poker; he's afraid that people will drown. He wipes his face on his sleeve.

On the other side of the wall, Sophie is silent; she continues to knit. He listens for her to say something, anything, but all he hears are waves rolling back and forth on the shore, the buzz of a mosquito near his cheek, and the damn clicking of those knitting needles.

"I'm going to topspin the two ball," he says. Then he leans over and does exactly that. The cue ball banks off one side of the rail and then another. The two spins its way into the pocket. Perfect. The nine ball, however, is still trapped.

"The three sits next to the six," he explains. "I'm going to try to ease it into the nine ball. Tap it in. That's the point, isn't it? Sink the nine. That's why they call it nine-ball."

Sophie doesn't respond, but he knows she's listening. Her knitting needles, like some sort of Morse code, click louder. Faster. So he keeps on talking.

"The problem is," he says, "if I don't tap the nine ball just so, it will either fly off the table or just get bounced around and go nowhere. It's trapped right now, sort of like Whit. You know what I mean?"

Apparently, Sophie does. Wilson can hear her stand up, gather her knitting. She's going inside. "By the way," Wilson says. "Derek left the hospital, but I suppose you know that."

She closes the sliding glass door behind her. Wilson takes the shot. He chips the nine ball hard. It flies off the table, off the deck, and rolls out into the surf.

"End of play," he says.

Chapter Fifty-seven

The overwhelming scent of jasmine surprises Sophie. She can smell it right through the door: heady and sweet. Abundant.

Derek, she thinks. Who else would it be? Wilson is still playing pool on the deck. Whit never comes. And who else would bring flowers? For a moment, she feels that maybe, just maybe, it was all a mistake. Or maybe he's sorry.

Or, maybe, I misunderstood or misjudged. Maybe the accident brought him to his senses.

She opens the door.

"Miss Sophie," Jimmy Ray says. "Just come by to see how you're doing."

Sophie recognizes his voice. Her disappointment is clear. Confusing. She doesn't know what to say.

Next door, Wilson shoots and there's that perfect sound. The clack. It's comforting. She listens as the balls roll into the pockets. Then says, "I thought you were—"

"I know."

"And I would have let him in, after all he's done. What's wrong with me?"

"Don't be so hard on yourself, darling," Jimmy Ray says gently. "The human heart is a wild and bruised beast and often acts accordingly."

"I don't like being this human."

Jimmy Ray looks into the condo—at the disarray, the stacks of plates, and the thick layer of dust that seems to have settled over everything.

"I'll tell you what. I'll help you clean up and we can invite your daddy over for dinner."

"I've made enough trouble for him."

Jimmy Ray shakes his head. "That's foolish talk. You're his girl and always will be."

Sophie shakes her head. A tear rolls down from behind her dark glasses. Jimmy Ray wipes it away with his hand, and says, "Tears are not going to get this house clean. Come on, I'll send him for Thai takeout and have him wrestle up a chilled bottle of Dom on his way over."

"Champagne?"

"Champagne. My mama used to tell me that a person sometimes just needs to celebrate being alive. You can't wait for an official day. You just have to jump in and be thankful with all your heart. So, champagne."

"But—"

"There are no 'buts,' " Jimmy Ray says, and gently places the jasmine branches in her arms. "You got to start living again, darling."

Sophie leans in, inhales deeply, and he says, "In Chinese, jasmine—*yeh-his-ming*—is the gift of good luck."

"Where did you get these? They're wonderful."

"Your daddy's yard. He doesn't know. He wants to be a Buddhist and Buddha says that we must practice the act of 'releasing attachment to things.' So I thought I'd help him release from these jasmine. I'd like to think that that new hole in his half-million-dollar landscaping will set him along the Right Path."

"Or drive him crazy." Sophie laughs.

"That, too," Jimmy Ray says. "Now, where's that vacuum cleaner? You dust."

Two hours later, Whit appears at Sophie's door with three chilled bottles of Dom Pérignon and the head chef and a busboy from the four-star Orchid Thai Cafe in Fort Myers. The staff has brought their knives, woks, and bags filled with banana leaves, pineapples, prawns, roasted ducks, rice noodles, and curries—everything needed for a feast.

Jimmy Ray laughs at the sight of him. "Son, have you *never* heard of takeout?"

"I thought it would get cold by the time I got back," Whit says.

And Sophie hugs him around the neck, hard, just as all lost children do.

Chapter Fifty-eight

Late that night, Danni wakes up from a dream about the mangrove forest. She hasn't been out there since Prescott died. Her heart can't bear it. It's not just because the Laguna Key Development Corporation has cemented over a good deal of it and burned a large portion of the rest. It's because she can't imagine the place without Prescott on the deck of that old boat of his. Reading. Smoking his pipe. Beached. Even when she thinks of the place, the memory of his tobacco—that sweet rum cloud—brings tears to her eyes.

Danni wakes in a panic. She can't remember what the dream was about, but she's damp from sweating. Her heart is pounding. Mandy is sleeping on the pillow next to her. She raises her head.

"It's okay," Danni says. "Bad dream."

The small dog burrows deeper into the down and goes back to sleep. That's when Danni hears bagpipes.

"Amazing Grace."

She looks out her bedroom window and Sòlas is standing in the surf. He's in his kilt. Shirtless. His steel hair catches the thin moonlight. The small wings on his back gently move back and forth with each note.

There's a storm out in the gulf; the night is bruised by it. The waves crash hard onto the shore, against Sòlas, rock his body, but he continues to play.

He looks more alone than Danni has ever seen anyone look. The sound of the bagpipes is like a wailing, a sorrow that runs too deep.

This has gone too far, she thinks, and has an idea, even though she knows that when she has an idea it's usually a dangerous thing. She jumps out of bed. Poe, sleeping on his perch, stirs.

"It's okay," she says, and gently runs her hand along his feet to calm him. She opens the hall closet and pulls out MR. P'S BIG BOX OF STUFF. That's what the box is labeled and that's what it is.

The song on the beach now seems distant, almost like a memory.

Inside the box is her childhood: beads and feathers and glitter and yarn and Popsicle sticks and white glue and sticky gold stars. And what she was looking for—rolls and rolls of plaster-casting tape. They are great for a broken arm and, more important, perfect for quick and easy puppet-making, she thinks, and blows off the dust.

"Circus time," she says to Poe. "After all, the pigs have flown."

Poe cocks his scarlet head. Mandy rolls over and snores again.

Outside, the bagpipes deflate; sound clatters to the ground.

Danni looks out the window. Sòlas is still there in the surf. But there seems to be something running toward him in the tall saw grass. Large and hairy, it looks like a man, but it's running wild like some sort of ape.

"Yeti," she says, and grabs Prescott's shotgun. Flings open the front door. Aims. The gun is loaded with birdshot; it's all about the noise.

Danni pulls the trigger. The noise is, indeed, deafening. The kick is worse.

She falls backward onto the hard wood floor. Poe is screeching. Mandy is howling. Sòlas comes running in, panicked, breathing hard. He drops the bagpipes at the door. Pulls her into his arms.

"Yeti," she says, and she can smell the salt of sweat on Sòlas's cold skin.

"Yeti? Buzzards, snakes, alligators, spiders of all sorts, and a thousand things in the water to kill you; the least of which are sharks—and now yeti? How do you people live here with all these beasts?" he says. Seems to want an answer, so she gives him one.

"Crazy," Danni says without hesitation. "It's a requirement. The Rorschach is actually part of the driver's license test."

And without another word, he kisses her.

Chapter Fifty-nine

At the turn of the century there were more than a hundred traveling circuses in America. Currently, there are about a dozen. They all claim to be the "Greatest Show on Earth," although Big Bertha—Ringling Bros. and Barnum & Bailey—has that phrase copyrighted.

Most are family-run. Some have one ring, some five. Some still use elephants to raise the tent, although few have animal acts anymore. Some practice the art form with an eye to circus tradition, like the Big Apple Circus. Some have re-created it, like the UniverSoul Circus, which replaces traditional calliope music with hip-hop and R&B, or Cirque du Soleil, which uses the big top and its traditions as a framework for avant-garde theater.

But at the end of the day, the brotherhood of the circus runs deep. So, the crones created an e-mail SOS with the subject line "Stars and Stripes Forever." The Sousa march has special meaning under the big top. It's a signal that there's an emergency, a call for the clowns to come running.

And so they came.

The next morning, a gaggle of Carson & Barnes "spec girls," showgirls who appear in the opening spectacle, arrived in an old red

VW Microbus. They were towing a trailer filled with straw and sacks of old coconut shells for costumes. Their circus is one of the few that still travels with elephants, and elephants like their snacks, so they had few coconuts shells to spare.

Two hours later, a family of famed high-wire aerialists from Tahiti, the Death-Defying Raapotos, pulled into Danni's parking lot. They came because they still know the Ai Kahiko, the ancient style of hula. They still understand the dance to be a form of prayer. Once they read the crones' e-mail, they knew they'd be needed.

Next came Girard the Samoan. He's the boss canvasman at the Big Apple Circus, a good man to have around. Part of his job is to make sure the Big Apple tent goes up properly and doesn't collapse, short of a major blowdown. Girard brought his five brothers. The boys always wanted to be in a circus. Since every circus needs a band, they brought their instruments. Drums, mostly. And quite an assortment, from the small sharkskin pahu pa'i, to the püniu—made from half a coconut shell and covered with the skin of the kala fish—to the traditional ipu hula, made of two gourds sewed together.

They also brought a conch shell to blow and the old calliope their father restored; he was a circus man, too.

Within two days, Danni's parking lot was filled with RVs, campers, and a tiny "big" top from a mud show, a small family-run circus, that the Shrine Circus had bought several years ago. It was faded and torn, but when the crones were done with it, it was a thing of beauty. They painted the underside of the tent in the style of Paul Gauguin's *Femmes de Tahiti*. Violent colors, intense and pure, illuminate the vision of an untamed world with sloe-eyed women looking off into an ultramarine sea.

"What kind of community circus is this?" Danni asked.

"Tiki!" the crones squealed. Then laughed. It was, after all, a stupid question.

Chapter Sixty

Danni has played a werewolf nuclear physicist, a mutant fashion designer, and a vampire soccer mom. Her world-famous face has been molded in latex, sculpted in silicone, layered with epoxy, and reconfigured into all manner of creatures.

But she's never been this nervous before.

She is lying very still on an inflatable raft, but she's not in the gulf. She's in her cottage. A two-inch-thick layer of Vaseline is smeared on her face, with a little extra over the eyebrows and the hairline, the tender spots. The crones are busy dipping the plaster bandage strips into water. They quickly wrap them around her nose, her mouth, and the furrow in her brow.

This mask will be of her. No character. Just Danni. There's something about that that makes her feel exposed. *It's easy to be a bloodsucking ghoul,* she thinks, *but being an aging actress really sucks.*

Sòlas is lying next to her, also on a raft. It was the crones' idea. "Sorrow and Joy," they explained, but Sòlas was too embarrassed to translate for Danni. The original Sorrow and Joy, the archetypal lovers locked in an embrace, was his tribute to his parents' love, and to all love.

You just can't say something like that to a woman who says she doesn't believe in love anymore.

It will take thirty minutes to dry the bandages, and Sòlas and Danni have to be absolutely still. They breathe through straws. The plaster is cold on their faces. When the drying begins, one of the crones places Sòlas's hand in Danni's.

At first the hold is tentative. Then their fingers twine.

The timer in the kitchen is set. The crones pick up their instruments and very softly begin to sing to help pass the time.

It's a song that Danni knows, and she knows she knows it, but she can't quite place it because it's slower, and sweeter, than what she remembers. And she doesn't speak Swedish. But the button accordion provides a profound sense of longing, which she remembers from the original. And, even at this speed, she thinks, there's a kind of Krazy Glue sort of hook.

Sort of soaring. Sort of heartfelt.

And then she remembers.

"Dancing Queen."

ABBA.

And now that that song is stuck in her head, Danni wonders if it would ruin the mask if she ran her breathing straw right through her brain.

Chapter Sixty-one

The charges against Bill are overwhelming. They include murder, assorted terrorist activities, and the theft of hurricane shutters. When Gayle Hennessey arrived at his house, she found the Taser, the pipe bombs, and the makings of a nuclear bomb—small, but dirty.

They also found a business card, which read BUDDY: POP AND RUN. And now Bill's sitting in the interrogation room at the FBI office in Naples and sweating hard.

"And how did you meet Buddy?" she says.

Wilson leans across the table. "You don't have to answer that, Bill. You shouldn't really answer anything without an attorney."

Hennessey had called Wilson because the old man asked her to. "One of your people is here," she told him.

"They're not *my* people."

But here Wilson is. And Hennessey is regretting it. It's not exactly by the book, she told him. Wilson understood. Hennessey's the kind of FBI agent with the stench of dead trees around her: paper-pushing and always by the book.

"Brian," she says, and tries not to sound shrill, "if Mr. Bryon wants to talk, he can—"

"When is Whit getting here?" Bill asks.

Bill looks like hell. His eyes are bloodshot. He shakes. He seems forgetful. Wilson says gently, "I told you already. You need a public defender."

"Whit's my lawyer."

"I know," Wilson says. Pulls Hennessey aside. "This guy is no terrorist. He's just a lonely guy."

"With nuclear capabilities."

"Fine," Wilson says. "Get technical about it."

"You don't have to whisper. I didn't kill that Buddy fella," Bill says.

Hennessey sits back down. "How did you know him?"

"I met him outside the educational seminar 'Real Estate Will Make You Rich!' They had a free buffet and an open bar. He was passing out cards to everybody in the parking lot."

"And you hired him?"

"I didn't kill him."

"What did you hire him to do?"

Wilson leans across the table. "Bill," he says, "this is the point where you shut up."

"Look, I didn't kill him. I just saw him that night. We talked. I was taking a walk and there he was."

"Where?"

"Over by the mangroves."

This is not good, Wilson thinks. "Bill, let's have Agent Hennessey leave a second. I'll be your attorney until Whit gets here. How's that?"

Hennessey narrows her eyes. "He waived his rights."

"I didn't hear that," Wilson says. "Did you say that, Bill?"

Bill shakes his head. "Could I have a minute with my attorney?" he says.

Agent Hennessey slams the door behind her.

"What the *hell* did you do?" Wilson asks.

Bill is frowning. "Nothing. It was serendipity. I wasn't going to hire him, but I ran into him again. He was in Laguna Key. He was just walking down the sidewalk. I figured he was doing some business with Whit."

"You seem to just run into this guy a lot. How'd you find out about this seminar?"

"This was back in November, before Sophie's accident. Whit's son-in-law got us the tickets. They had free prime rib, much as you want. Carving station and everything. Really classy."

What rich guys won't do for a free meal, Wilson thinks. *And Derek knew that. Nice setup.*

"Did Derek go with you?"

"No," Bill says. "I've never met him. Whit thought he was coming, but he never showed. Shame. It was really good prime rib."

"Bill. Focus. Just tell me. You kill Buddy?"

"No."

"Peter?"

Bill looks confused.

"The homeless guy," Wilson says, and hates having to call him that. "You kill him?"

Bill suddenly breaks down crying. "Just Prescott."

"Shit." Wilson leans back hard in his chair.

"I didn't know his heart would stop forever. He came at me

screaming all sorts of things. He was hallucinating. He went on and on about how the ghosts of slaves were going to get me, like they got him. And he was talking about bones. Bones everywhere. So I Tasered him. He fell. I ran."

"Damn. Okay. How about Buddy? Did you zap him?"

Bill is now crying so hard he can hardly breathe. It breaks Wilson's heart.

"I tried," Bill says. "But he took the Taser from me. He was threatening me, but he was alive when I saw him."

Wilson shakes his head. "I don't know, Bill."

He leans across and grabs Wilson's hand. "You have to believe me," he says. "That fella on the motorcycle. He knows. He pulled up when we were talking. Buddy seemed to know him. I figured he was meeting him."

Derek has a Harley, Wilson thinks. "Why didn't you tell the police this?" he says.

"Because then I would have had to tell him that I hired Buddy—"

"—to burn the Hummer."

"No," Bill says. "To impersonate Barry Manilow. He said he was a music lover and could fake it. He suggested it. I figured people would be running from the bar in droves if he played there. So I sent him over and Danni hired him. I knew she would. She was desperate after her truck blew up."

"And so you and Whit hired him to pretend to be a singer?"

"Whit didn't know about it. I didn't tell anybody. I didn't want people to know that I hired Buddy because Sir Edmund Hillary wouldn't have hired Buddy. Do you know what I mean?"

"I do," Wilson says. "And that sort of frightens me."

"I didn't do anything wrong, except for the Prescott thing, and those couple of bombs, but other than that—"

"This guy," Wilson says. "The guy on the Harley. Would you know him if you saw him again?"

"Well, sure," Bill says as if Wilson has just asked him a stupid question. "How could I forget him? He's the guy who's blackmailing me."

"Blackmail?" Great, Wilson thinks. "Let's just start at the beginning, shall we?"

Chapter Sixty-two

Electric violet, deep orchid, aubergine—no matter what the puppet is, no matter whose face is used as a mold, or what animal it represents, Sòlas has decided that they will all be painted in memory of those eyes: his mother's eyes, Peter's eyes.

They will be watching, he thinks, which somehow gives him comfort.

Aunt Bee has put herself in charge of finding volunteers to make the puppet menagerie. In most traditional circuses, the menagerie of animals is crucial. They walk in the parade and take center stage under the big top. In the Rose and Puppet Circus, the menagerie consists of puppets, which can represent fanciful beasts or real beasts or beasts that are now extinct. They can be hand puppets, marionettes, masks worn with costume, or towering-rod puppets—but there must be beasts.

"And they must represent the dreams, the darkness and joy, of each member of this community," Sòlas says to her.

Sòlas, Danni, and Aunt Bee are standing on the beach in front of the bar, the same beach that just a few days earlier held the Santa

Lucia celebration. The long tables are back, but they are now covered with the makings of puppets—plaster, chicken wire, gallons of paint, long rolls of white paper, and bamboo poles. Danni and Aunt Bee cleaned out the nearest Ace Hardware.

"I understand completely," Aunt Bee says. She takes off her white lace gloves and paints a huge banner that reads BEASTS OF DESIRE MADE HERE.

While the banner dries, she and Danni make cookies in the kitchen of the Bad Girl's Bar & Grill. The scent of warm chocolate soon fills the streets.

By the time the cookies are finished, the two women have found a comfortable silence together.

Aunt Bee says simply, "I had always wanted to have a daughter."

"I know what you mean," Danni says, and does. She pours them both a cup of coffee.

When the cookies are laid out on the tables, the banner is raised. The line of volunteers soon wraps around the bar.

The crones, Sòlas, and Danni make sure everyone has all the supplies that they need. They help when they can. The range of beasts is surprising. Aunt Bee makes a swan mask, the color of irises, with a rhinestone tiara perched on the very top of its towering head.

Jimmy Ray and Whit work on transforming themselves into twin crocodiles in tuxedos. "We are nearly extinct, but elegant," Jimmy Ray explains to Sòlas.

"I understand completely," Sòlas says. He is trying to help the men create their vision exactly as they imagine it, but it's difficult. Whit wants the masks be the color of a Côte de Nuits, specifically the Saint-Julien, Maison Champy. He even brought several bottles along for reference.

Sòlas does his best, but when the paint dries, the final shade is lacking the depth and intensity that the rare wine is noted for. In fact, it sort of looks like grape pop.

"I like grape pop," Danni says.

The hint of a suggestion, no matter how slight, that somehow the Saint-Julien, Maison Champy is even vaguely related to "pop" makes Whit start to twitch. Before he can deliver a long and convoluted lecture on the particulars of the God-kissed grapes of the Côte de Nuits, before he can say a word, Jimmy Ray whispers to him, "Fling your heart into the world like a Frisbee."

Whit understands. He takes a deep breath. "Grape pop is lovely. Fanciful," he says. "It's so very much not like anything that nature ever intended."

And he means this as a compliment; it's the best he can do. Then he pours everyone some wine.

There's also a marionette trio of golfing dinosaurs—two T. rex and a brontosaurus. Their puppeteers wear knickers and shout, "Fore!" everywhere they go.

They see it as a statement of protest that Laguna Key is still one of the few developments in Florida without a golf course. Most people just think it's cute.

Wilson, wanting to keep a close eye on things, decides to be "the human animal." No mask for him. He'll wear his uniform. Aunt Bee thinks that's cheating, but since he's nearly a police officer, she doesn't want to argue about it.

And then there's Jim, who once a month had transformed himself into Deputy Barney Fife but now can't imagine ever doing that again. He just can't shake the nightmares of Buddy's body. Jim wants to be an egg—a six-foot-tall egg. It takes plenty of chicken wire and plaster. He paints it the lightest shade of violet that he can.

"What kind of an animal is that?" asks Aunt Bee.

"Evolving," he says.

It is surprising to Danni that the residents of Laguna Key seem to be particularly adept in the field of puppet production. The crones slather their faces with Vaseline and then the cold plaster, and they don't complain. The Beasts of Desire are made real within hours.

And so, less than weeks after Peter's body was found, a circus in honor of him is ready. Tomorrow morning the festivities will begin.

There's only one problem: no audience. Everyone is in the circus.

At least, it appears that way.

Chapter Sixty-three

At dusk, Whit stands on the beach where it edges the mangrove forest. It's the predetermined spot. It's away from the house, away from the streetlights. Derek is late—*As usual,* he thinks. The salt air is humid, near rain. The waves are inconsistent, not like they are on his *Ocean Surf* CD.

Short, long, short, he thinks. *Chaos.*

The idea gives him a chill. He flips up the collar of his leather bomber jacket. A flock of seagulls caws overhead. He's holding a leather satchel filled with bills. It's not as much as Derek wanted, but plenty to live a good life somewhere far away from Sophie.

Jimmy Ray's plan was simple—call the FBI. "Don't mess with crazy," he told Whit.

And that seemed reasonable, so Whit called Agent Hennessey's office to arrange a meeting, but she wasn't there. Her voice mail said she was out of the office until tomorrow morning. That would be too late.

So they have to go it alone. Whit decided that Wilson was not to be told any of this. "If something happens," he said, "who'd take care of Sophie?"

Jimmy Ray understood. Daughters make a man brave—and foolish.

And so a voice-activated microcassette recorder is taped to Whit's chest, right underneath the V-neck in his cashmere sweater. It isn't high-tech, but it should do.

Jimmy Ray stands on the roof of Prescott's boat and watches with an ancient telescope. He has Whit's cell phone, in case anything goes wrong. He can call Wilson for help or the sheriff.

He hopes nothing goes wrong.

This is not a venture for old men, he thinks. The son-in-law has killed. Will kill again. Those kinds of people always do.

Jimmy Ray's heart beats hard like a fist, rattles his bones. Soon, it will be completely dark. He won't be able to see Whit and can't help him if something goes wrong.

The sun sinks slightly lower into the gulf. Suddenly, it's eye level with the telescope, blinds him for a moment.

On the beach, Derek finally appears. He is limping. His leg is in a full cast. His chest is taped. He speaks into Whit's chest to the tape recorder that he assumes is planted there, "Testing. One. Two," he says raspy and grabs the satchel. Then laughs like some fifth-grade bully.

It's a game to him, Whit thinks. *All a game.*

Jimmy Ray can hear voices, laughter, but his eyes are slow to adjust.

"This doesn't look like forty-seven million," Derek says.

Whit is shaking. "Get out," he says. Even though Derek is clearly hurt, he's afraid of him.

How did I get so damn old? Whit thinks.

Derek speaks into the tape recorder again and looks, unblinking, at Whit. "You're a fool."

Whit suddenly feels as if he's on fire.

Jimmy Ray looks into the telescope again. The beach is too dark. He can't see. It's then that the bats come screaming over his head. He ducks and suddenly there's there the sharp-edged sound of snapping and the flashing of blue-white light, like a strobe, like lightning. Then he hears it.

It's not so much a scream as a wail. A horrible wail: hardly human. "You made my daughter blind."

Then the words run over each other, choke and claw.

"She loved you/trusted you/you killed a boy/God knows what else."

Just then, something catches Jimmy Ray's eye. Something in the brush is running toward Whit. The high grass parts as it goes. Banana trees bend.

Maybe Wilson, Jimmy Ray thinks, and scrambles down the ladder, off the boat, and through the dark forest toward Whit, the explosive light, the screaming, and the beach.

That damn Taser, Jimmy Ray thinks. He didn't pat Whit down. Didn't think him capable of something so stupid. But he is. He's firing it over and over again.

He'll stop his heart.

Whatever is running in front of Jimmy Ray veers off to the right. He has no time to go after it. When he reaches the beach, Derek has collapsed into a heap on the sand. Unmoving.

Too late, Jimmy Ray thinks. *I'm too late.*

Whit bends over the man again. Fires the Taser one more time.

Jimmy Ray screams, and the sound of his voice shocks Whit

back into his own skin. He looks dazed. "He hurt my baby," he says, and starts to cry, falls to his knees. Spent. The Taser tumbles from his hand.

This is not good, my friend, Jimmy Ray thinks. A sick feeling comes over him as he leans over Derek. The man's face is scarred, bruised from the crash. One eye is still swollen shut. His body is broken. He looks more pathetic than dangerous.

Jimmy Ray feels for his pulse. It's there. He nudges him in the ribs. "Boy, get up," he says. Throws the satchel onto his chest. Derek's eyes open. They are dull. "Listen," Jimmy Ray says. "You go far and fast. Don't you ever turn back here."

Derek is groggy. "He cheated me," he says. "There's less than a million in here."

Jimmy Ray picks up the Taser. "If you don't leave now, I will finish this job."

The young man looks at him, unbelieving.

"Don't let these old bones fool you," Jimmy Ray says. "That could be a fatal mistake."

Unsteady, Derek gets to his feet. He has a wild-eyed, beaten look about him.

Jimmy Ray snaps a warning shot over his head and is surprised at how hot the gun feels in his hand and how loud it is. Then he aims at Derek's heart.

"Try me, son. It would give me great pleasure."

Derek meets his eye and there is no doubt that the old man will make good on this threat, and enjoy doing it. Derek picks up the satchel.

"I'd hurry up if I were you," Jimmy Ray says. "I might just give you a jolt for old times' sake."

But Derek makes his way slowly, deliberately, into the mangrove forest. *Probably parked his bike somewhere nearby,* Jimmy Ray thinks. *Lots of places to hide in a swamp.*

Jimmy Ray sinks down on the sand next to Whit. "It's okay," he says. Whit nods.

For a while, the two men sit together, silent, and watch the stars come out. After a time, deep in the forest, there's the distant sound of a struggle, the sharp intake of surprise. Then a howling, long and low.

"Wild dogs," Jimmy Ray says, but it doesn't sound like a dog. *Not at all.*

And so he smiles.

Chapter Sixty-four

At dawn, Jimmy Ray and Whit are deep in the mangrove forest. Neither one could sleep, not knowing.

"Derek?"

"Derek!"

They seem to be walking in circles. Not lost—Whit took his handheld GPS—but not getting anywhere, either. In the daylight, the forest doesn't seem like a swamp at all. It's too cold for snakes. Gators are hibernating. Everything looks silver in the sunlight. Flamingos pick at shrimp swimming in and out of the "knees" of ancient cypress trees. They cock their heads as the men pass, curious. Flutter their wings.

"He could have got away," Jimmy Ray says.

Whit sees something shiny in the distance under a patch of flowering white dogwoods. "Have we been that way?"

"Not sure."

When they reach the stand of trees, it's actually a clearing. It's quiet. Calm. Underneath the delicate canopy is what seems to be an overgrown garden. It's as big as a room, surrounded by a low wall, made of seashells and some sort of sandy mortar. Old, it crumbles to the touch.

The garden itself is a tangle of white: wild white roses, star jasmine, and orchids dug into the crooks of the trees. Kudzu crosses over it and back again, wraps around the things left behind—a brass bed frame, glass hurricane lamps, and mirrors of all shapes and sizes. Some are hand mirrors, some from dressers. All of them are planted in this place.

As soon as Whit sees this he knows that Prescott was not crazy. This is, indeed, a slave graveyard. The old man described it in great detail. And here it is.

From where they are standing, it looks as if there's been some recent digging.

On top of a new mound of sand, there's Whit's shovel and satchel.

Whit starts to dial Hennessey; he brought her number just in case. "We can't screw around with this," he says.

Jimmy Ray gently closes his phone. "Let's take a look first."

And so they do.

The two men stand over what they now know is a newly dug grave. The hand that last held Whit's satchel still holds it. The long elegant fingers, now a shade of pale, are locked in rigor mortis around its handle and stick up from the smoothed sand.

Jimmy Ray gets down on his knees. Says a prayer for lost souls. Whit doesn't know what to say. He prays along.

Next to the mound is a piece of broken marble under a tangle of weeds. It's been there for a very long time. There is only one word inscribed: "Free."

Whit understands what that one word means in this place. He knows that it's proof of where he is and what he's seeing.

And he knows what that means to Laguna Key and his dreams of developing it until it has its own zip code.

But he also understands the need to cherish your dead. And mourn them. *Damn Buddhist stuff is wearing off,* Whit thinks, and begins to dial Hennessey again.

"I don't think that's such a good idea," Jimmy Ray says. "Maybe we should try to find out who did this first. People don't bury themselves. Somebody could think it's us."

Whit looks down at the hand still holding his satchel. The wedding ring is still on it. It's a Möbius band: a ring designed on a mathematical concept, it appears to be a thin strip of gold with only one side, one edge. Sophie had them made.

"The perfect symbol for marriage," she told Whit.

Unless you're making a mockery of it, he thinks now.

"You're right," he says to Jimmy Ray. "Not like he's going anywhere."

Chapter Sixty-five

At 9:00 a.m., the circus parade is ready. Everyone is in place. Wilson, as security, clears the streets with his bright yellow golf cart.

Sophie sits next to him, poised and waving. Danni loaned her the Hawaiian-print sarong she wore in *Vampiria Meets the Volcano*. It's lava red. Smoldering. The crones oiled Sophie's long black hair and braided it with tiny wild orchids. She looks like a sacrificial virgin on her way to the fourteenth hole, hoping for par.

The crones, in their white dresses and red clown shoes, jog alongside. Klara holds a basket bearing Mandy. Her twin, Marie, has Poe lashed to her arm. All are wearing flower leis, although Poe thinks his is some sort of snack.

Behind them is the circus band—Girard the Samoan and his five brothers perched atop their father's old calliope. It creaks under their weight, leaning to one side and then the other. The steam from its whistles makes it seem as if the men are riding on a cloud.

The brothers are wearing the traditional clothes of hula: fern crowns on their heads, pressed white shirts, and long black pants.

That surprises some. They expected half-naked warriors, but that's just for the tourists. Many years ago, Girard and his brothers started the praise and worship hula ministry at Po'okela church. And so they beat their drums the ancient way, and dress accordingly.

As the parade moves through town, the men drum in time with the calliope and its old-fashioned circus siren song. The music is so loud it feels like a series of shock waves. Whistles and pops.

Behind them, Jimmy Ray and Whit, dressed as twin grape-pop alligators wearing tuxedos and waving American flags, are walking on stilts. They tower over it all. They wave at the empty sidewalks as they pass and imagine cheering crowds.

Next comes the gaggle of "spec girls" from Carson & Barnes. They have death-defying hair—dyed violet and piled high on top of their heads. They juggle flaming tiki torches and laugh that toothy showgirl kind of laugh, all blinding teeth and ruby lips. Once under the circus big top, they plan to take the high wire. Dip and tumble. Try not to set the place aflame.

After that comes the menagerie of Laguna Key. There are beasts of fancy, beasts of darkness, beasts of dreams and desires: they are the heart of this place. Each puppet, each costume, and each mask is painted so many shades of violet that they make their way through the whitewashed streets looking like wisps of storm clouds.

Behind the menagerie of townspeople, the high-wire aerialists from Tahiti ride in their rented convertible. The top is down. Each holds in his or her hand a tiny marionette fashioned after the rulers of their native land. There's Queen Pomare Vahine with her head made entirely of eyes. It was her custom to eat the eye of her foes. Then her son, King Pomare, who gave the islands to France and died the same year Gauguin arrived. And finally, the last queen, the artist Marau Salmon, half Jewish and half Tahitian, who some say died of a broken heart.

At the end of the parade walk Danni and Sòlas. They are dressed in the tradition of Bunraku puppeteers in Japan: completely in black. Vented hoods cover their heads, black gloves on their hands. They are not to be seen.

They hold Sorrow and Joy, their two puppets, high above them on bamboo poles. The puppets seem so real, with their sad faces and their hands intertwined. As they make their way through the streets, they dance a slow waltz to music that only they can hear. Every now and then their lips touch, as do the puppeteers'.

When they stop for an embrace, the parade moves ahead without them.

They do not see him hiding in the sea grass. Crouched. But he sees them. For a moment, he remembers Sorrow and Joy from long ago. Knows that they are not the same. The faces are different.

They kiss.

There is a roaring inside his head, like that of a wounded animal.

They kiss again.

Devil is all he can think. The word pounds against his brain.

They kiss once more, and this time they linger. The world around them seems to fall away.

He could have killed them then. It would have been easy. Then bury them next to that man who killed his friend and threw him in the Dumpster like trash.

He wanted to kill them. After all, he was a warrior, born of the warrior clan. But it was too public.

Chapter Sixty-six

After the parade, no one can find Sòlas. Danni has looked everywhere: in the performer's tent, in the bar, in the cottage. She can't find him at all.

"Maybe he's on the beach," Sophie says.

Danni has changed into her hula outfit, the tourist version, which is hardly the kind of thing to wear when you're trudging down a beach. It's a coconut bra, a fake grass skirt, and a lei of gardenias around her neck. The day has turned bone damp. The wind has kicked up. She's cold right down to her coconuts. Shivering.

"I thought we were in Florida," she tells Poe, who has eaten most of his lei and now looks less than festive. He hisses.

"I agree," she says. Hisses back.

She gets all the way to the mangrove forest before her cell phone rings. Hennessey says, "Ms. Keene, do you feel as if you're hallucinating?"

Danni takes a moment to evaluate. She's pretty sure that she is standing on a cold and windy beach wearing a coconut-shell bra and grass skirt and leashed to her pet vulture, Poe, who—thanks to the crones' handiwork—has remnants of a tiny pink plastic lei around his flesh-eating head.

"No more than usual," she says.

"Have you been drinking the well water?"

"Ick. No. Smells like rotten eggs. I hooked up to city water as soon as I moved in. Nobody drinks that anymore." Then she thinks a minute. "Wait. Peter. The one Wilson found. He was drinking it before he died."

"Nobody should. It's tainted with digitalis," she says. "Causes hallucinations and can kill you. I'm stuck in traffic. I'll be there soon—"

"Great," Danni says, and hangs up, even though Hennessey was still talking. She couldn't help it. The hairy back. The wild hair.

Yeti.

The huge hulking beast is off in the distance. She can see it turn into the mangrove forest at the edge of the beach. She turns off the phone, so it won't startle the creature. Then goes after it.

It never once occurs to Danni that this is not a movie.

Unfortunately, it's not a yeti, either.

Chapter Sixty-seven

When Wilson's cell phone rings, he's surprised that it's Hennessey.

"She hung up on me," she says. "That Danni Keene hung up on me in the middle of an important conversation."

"Welcome to Danni's World," Wilson says. "I told you that the son-in-law was good for it."

"So I owe you a beer," Hennessey says. "I'll be there in about half an hour. Is she there?"

"Hang on," he says and looks around the crowd milling about in the parking lot. The parade is over. This afternoon's performance will, as the sign says, "Commence at 3:00 p.m., more or less." Near the Tahitian-themed big top painted with Gauguin's *Femmes de Tahiti* are the crones, with their Pippi Longstocking hair, white dresses, and red clown shoes. They're serving glogg to a six-foot-tall violet egg.

Just another day in Paradise, Wilson thinks. "Nope. I'll go look for her."

"Thanks," Hennessey says, and actually sounds thankful.

She should, he thinks; she almost blew it. But there's still something nagging at him.

"Hey, wait," Wilson says. "Peter . . . the guy I found."

"You need to find Danni."

"I know, but something's been bothering me. How did you ID him?"

"He had ID."

"Nobody identified the body?"

"You saw it."

"Right," Wilson says. He still sees it in his dreams.

"When that Suny woman told us about the boy, we ran some DNA to check the story, but there was no match to anything in our files."

"Makes sense," Wilson says. "Was there stray epidermal—hairs, that kind of thing?"

"Of course. "

"You run DNA on those, too? Or just the body?"

"Brian, don't start—"

It's clear from the whine in her voice that she didn't. "I knew it," he says. "Check the lungs, too. I suspect they look like a tar pit."

Then he tells her why.

"How did I miss that?" she says. Wilson can hear the panic in her paper-pushing voice.

"Don't feel bad," Wilson says. "Details will always bite your ass."

Chapter Sixty-eight

The night before, Sòlas saw what Whit and Jimmy Ray had done.

He was walking along the beach when he heard the screaming and then saw the snap of the Taser up ahead. When he came upon the old men, spent on the sand near the edge of the mangrove forest, he hid and watched them for a long time. When he heard howling, he knew it wasn't a pack of wild dogs.

It's over, he thought.

The old men had done the one thing Sòlas couldn't bring himself to do—they had avenged his kin. They had their own reasons, but the outcome was the same. The man who killed his brother was dead.

Sòlas knew that the unburied body would eventually be found, and maybe found sooner rather than later. And maybe it would be traced back to the old men. *That would be wrong,* he thought. *Old men have no place in prison.*

And so, the last of the warrior Clan MacKay, the last living relative of King Macbeth, became duty-bound to them. *Tomorrow,*

Sòlas thought. *I'll make it right for you tomorrow, when daylight comes.*

Sòlas MacKay is a man of his word. As soon as the circus parade is over, Sòlas changes into his kilt, leaves his shirt and shoes behind, and runs. The circus begins in ninety minutes. *If there's blood,* he thinks, *I can take off the kilt. Jump in the gulf waters. No one will know.*

He takes his sword, just in case.

Sòlas runs all the way down the beach to the mangrove forest. He knows he doesn't have much time before people will notice he's gone. He is kilted and yet shirtless. Barefoot. His clan would be ashamed of how he wears the tartan, but he doesn't care. He honors his dead the best way he can.

Inside the forest, he's not sure where he's going. He runs wild, sometimes in circles. He cuts through the tough undergrowth with his sword, searching for what's left of his brother's killer. Feels the ancient blood within his veins.

When he comes to the clearing, he is breathless. It is other-worldly. The beauty of it, the sorrow, is so profound. He sees the freshly dug mound and it is clear to him that the old men have already been here.

The dead are buried, he thinks. When he looks carefully, he can see that there are mounds of sand everywhere, nearly every one untouched. But there is also a shovel and a pile of bones. This is some sort of a graveyard.

He wonders about the bone that Danni hid from him. Wonders if someone knew of this place, dug it up. Put it under the bar to scare her away.

Sòlas puts down his sword at the edge of the seashell-and-mortar wall out of respect. Gently walks into the tangle of lost lives.

Petals of white dogwood fall all around him like snow. Cover his hair, his arms, and his small, useless wings. Sòlas thinks about all the graveyards he's ever been in. How they often have winged angels sculpted in marble standing watch. Silent. That's how he feels, like some sort of stone angel. So he gets on his knees and prays aloud for all the souls buried around him.

That's why he doesn't hear the man or see his own sword come down across his back.

He doesn't see his wings, useless, always earthbound, sever and then tumble like wax petals onto the white orchids, the star jasmine, and the now-red earth.

He doesn't see any of it. It happens so fast.

Blind with pain and rage, and acting on pure instinct, Sòlas pulls the *sgian dubh* from the place in his kilt, turns, and thrusts it upward into the man's heart.

His brother's heart.

The look of surprise on Peter's face is something Sòlas knows he will never forget.

"God in heaven forgive me—" he screams. Everywhere there is blood.

Peter says nothing. He touches a single finger to the corner of his own eye, his mother's eye, and then to Sòlas's. At the same time, and at the same speed, he traces an imaginary tear on each of their faces. *The Harlequin's Sorrow.*

And then the roaring in Peter's head stops.

Chapter Sixty-nine

The vultures tip Wilson off. It's not uncommon to see a kettle of vultures circling, but when one has a bright pink leash you know that Danni Keene can't be far behind. Neither can Sòlas.

As Wilson runs though the mangrove forest, he calls Hennessey.

"You were right," she says. "The DNA on those stray hairs matched the hit-and-run."

"So Jason was Peter's son," Wilson says. "But it wasn't Peter in the Dumpster."

"You got it."

"Choo-Choo was in the Dumpster?"

"More than likely; awful lungs. But the important thing you need to know is that Peter isn't dead. At least, not that we know of."

"That's exactly what I was worried about."

Wilson's stomach goes sour. He seems to be running in circles, trying to track those birds. It feels as if he's out of time. Out of luck. Again.

"Look," Wilson says. "We probably need an ambulance. Just follow the vultures."

When he says this he knows just how horrible it sounds, so he hangs up the phone.

"Danni! Sòlas!"

Wilson isn't sure if Peter plans to kill Sòlas—driven by greed and power like that Macbeth guy in the play—and inherit his money, but he's pretty sure Peter planted that old ID and Sòlas's phone number on his dead friend to set up some sort of family reunion. And he's pretty sure that the vulture Poe and his pals aren't circling around waiting for the circus to start. And that makes his hands sweat.

Hang on, Scottie, he thinks, and follows the hissing of the birds.

"Danni!"

There's no answer. But there's no screaming, either. That's good, he thinks.

Then he sees the clearing. Runs to it. Stops. The moment takes his breath away. It looks like a snowstorm. The wind has kicked up, sending dogwood petals everywhere. White flowers, fat and fragrant, cover everything. But it's not a beautiful sight. It's stark.

In the center of it all, vultures dive low, hiss, peck, and scream away. Peter's body rolls back and forth under the force of them. Their iridescent black bodies cover him, greedy.

A leather satchel is on the ground; the hand holding it is pecked to the bone.

The vultures keep coming, Poe included.

In the midst of it all, Danni is in shock. She's on her

knees bent over Sòlas, holding him in her arms. His body shakes uncontrollably.

His wings are gone.

"Danni!" Wilson shouts. The birds scatter.

She turns slowly, holds up her hand as a child would, to show it to him. It's covered in blood.

In a very small voice she says, "It's real."

Chapter Seventy

Two weeks later, it's Thursday night and it is, indeed, Tongo-riffic Mai Tai Night at the Bad Girl's Bar & Grill. Don Tiki is blasting on the sound system. The bar is packed.

Everyone in Laguna Key is trying hard to have fun. Their laughter is a little louder than usual, a little forced, but that's okay. Nobody seems to mind. They all want things to return to normal. Helping the Bad Girl's Bar & Grill stay in business seems like a good place to start.

Plus, the mai tais are great.

Mandy, the small dog that bears a striking resemblance to Barry Manilow, is curled into her new Hawaiian-print bed. Guarding the cash register. The ancient twin crones are dancing hula on top of the bar again. Their coconut bras are chaste, but mesmerizing.

"How do they do that?" Whit says.

"I just don't want to think about it too hard," Wilson says.

The two have come to an understanding. Wilson has a huge raise. And somewhere in northern India, in a village whose name he can't pronounce, there's a couple of water buffalo, a father and son named "Ray" and "Brian." Wilson's pretty sure that neither can carry a tune.

Danni serves a round to the table. It's the first time she's been back since Wilson found her. She's spent the last two weeks at the hospital with Sòlas. What was left of his wings was removed; it's something that neither one of them talks about.

Since Danni's been busy, the crones have completely taken over the bar. With a new marketing strategy, which includes authentic luaus featuring the five drumming brothers of Girard the Samoan and free pupu platters for early bird diners, the place is jumping. They had to hire Aunt Bee to give them an extra hand.

Wilson is glad Bee is not waiting on him. He knows that if she served his mai tai with that Playboy bunny dip of hers, wearing that grass skirt and coconut-shell bra over her prim cotton dress and white crocheted gloves, it would give him nightmares for the rest of his life. The crones are bad enough. They're shaking their hips so hard to the Mondo Exotica sounds that grass from their skirts is flying all over the room.

"You know what they need?" Whit says to Danni.

"Clothes?" Wilson says, and as soon as he says this Sophie appears behind him—wearing a hula outfit, complete with a coconut-shell bra.

"This is for my physical therapy," she explains. "Stage two." Wilson is speechless. Whit clears his throat.

"Daddy?"

Sophie is waiting for a reaction—and Whit has one. He leans over and takes her hand. Kisses it gently. He's so proud of her standing there nearly naked in a grass skirt, without gray sweats, that there are tears in his eyes.

"Wish me luck," Sophie says, and Danni hugs her.

"Hey, aren't you cold?" Wilson says. "Where's your shawl, that knitting thing?"

"Threw it away."

Sophie makes her way slowly through the crowd to the bar. Every now and then, someone tries to help her, but she pushes whoever it is away. When she reaches the bar, the crones stop dancing. They signal for the music to stop. Everyone is watching.

The crones help her up. And then shout, "Ta-da!" and the Mondo Exotica sounds begin again. And so does the hula.

The music transforms the women. Lost in the ancient ritual of the dance, they are glowing, laughing, filled with pure joy. Sophie's dark glasses fly off her face; she doesn't seem to notice.

"That's nice," Danni says, and for a moment seems to be her old self again.

"You know what you need?" Whit says. "Live music."

"What about *Wheel of Fortune*?" Danni says.

"Look," he says. "I know this guy. Great guy. Looking for a gig. All you have to do is put a sign in the window and he'll be here."

Danni leans in. "This guy is good?"

Whit smiles. "He is the dharma within."

She looks at Wilson for clarification. Wilson shrugs. "I think that means he rocks."

Chapter Seventy-one

Sòlas said he'd come by, that the hospital was releasing him, and he does. Finally. When it's time to close up for the night, Danni finds him sitting on the back deck by the Dumpster.

"You need to forgive yourself," she says, and sits down next to him. He pats her hand, like old couples do. She takes it in hers.

"That's going to take some time," he says.

The moon overhead is full again. Silver as a lost nickel. *One month,* she thinks. *That's not a very long time to know someone.*

"I've never been to Vermont," she says. "Ice cream, right? All those cows."

He smiles. She smiles. The shyness between them is raw, new.

"It's very hot in Florida in the summer, isn't it?" he says to her.

Danni looks at Sòlas closely. His violet eyes are now a deep shade of ultramarine, not violet at all. Just dark.

"Awful," she says. "Lots of places close up after Easter and open again in October."

"That seems very civilized," he says, and their shoulders touch, then their lips.

The kiss does not feel like good-bye, although it could be. It's difficult for Danni to tell. There's so much that's unsaid between them.

Sòlas stands. Pulls her up and into his arms. Kisses her again. This time it's filled with longing.

Then he walks away. Doesn't turn back.

Danni follows until he reaches the parking lot and gets into a small white rental car. Their puppets, Sorrow and Joy, are posed in the backseat as if they are lovers locked in an embrace. When Danni looks at them, she sees her face and Sòlas's. Wonders if Sòlas sees that, too.

He looks back at her for a moment. Danni raises her hand in a wave. He nods.

As Sòlas pulls out of the parking lot and turns onto the long whitewashed street, Danni realizes that she's not alone.

"Ta-da," the crones sadly say. Put their arms around Danni. Hold her close.

"Ta-da," Danni says.

Chapter Seventy-two

The HELP WANTED sign lasts only two hours in the front window of the Bad Girl's Bar & Grill.

"I'm here for the job," the man says. She recognizes him from the parade as Whit's friend. His voice is gravelly. He has the air of a deposed king, with his brilliantined hair set in a perfect Marcel wave. The pin-striped suit is immaculate, but the hem is slightly frayed.

When he sings, his voice is strong.

"Breaking my heart, woman. You breaking my heart. Mamma, let me be."

He growls, shakes under the weight of the words. His hands coax the notes from the old piano. Danny's never been much for the blues, but there's something about his sorrow that makes her want to hear more.

"Where's home?" she asks when he's finished.

"Last time up, New Orleans," he says, and the way he says this makes it all he needs to say.

"I only need somebody to play during happy hour," she says. "The tips are very good."

It's the biggest lie she's told since third grade.

"It's all good," the man says, and smiles the kind of smile that says he knows she's lying but it doesn't matter.

"Welcome then, Mr. Ray," Danni says, and holds out her hand to shake on it.

He takes her hand in his but doesn't shake it. He holds it gently. "Jimmy Ray is my first name," he says. "But you can call me 'darling'—most ladies do."

Danni is clearly charmed. For the first time in a long time, she feels a little like herself again. "You're quite a flirt," she says.

Jimmy Ray smiles. "Buddha says that there are three things that cannot be long hidden: the sun, the moon, and the truth."

This is probably not a good time to ask if he knows any Jimmy Buffett, Danni thinks.

Acknowledgments

First, and always, I thank my irreplaceable husband (also known as "the Hardworking Staff"). Steven is my compass and humanity. He makes all things possible through his love.

Next, of course, is my glorious editor, Shaye Areheart, and wise agent, Lisa Bankoff. I must also thank Susan O'Neill, a wonderful writer and dear friend, who takes the time to read my manuscripts and asks only for chocolate in return. Sure, it's a lot of chocolate, but editing is a thankless job.

Many thanks also go to Dwight Yoakam; his friendship and fierceness about art touches and inspires me. God bless his unruly cowboy heart.

This book began when I ran across a blog by Kevin Barbieux, aka "the Homeless Guy." Although this work is not about him, I was so moved by his plight that I felt compelled to write about homeless people in Florida. His line about abandoned cats and dogs being homeless is echoed here and expounded upon. After reading that, I felt the need to explore the subject more closely. I hope I did that with honor and dignity.

Acknowledgments

Much of the spirit of this book was inspired by the brilliant vision of Peter Schumann and his Bread and Puppet Theater in Vermont. His profound landscapes of puppets and wild re-creations of the idea of "circus" are amazing. I have had the good fortune to spend time with him and enjoy the hospitality of his home on a recent winter's day. Sitting in the kitchen of his tiny handmade house, the fireplace ablaze, talking to him and his wife, Elka, about art and beauty and the undeniable pleasure of well-made bread was an experience I will never forget.

Schumann's art has directly and indirectly influenced my own vision of the world for as long as I can remember. In the 1980s, I worked with his student Sandy Spieler and her In the Heart of the Beast Puppet and Mask Theater in Minneapolis, Minnesota. It was an amazing experience. Sandy is a positive force in the world, and her theater provides the Twin Cities with a vision of community that ennobles and strengthens.

I would also like to thank Web guru, marketing genius, and bestselling author Seth Godin for being his determined self and thereby introducing me to the world of tireless entrepreneurs. Whit could not have been written without him.

And so many thanks to famed pool expert Robert Byrne for writing *Byrne's Complete Book of Pool Shots* and taking the time to talk to a hack like me.

Finally, I must thank the entire state of Florida. Without its rampant beauty, unrelenting heat, and wild-eyed insanity, I would have grown up to be a normal person. What fun would that be?

About the Author

Novelist N. M. KELBY is also the author of *Whale Season, In the Company of Angels,* and *Theater of the Stars.* She spent more than twenty years as a print and television journalist before she began writing fiction and poetry. Her poems and short stories have appeared in more than fifty journals, including *Zoetrope All-Story Extra, One Story, Southeast Review,* and *The Mississippi Review.* She is the recipient of a Bush Artist Fellowship in Literature, the Heekin Group Foundation's James Fellowship for the Novel, both a Florida and a Minnesota State Arts Board Fellowship in fiction, two Jerome Travel Study Grants, and a Jewish Arts Endowment Fellowship. She grew up in Florida, where she currently lives. Her website is www.nmkelby.com.